ANDREW LADD grew up in Edinburgh. He studied sociology at McGill University in Montreal and has a Master's degree in Creative Writing from Emerson College in Boston, where he also taught for three years. Currently he lives in London. *What Ends* is his first novel.

What Ends

ANDREW LADD

ONEWORLD

A Oneworld Book

First published in Great Britain & Australia by Oneworld Publications, 2014
First published in America by New Issues Poetry & Prose, 2014

A CIP record for this title is available from the British Library

ISBN 978-1-78074-498-8
ISBN 978-1-78074-499-5 (eBook)

Text design and typeset by Tetragon, London
Printed and bound in Denmark by Nørhaven

Oneworld Publications
10 Bloomsbury Street
London WC1B 3SR
England

For Betty, Dwight, Leonas, and Maria –
I know you're reading somewhere

1980

I

THE ISLAND'S FINAL CHILD was born on a bleak, October evening: a boy, Trevor Alistair McCloud. At the time no one knew he'd be the last, of course, and so his birth was noted much as any other; even years later his brother and sister would remember less the event itself than the weeks before it, how their parents had shut the guesthouse early for the season, and the way the closing days of summer had left the island strangely muted. They'd revelled in the difference of those gravid afternoons, the pub downstairs completely empty and their father cooking all the meals, and their mother, usually so busy, spending her days on the sofa or in bed, exhausted but serene.

The family's first son, Barry, was seven, with coal-black hair and a splash of translucent freckles that stretched from ear to ear. He was a quiet boy, his manner unassuming, but to Flora – his sister, three years younger – he seemed practically omnipresent: a face behind her birthday candles, and the hand she held on walks, and the warm bundle by her side during their mother's stories on the sofa. His laugh, as their father tickled them by the fire one evening, was the first memory she had.

They lived on Eilean Fìor, an island three miles long by one across, and nestled in a cluster of four others off Scotland's north-west coast. Of its twenty-eight inhabitants Barry and Flora were the only children, so from necessity, if not fondness, they were rarely far apart; they played together, and pooled their labour to get through chores, and with Trevor arriving had given up their separate rooms, too, to make way for a nursery. Flora squeezed in with Barry now on a just-built set of bunks, and despite their endless bickering about the dolls she left in his toy box, or the intricate wooden train tracks he set up across the floor, they found they liked the new arrangement. In the quiet after lights out they could whisper to each other for what felt like hours, until their breathing drifted into unison and they fell asleep contented.

Their room was on the second storey in their family's sprawling, sandstone guesthouse, across the hall from their parents' bedroom and a bathroom, and flanked on either side by the new nursery and a study, where every weekend their father would curse his way through the accounting. All of it was hidden behind a wooden door off the main staircase, with *Do Not Enter* stencilled in cracked black letters across its middle. One floor up was a converted attic containing five small guest rooms, and one floor down was everything else: the kitchen, the pub; the lobby, the lounge; the heart of the community. The pub, especially, was always busy, in summer with guests from upstairs and a steady stream of campers, and year-round with a friendly group of local drinkers too, complaining about the weather, or trading gossip, or occasionally discussing the mainland's politics and football. And since most visitors found that atmosphere impossibly inviting, few ventured to the lounge at the front of the house – ostensibly for public use as well – which instead became a family sitting room, filled with photographs of relatives, board games for the children, and the old wood-cased wireless that once they'd kept upstairs. (There was no television, the children's father having inherited his own parents' stubborn distrust of the things.)

That life revolved so completely around the guesthouse was mainly an accident of circumstance – the islanders all knew it, despite their fondness for the place. The old general store was derelict; the granite chapel towards the jetty had been padlocked shut for years. So where else could they go? The ferry to Mallaig, on the mainland, took two hours, and even at the height of summer there was only one crossing a day – two on the weekends – so the nightlife there, such as it was, was hardly worth the trip (doubly so in winter, when the ferry ran just three days a week). And while the other islands were close enough, the smaller boats they used to hop between them, for visiting the post office or the doctor or the farmers' market, struggled when the sea was even moderately rough – and when a full-blown storm descended it was the ferry or nothing. Sometimes not that either.

For a long time none of that had seemed to matter, to the McClouds or to the rest of Eilean Fìor. They always had enough food, in their vegetable plots and larders and sheep pens, to survive heartily even if the ferry never returned; they had enough water, tapped from a well near the centre of the village, to last them far beyond what they could ever need. They even had a school for the children, set up by the board of education long before Barry became its only student, back when its single classroom was regularly filled to bursting. And most importantly they still had each other, and their livelihoods, and the guarantee at almost any time of day of a warm welcome in the pub.

Or, at least, they'd had all that once. By the eve of Trevor's birth, though, that older way of life had begun to falter, and a skulking sense of the end impending – however optimistically ignored, however strong their sentimental bonds – was slowly beginning to take hold.

*

The birth itself, that evening in October, took place in the guest-house master bedroom and was attended only by Oonagh Kilgourie, a crofter's wife from the island's other side. It was an arrangement that the children's mother, Maureen, had insisted on.

'I'm tired of going all the way to Fort William to get gawked at by a load of teenage nurses,' she'd told her husband one night, Flora at their feet and surrounded by crayons. 'Oonagh and I can manage just fine on our own.'

'But Reenie,' he'd started to reply. 'What if there are complications? At your age...'

'My age! I'm only thirty-nine, George, and it's not as if I haven't done this before. People have been having weans here for hundreds of years without having to scurry off to the mainland. I don't need anyone to hold my hand.'

Rubbing absent-mindedly at his bald spot and thinking that he'd rather like some hand-holding, actually, George made some last-ditch point about the children being upset by the sight of her in labour.

'Nonsense,' she clucked, reaching down and patting Flora on the shoulder. 'Poppet, will you be all right if your new brother or sister is born at home?' Flora murmured yes, barely looking up, and with a curt *Hmph!* Maureen nodded in triumph.

The night of the birth, though, George called the region's doctor anyway: a plump, officious man from the largest island in the group, who arrived an hour later – relatively swift, given his small speedboat – and rushed up to the bedroom to take charge, his shirt straining to come untucked beneath his belly. Almost immediately he was sent back downstairs.

'Everything seems to be in order,' he said, as he reached the bottom landing. 'The ladies are, er... *confident* that they have the situation in hand.'

George nodded, unsurprised; he'd been scolded for even summoning the man. Instead, he suggested a whisky.

'Well,' said the doctor, puffing out his chest. 'I should stay, of course.' He glanced towards the ceiling, and his shoulders sank. 'But perhaps I had better stick to tea.'

'I'll put the kettle on,' said George, and told the doctor to make himself comfortable in the sitting room. When he brought the tray through a few minutes later, though, he found the man looking decidedly uncomfortable, Barry cornering him in an armchair and quizzing him on the finer points of childbirth.

'You see,' the doctor was saying, 'the baby can't come out until… Your mother needs to be fully… prepared.'

Barry leaned in. 'But *how* did it get *inside* her in the first place?'

'Ach, wheesht,' said George, setting down the tea on the centre table. 'Leave Dr Nicol in peace. He's not an encyclopaedia.' He poured out a cup and carried it across the room. 'There you are,' he said, winking, while Barry reluctantly returned to the board game he'd been playing with Flora. 'Not a moment too soon, eh?'

The doctor laughed nervously and said thank you, taking the teacup and a first, wincing sip. He swallowed. 'The McKinleys are moving away from Rum,' he said. 'I just heard.'

George settled into his chair across the room. 'Oh?'

'Aye, somewhere near Aviemore. The Post Office is relocating him.'

'Hmm,' said George, smiling gravely. 'All change these days, eh? We've three more couples leaving here in the spring, too.'

The doctor set down his cup on the arm of his seat. 'It's been worst on Fìor, hasn't it? How many in the past year?'

'More than two dozen,' George sighed. 'Six families.'

'Such a pity,' said the doctor, looking wistfully at the steam still rising off his tea.

Upstairs, suddenly, Maureen let out a cry, and the children both snapped to attention.

'Now now, you two,' said George, lowering himself from his chair to the floor. 'There's no need to look so worried.' He shuffled over to where they were sitting and put an arm around each of them. 'She's okay. I promise.'

The children nodded but still looked uneasy, so George pulled them both a little closer. 'Listen,' he began. 'Have I ever told you what happened the night Barry was born?' He winked at the doctor over their shaking heads. 'It's quite the tale.'

When their mother went into labour that first time, he explained, she'd been baking a birthday cake for Mrs McKenzie, the woman who'd run the general store; it was as she stood up from putting the tin in the oven that she felt the first contraction. But then, because she couldn't bear the thought of the food going to waste, she'd convinced herself it was nothing more than a spot of indigestion. 'She ignored it for a full three hours!' George laughed. 'It was only once the thing was iced, all three layers, and a pound of strawberries sliced on top, that she told me the baby was coming.'

'So he called me,' said the doctor, cutting in, 'and I hurried over to take them to the mainland. Except by now your father was in such a tizzy he tripped over his own feet when we got to the jetty and fell head first into the water.'

'I think I swallowed some seaweed,' said George, his voice plaintive but his face a giant grin. 'It was about as tasty as your Auntie Susan's Brussels sprouts.'

Barry and Flora giggled, and the men waited for them to settle before continuing. Dr Nicol told them how he'd taken off his coat and used it to fish their father out; George explained how Maureen had grown so impatient – afraid, after so much waiting, that she might end up having her first child right there in the doctor's boat – that she'd refused to let George go home and change. How he'd spent the entire crossing wrapped up in a blanket and shivering in the stern.

'And when we finally got to Mallaig,' said the doctor, 'your dad was still so sopping wet that the paramedics wouldn't let him into the ambulance.'

George shook his head. 'I had to spend an hour and a half waiting for a train to take me to Fort William – and when I got there I ended up walking to the hospital because no taxi would take me either.' He smiled. 'I still made it, thank goodness.'

He paused for a few seconds, and Flora asked what had happened when she was born.

'Ach, you were easy,' he said, with a dismissive wave. 'We were so traumatized by Barry we had everything planned to a T.'

Her face fell. 'Oh.'

'But your first birthday,' he continued, not missing a beat, 'was a total mess.' And then he was off again.

The children were used to their father telling stories this way, each word seeming to give him the energy to say another five. Mostly it happened on the walks they took on mild afternoons, once Barry was home from school; they'd set out along the village road and quickly veer into the heather, hiking up hills to watch for boats across the water, or wading into sheltered dips and glens, to play hide and seek in the long grass or chase after mice and rabbits. Throughout it all George would tell them his countless, gleeful tales, filling in his childhood on the island, and their family history, and a timeline of the place's ample past.

Fìor's first inhabitants, he'd explained, were Picts, the only signs of their existence now a few wrecked foundations in the hills. Their most likely executioners, sailing through a few centuries later, were the Vikings, whose strange runes George had shown them once, carved into a cliff face along the coast. Then, another millennium after that, though the children could hardly conceive of so much time, there were the farm and fishing families who'd settled to serve their feudal laird – and finally came the village, after an eccentric new owner bought the island with the dream of making it a holiday resort. He was the one who had built the guesthouse, in the late nineteenth century, along with the newer cottages and the jetty on the island's southern tip. He was the one who had persuaded dozens of entrepreneurs, George's grandparents among them, to move to the island with their families, and cater to the tourists he was sure would soon arrive.

And arrive they did, hundreds each summer – thousands, even, in the best years – on an endless stream of cruises up the coast. The ships would drop anchor early each morning and their genteel passengers would swarm ashore, buying woollen souvenirs at the village craft shops, sending novelty postcards from the general store, and wrapping up the afternoon nibbling on scones and sandwiches in the guesthouse tea room. (The pub came much later.) Then, in the evenings, they'd disappear just as quickly, back to their ferries and away to sea, leaving behind the island's few hundred inhabitants and a handful of wealthier tourists, usually, who'd paid to spend some time ashore.

With the Great War things changed, of course. It simply wasn't safe to gad about the Atlantic any more, even in the relatively sheltered sea around the Hebrides. *Your grandfather*, George told the children, while sitting at the island's highest peak one day, *used to come up here and look for submarines*. He pointed out across the ocean. *You could see their shadows beneath the water, he used to say – like little black slugs, slithering along*. He put extra emphasis on *slithering* and leapt towards the children as he did so, his fingers wiggling; they laughed and shrieked, and scattered for the path.

After the war things started to pick up again, but then the thirties came, and the Depression, and after that the tourists increasingly stayed away. The population shrank; the island's owner was forced to sell. And at that point George would always change the subject, or gloss over the details, refusing to say more even when the children asked. It was only from Mr Lewis, the island's schoolteacher, who'd been there just eight years himself, that Barry learnt the truth: whereas the old owner loved the place for what it was, the new one was simply an investor, convinced the island would be a lucrative source of peat. When that came to nothing he raised the rents instead, and while the few who could afford to buy their homes and land outright at that point did so – the McClouds and their guesthouse among them – the poorer families were forced to leave. *And they never stopped leaving*, Mr Lewis explained to Barry, sitting on the edge of his desk with his glasses sliding down his nose. *Even after the old crab died and his children donated the land to the Trust, they didn't want to stay*. He pushed his glasses back up as Barry, straining forward in his seat, asked: *why?* The teacher had shrugged. *Who knows? Sixty people left in five years. It was half the island. Probably the rest of them just couldn't bear to see it*.

Barry later passed the story on to Flora, though in his retelling the details were inevitably smudged. The parts he'd failed to understand (rent, wildlife trusts, nostalgia) were left out altogether, while the landlord became a literal crab – a seven-foot-tall one who'd chased away the other islanders. His pincers cut people clean in two in Barry's version, and Flora hid beneath her blankets as she listened.

This was their habitual way of absorbing the adults' stories: as jumping-off points for their own, inventing whole sagas around the tiniest of details. In their universe, the runes along the coast had been carved by a Viking murderer who'd been exiled to the island as punishment for his crimes; before him came a Pictish sorcerer, who'd conjured the island from the sea. There were winds so dreadful, they imagined, they could blow children clean away, and thunderclaps so booming they left others briefly deaf. And then there were all the ships they imagined sunken just offshore, whose contents would have washed up for days following a wreck: enormous jewels and treasure chests fit to burst, and exotic, long-extinct animals, who would have shook their long fur dry as they'd lumbered up the beach.

If the two of them were often lost in imagination, though, they hadn't failed to notice the island's population still trickling away; they had grown accustomed to the procession of tearful goodbyes in the pub, the postcards from expatriates in mainland cities, and occasionally the strangers they'd see knocking on village doors. *Why are all those people going to the Leslies' house?* they asked at dinner one night. Their mother snorted. *They're thinking about buying it*, she said. *I doubt they will*. And she was right. Except for the old laird's manor, which sold to a Glaswegian woman the year before Trevor's birth, the rest of the village homes ended up abandoned.

Still, the children weren't bothered by the constant departures; if anything they liked the island emptier, as it gave them more scope to play. There were fewer extra eyes to report their bad behaviour to their parents, and fewer spots off limits – and increasingly they roamed as they pleased around the silent houses, and the empty churchyard, and the musty old barns in the hills. Or else they would run off along the road, a mud track mixed with gravel and crushed shale that ran straight across the island, following it to the crofts on the north shore or, more often, to the jetty on the south. From there they could watch for seals around the distant skerries, or carry on down the coast, searching for shells along the island's pebbly, seaweed-covered shores.

On a map, they knew, those shores followed an outline like the wing of a maple seed; their father had shown them one on a Christmas visit to their cousins' house in Perth. *Look*, he'd said, pointing to the seed compartment with his pinkie. *This is where the puffins nest*. He moved his finger towards the centre of the wing. *And this is where we do*. The children nodded, picturing the map of the island that their father displayed proudly above the bar, acknowledging the similarity – but for some reason the image failed to resonate. Perhaps, with the island's only trees marooned in a plum orchard behind the laird's manor, the seed itself seemed too foreign to relate to home. Certainly the yellowing, dried-out pod seemed a world away from their own experience of scrabbling around the coast, and over the island's pea-green hills and concertinaed, basalt cliffs, leaping the tiny burns that crossed the path every few hundred feet.

More than that, though, there was the Stùc, the tiny spur on the island's north coast that ruined the maple seed outline. Once upon a time it had formed a natural harbour, their father told them, which the Vikings would have used in the centuries before the jetty. *You see how it looks like an arm, ready to give someone a big hug?* he explained, sticking his left hand out in front of him as they gazed down at the Stùc from a nearby cliff, then wrapping his outstretched arm around his right shoulder. *Well, that makes the water in the middle calmer, so boats could have docked there when the seas were rough*. He stuck his right hand in the crook formed by his awkward self-embrace, and waved his fingers at them. *See how comfy they are in here?*

The children laughed at the analogy, though like the seed pod it wasn't perfect: the Stùc was an arm only when the tides were low; the rest of the time it was a separate island, connected to the north shore by a small causeway and nothing else. *The old laird built the bridge*, George told them one afternoon, as they watched the wide, sandbar isthmus disappear beneath the water. *He wanted his house over there so he could holiday away from the riff-raff – he just didn't want to wait for the tide to go in and out.*

Barry frowned at that and asked why, if he'd wanted to be left alone so badly, he'd built the school on the Stùc as well. George grinned and ruffled the boy's hair. *Don't miss much, do you? It wasn't a school to begin with – it was the old servants' quarters.*

Then it was Flora's turn to frown, and ask why the laird had needed servants, but this time George only shook his head, chuckling to himself, and told her that was a story for another time. *Now come on*, he said, turning towards home. *Let's go find some dinner.*

By eleven o'clock, the lounge's campfire atmosphere had largely vanished. The children had finished their first board game and had already played another, and now Flora was back to her usual drawing while Barry, nodding off every few pages, struggled through a Roald Dahl book on the sofa. Dr Nicol, in the meantime, had given up the fight and was snoring softly in his chair, while George, chewing at the end of a pencil, muddled through *The Scotsman*'s cryptic crossword.

Against that quiet, Mrs Kilgourie's footsteps on the stairs were practically thunderous, and George's head jerked up at the sound of them; by the time she reached the sitting room door he was already half-way there himself, and when she announced the baby boy's arrival Flora jumped to her feet, too, asking loudly if they could see him, and jolting Barry and the doctor awake.

Mrs Kilgourie nodded and led them all upstairs, to where Maureen lay clutching the baby, her hair matted and a few streaks of red on her bedclothes. George approached her first, sitting down on the edge of the mattress and planting a kiss on his wife's cheek as he leaned in for a better look at the bundle in her arms.

'Another chip off the old block, eh?' He gave the blanket a gentle pat.

'I bloody well hope not,' said Maureen, smiling.

Barry stepped forward, his eyes flitting between the baby and the bloodstains. 'Are you okay, Mum?'

'Aye, Barry,' she said, looking away from George. 'Just a wee bit tired.'

At that, the boy edged closer still, eventually reaching his mother and, with some encouragement, pulling back the edge of the baby's wrap. His eyes widened. 'He's all purple, Mum!'

In the doorway the doctor cleared his throat. 'That's normal, Barry.' He glanced at Mrs Kilgourie. 'Sometimes being born can be just as hard on the baby as it is on the mother.'

At the sound of the doctor's voice Maureen looked up at him, and then to his right, where Flora was still fidgeting with a crayon she'd carried from downstairs. 'Come on, dear,' she said. 'Come and see your brother.'

Nodding silently, Flora walked across the room, Barry moving aside to make way for her by the bed. And as she finally looked down at Trevor – at his tiny, puckered eyes, and his dab of a nose – the frown on her face softened, and she reached forward to stroke his cheek. 'He looks nice,' she said, glancing up, and Maureen smiled back in approval.

After a few more seconds, Mrs Kilgourie bustled forward again. 'Right,' she said, placing a hand on each of the children's backs. 'That's enough. We've things to do.' She ushered them to the door, where the doctor was still standing looking gormless. 'You too, Mr Nicol,' she said. 'George will make up a guest room for you.'

'I... yes,' said the doctor. 'Thank you.' He stepped into the dark hallway with the children.

'And you bairns,' Mrs Kilgourie added, already closing the door behind them, 'get yourselves to bed. I'll want your help with breakfast.'

Behind her Maureen called out goodnight, but the door was completely shut before they could reply – leaving them to share a look of confusion with the doctor before brushing their teeth in silence and putting themselves to bed. It was the first night they could remember not having their mother tuck them in, and the first of many repercussions that Trevor's birth would have: his arrival on the small, declining island was a pebble dropped in a pond. A dying stillness, momentarily disturbed.

2

No one would ever know how the rats made it to the island, or when exactly they first arrived. For months after Barry first claimed to see one, his parents wouldn't even consider that it might be true, and once the situation had at last become impossible to ignore – once whole harvests sat ruined, and countless gnawed-through power lines had been replaced, and the seabirds that usually blanketed the island were gone – by then the only thing anyone could think was: *how will we get rid of them?* Or, in bleaker moments: *will we?*

That came much later, though, after many more years of diaspora and disappointment, after Trevor's first steps and words – and after those early weeks following his birth, when his siblings realized that their lives, like that, had changed.

At first the children blamed Mrs Kilgourie: once she'd shooed out the doctor that first morning, after allowing him a hasty breakfast and a token examination of mother and child, she seemed to take up permanent residence. A small bag of her things appeared in a guest room upstairs; the dial on the sitting room radio moved to a classical station that the children hated. She crowded visitations with their mother, and talked over them at dinners with their father, and at night, when they tried to take shelter in their room, she would appear at the door without warning (or cause, they thought) with a stern *Hush! You'll wake the wean!*

Just as present that first week, though less annoying, was Mr Kilgourie, who arrived on Saturday morning before the doctor had even left. He made little effort to disguise his motives, not even visiting Maureen upstairs – he just pulled off his green wellies in the hall and gave George a pat on the shoulder, then padded towards the kitchen and the smell of sizzling bacon. Unlike his wife he brought no luggage, but he stayed for lunch and returned for dinner, and was back the next day too – and soon the faint whiff of his pipe smoke lingered in the sitting room, even when he wasn't there.

The first morning after Trevor's birth, they also had a visit from the schoolteacher, Mr Lewis. Better mannered than Mr Kilgourie, he at least stuck his head in the bedroom to say congratulations, and to make a crack about his next pay cheque being guaranteed – but after that, and a few quiet words with George, he spent the rest of the morning in the sitting room, trying to chat with Flora but mostly being monopolized by Barry. Not used to seeing his teacher outside the usual context, the boy had developed a sudden exhibitionist streak, and bombarded Mr Lewis with endless show-and-tells. *This is my favourite place to read, sir! And this is a picture of my cousins in Perth! And – oh! Would you like to see my room?*

More exciting still was who turned up after Mr Lewis: Bella, the Glaswegian woman who'd bought the laird's manor, and the Stùc's only other resident. That she was the only person to move to the island in the children's lifetime was fascinating enough, but in the year since then she'd kept mostly to herself, and had returned to the mainland for the winter months when the island's farms were dormant and the social scene at its peak – and so still no one knew anything about her. She was in her thirties, they'd divined that much, and an artist, and apparently not a struggling one if the amount she'd spent on the manor house was any indication. It wasn't just the cost of the property, though they knew she'd paid the asking price without much negotiation: it was her subsequent renovations. She'd never invited anyone to see them, but they'd been hard not to wonder about with the workmen going to and fro for weeks, and the steel beam she'd had shipped over, and the giant bags of masonry dust and other rubbish she'd then had shipped back out. She was a mystery. And now here she was standing on their front step.

'Miss Fowkes,' said George, opening the front door while Barry and Flora hid just beyond the vestibule. 'What a pleasant surprise.'

'I heard congratulations were in order,' she said stiffly, standing well away.

George nodded and thanked her, and asked if she'd like to come in.

'Oh no,' she said. 'I wouldn't want to intrude. Perhaps another time.' She handed him a card, thick and grainy with an ink design of an angel on its front. 'But please do give this to your wife.'

George took it, with more thanks, and then moved slightly to the side. 'Are you sure you won't come in? It's really no bother.' Once more she demurred, though, mumbling goodbye and turning to walk home.

Barry and Flora immediately galloped upstairs to watch her from their bedroom window, hypnotized by the loose-knit orange scarf whipping around her in the wind, while downstairs George studied the card she'd left, bemused. It contained only five words, carved in loopy black calligraphy. *All the best*, it read. *Bella Fowkes*.

After that the remaining visitors, arriving in a steady stream through Saturday evening and Sunday afternoon, were a bore – at least as far as the children were concerned. Each of the island's other households turned up bearing the usual array of gifts – pots of stew, jars of preserves – and with so little overlap it seemed as if they'd all sat down upon hearing the news and drawn up a plan. The timing of their visits displayed that same military efficiency: they would arrive and troop up to the bedroom, cooing and fawning as appropriate, and then Mrs Kilgourie would swiftly herd them back to the pub, where they'd sit and tell George what a splendid little boy he'd produced, and then be on their way within an hour. It was eminently pleasant. But beneath that warmth there also seemed to lurk some deeper feeling of reproach. Of disappointment. As if, at that same meeting where they'd assigned gifts and divvied up the schedule, they'd all agreed that giving the island another child was a futile thing to do.

Finally, at the end of Trevor's first week, Mrs Kilgourie returned home, and the children briefly entertained the hope that their lives might return to normal – but even then, the household's rhythms faltered. The occasional family storytelling nights ceased entirely; their mother still wasn't tucking them into bed. And, worst of all, Trevor crowded out their meals each evening, perched in a battered plastic baby carrier at the table's head, their parents smiling and burbling at him as if Barry and Flora weren't even there. While in the past they'd often lingered at the table after dinner, now they ate in glum silence and asked as soon as they'd finished to be excused.

Meanwhile, during the day while Barry was at school, Flora grew increasingly lethargic. For a while she spent the hours with her mother, as she'd done before Trevor's birth, but when Maureen wasn't tending to him she didn't have the energy for much else any more – and when Flora attempted to play with her new brother she was only left more frustrated. He wouldn't respond when she called his name – wouldn't even turn his head at the sound, half the time! – and when she tried showing him her pictures he just grabbed at them with drool-slicked fingers and left them smudged or crumpled. She tried making faces at him, the way Barry sometimes did with her, or tickling him, or waving his toys in his face, but still he'd only lie there gurgling – and Flora, having never seen another newborn, took his lack of sentience personally, as if he were withholding some more meaningful response. Worse, when she tried to coax more out of him, crushing his fingers around a crayon or grabbing his head and turning it towards her when she spoke, it would only start him crying – and then she'd be sent away to help George with the chores. Eventually she gave up leaving her room at all, and would sit and make up half-hearted worlds for her dolls or flip through the pictures in Barry's books, until three o'clock arrived and she moved to the window to watch for him walking home.

At Christmas came another change: rather than visiting the mainland relatives, George and Maureen decided that Trevor was still too young to travel and that they would have to stay at home. That, at any rate, was the story Maureen gave to the relatives. In truth, Trevor was a calm baby, and travelling would likely have been painless – but Maureen had long wanted to spend Christmas at home, and she wasn't sure when she might ever have another excuse so impossible to challenge.

It wasn't that she didn't like her cousins in Perth; on the contrary, she'd been happily spending her holidays with them since she was a girl, when they were still her neighbours on the island. Indeed, from the earliest Christmas Maureen could remember – she'd been four, maybe – they'd gone next door on the twenty-fourth, returning home only around one or two in the morning for a few hours' sleep, and then marching straight back over for the meal on Christmas Day.

It was different after Auntie Moira's side of the family left for Perth, of course, when Maureen was eight or nine, though they hadn't moved the Christmas celebrations to the mainland immediately – instead, the émigrés returned home. It was only when Maureen's mother passed away a few years later – a complicated birth after years of miscarrying, which also robbed Maureen of what would have been a sister – that she and her father were glad, suddenly, for the chance to get away.

After she'd married George, another change: Auntie Moira's family began to spend Christmases on the island again with the McClouds, especially as Maureen's father grew frailer. But once he was gone, and George's parents as well – and George too upset to spend Christmas at home without them – the annual visit to Perth had become the norm. It had been four years in a row, now – and it increasingly struck Maureen as a shame. She wasn't a particularly sentimental person, and certainly she wasn't that attached to the guesthouse, which had always been the McCloud family home, not hers. But her fondest memories as a girl were of those few Christmases when her mother was still alive, and when she'd first discovered the joy in their peculiar family customs – spending the day with her cousins, yes, but more private ones, too, shared only between her and her parents. Once, she remembered, if not four years old then five, she had woken from a dream in the middle of the night and found her parents cross-legged on the sitting room floor, candles all around them as they cut out chains of paper angels. The sound of the waxy paper between the scissors still stuck with her from that night, that gritty squawk and the warm, undulating candleglow on the walls. She couldn't remember much more from that year – or perhaps the years had all blended together after so much time – but from later holidays she remembered taking the angels to Moira's on Christmas Day, and stringing them around the table with her cousins while the women cooked and the men tended to the fire.

The midnight angels were only one of her parents' many rituals, too: there was also their Christmas morning prayer, gathered around the previous nights' spent coals; there was the spiced lentil soup they made for lunch on Christmas Eve; and there were the tiny mincemeat pies, borne of a fingertip-to-fingertip production line, her mother pressing the dough into old warped baking tins, her lips between her teeth, and her father placing a gentle scoop of fruit inside.

Moira's family also had its customs, of course, which the cousins continued after she was gone – and Maureen thought almost as fondly of them. But after everything, and in the midst of so much departure from the island, she had lately begun to feel a desperate need to grow her own; to leave something for her own children to remember, warmly, long after she had left them. And that was why she was so glad to stay at home that year, so glad to send Barry and George to the jetty, twilight well entrenched, to fetch their first Christmas tree, ordered specially from the mainland. So glad to start Flora making not paper angels but paper chains – her own mark on the tradition. It would be perfect, she thought, standing with Trevor in her arms, and watching Flora sprinkle glitter onto a paste-soaked piece of construction paper on the sitting room floor – all she needed to do was get this one, unpleasant conversation out of the way.

'I'm glad you stayed, poppet,' she said, stepping all the way into the room and making for the sofa. She made a show of admiring Flora's handiwork as she sat down, cooing over how handsome they'd look on the tree, planting the suggestion that they'd have to do this every year – and then she told herself to stop stalling. Letting her voice harden, she told her daughter there was something else they needed to discuss that night, and when Flora only nodded absentmindedly, continuing to frantically cut and glue, Maureen tried to sound even sterner. 'Flora,' she said. 'Pay attention. This is important.'

At last the girl reluctantly looked up, and with a resolute stare Maureen began to explain that, given how much of their time the baby had been taking up lately, and how unhappy Flora had seemed about it, they had decided that she would be starting school a few months early.

Flora, whose eyes had been gradually shifting back to her paper chains, now jerked to attention. 'What!'

'You're starting school early,' Maureen repeated. 'As soon as the Christmas break is over.'

'But, Mum!' Tears were already filling Flora's eyes, and Maureen found herself wondering how, of all the household tasks, she'd let George give her this one.

'I don't *want* to go to school! I just want Barry to stay at home!' Flora glanced at Trevor, who only hiccupped. 'It's not fair!'

'Flora—'

But the girl was standing up now, screaming at her mother that she hated her and hated the stupid baby, and was galloping upstairs just as Barry and George reappeared with the tree and Mr Kilgourie – who had kindly agreed to help carry it home. 'Where's young Flora off to?' he asked, as her feet vanished over the edge of the top landing.

He turned and began shuffling sideways down the narrow hallway, the top of the tree in his hands. 'She'll want to get a look at this fine specimen!'

'She's in one of her strops,' said Maureen, standing to one side to let them past. Then, glancing at George, 'I told her.'

Mr Kilgourie seemed not to register that second remark as he backed into the sitting room, or the look that George and Maureen shared – or perhaps he simply chose to ignore it. 'Well,' he said, huffing as they finally set down the tree and steadied it by the hearth. He petted one of its branches, and the thing sprung back eagerly. 'This will bring her out of it, I'm sure!'

Maureen told him she rather doubted that – and indeed, when George went upstairs to try and reason with Flora he returned after barely five minutes, a door slamming overhead. 'She says' – he cleared his throat – 'that she doesn't care if we decorate the whole stupid tree without her.'

So that was what they did, in the end, Mr Kilgourie making his excuses and his way out, while Maureen set Trevor in his baby carrier and George, after a deep breath, fetched his parents' old decorations from under the stairs. Only Barry seemed unsure what to do, rooted in the middle of the sitting room and glancing towards the ceiling at every stomp and bang. *Some memory*, Maureen thought to herself, even as outwardly she put a hand on Barry's shoulder and told him he shouldn't worry. That Flora would come around soon.

They'd reached the bottom of the decorations box, though, before she reappeared; Barry, hoisted up in his father's arms, was fumbling the angel into place on the bough when they heard the sniff behind them and saw Flora in the doorway, her eyes red and her lashes still damp. Now it was Maureen's turn to take a deep breath, blinking back what felt like tears of her own. Was it anger she felt on seeing her daughter there, the evening so thoroughly ruined? Sorrow, maybe, at her own part in ruining it? Or was it simply relief? Happiness, perhaps, that all was not lost?

'We saved your paper chains for you,' she said at last, kneeling down to pick one up, and holding it out in front of her.

Saying nothing, Flora sniffed again and stepped forward with her arm outstretched – and then, with Maureen still holding the other end, they wrapped the chain around a few of the lower branches. They did another after that, and soon Barry joined in, and before long the only bare spots were the higher ones that the children couldn't reach, which George and Maureen filled in quickly, as if slowing down might scupper the detente.

'Wonderful,' said George at last, stepping back to admire the finished tree, and putting an arm around Maureen – which he hastily retracted, mumbling that they ought to get a picture. He hurried upstairs to fetch his camera, and after he'd returned and balanced the thing on a pile of books on the coffee table, the rest of them watching, Maureen finally convinced herself that it had turned out all right. George set the timer and took his place with the rest of the family in front of the tree, he and Maureen in the middle with the baby in their arms, and Barry and Flora standing one on either side – and suddenly there was that sense again that everything could be perfect. That they might remember only this. And indeed, when she saw the printed photograph a few weeks later, the quizzical stare on Barry's face as he glanced at Flora was the only slight sign of anything the matter.

Despite Flora's tantrum that night, and several more to follow, she did start school in January just as Maureen had announced, walking there with Barry on her first morning under a sky the colour of pencil lead. Barry tried his best to lift her mood but the truth was he didn't really want her there either; the school had become his sanctuary over the past year, especially in the months since Trevor's birth, and he didn't want to share it, not even with his sister.

The school, housed in the old servants' quarters on the Stùc, was two floors high and built of stone. (*That fellow didn't want for help*, their father liked to laugh.) Inside it was divided in half, with the ground floor devoted to the classroom, such as it was, and the teacher's flat above. With so few students in recent years, though, Mr Lewis's space had begun to encroach downstairs as well: what was supposed to be a storage closet for the pupils' coats was filled mostly with his own; what was supposed to be his office had now become a lounge, with the old teacher's bureau hidden under a mess of potted plants, and a sofa and several chairs moved in around the hearth.

The classroom, meanwhile, had grown emptier, with most of its thirty desks stacked against the rear wall and just four still facing the blackboard at the front. Even they were largely for show; for almost a year and a half Barry had been the only student, and Mr Lewis, of course, the only teacher – and as the two of them had grown to know each other better they'd fallen, like an old married couple, into their own set of peculiar routines. Mr Lewis had given up writing on the board, instead pulling a chair to Barry's desk and demonstrating the day's lesson with pen and paper, and soon they were wondering why they even bothered with that. So on a particularly cold day during Barry's first February alone, they'd moved to Mr Lewis's sitting room, Barry practising his reading in the fire's flickering glow, and before long they were spending half the school day on the sofa. After dropping his bag in the classroom every morning Barry would wander across the hall, where Mr Lewis would be waiting with a cup of tea and the morning's agenda.

It was that closeness Barry feared Flora would disrupt, and his worry was a prescient one: his sister was an intrusion from the start, throwing off the balance in the classroom just as Trevor had at home. On that first, gloomy morning, Mr Lewis was waiting in the classroom again when they arrived, a long-forgotten necktie looped beneath his collar.

'Good morning,' he said, the phrase crisper than usual. 'Please take your seats and we'll begin.'

He did, at least, pull up his usual chair as the day went on, to sit with Barry and explain things one-on-one, but their camaraderie seemed to have dried up somehow, turned brittle; when Barry faltered on a problem now, or wondered how to spell a word, he was no longer guaranteed an immediate response. Instead, hunched at Flora's desk, Mr Lewis would say a quiet *I'll be with you in a moment, Barry*, without even looking over.

It didn't help, either, that Flora was so openly opposed to being there. It took twice as long as necessary to get her started on even basic tasks, and after five minutes she'd give up anyway and throw whatever it was to the floor; she butted into conversations, and demanded almost hourly to be sent home, and sometimes, on especially bad days, she would ask to go to the bathroom and not return until someone went to find her. Most of the time she had hidden upstairs, drawing on some scrap of paper she'd filched on her way out, but as spring blew in she began to venture further: down to the beach, or climbing on the rocks around the water, or once even all the way home, where Maureen scolded her until the baby woke and then sent her to her room. After that she took more care, vanishing to a place Mr Lewis could never find – at least, not until Bella returned in April that year and appeared at the school's front door one morning with Flora gripped firmly by the bicep.

'Lose something?' she muttered, pushing the girl forward. 'She walked right into my living room.'

Meanwhile, as spring opened into summer and two more couples fled the island, Barry saw the first of the rats; he was on his own, walking to the beach on a sunny weekend afternoon, when one of them scurried without warning from the high grass beside the trail. Startled, he let out a cry and ran home to tell his father – but George, tending to a row of carrots in the garden, was unmoved.

'Don't be daft, Barry,' he said, not even turning around. 'There aren't any rats here, only mice. You know that.'

'No, Dad, no. It wasn't a mouse, I'm sure! Mr Lewis showed us a picture of a rat once, and—'

'Barry,' said George, finally looking up. 'I've lived on this island my whole life, and not once have I even *heard* of someone seeing a rat. It must have been something else.' He shook his head. 'Now go on, away with you. I think your mum wanted help with dinner.'

Barry might have been more insistent, but as the afternoon wore on the less clearly he could even picture what he'd seen, and by dinnertime he'd convinced himself it *had* been just a mouse. Besides, a few days later was the start of the summer break, and he had a more pressing thing to ponder: Flora's disappearances. At school Mr Lewis had finally put an end to them, accompanying Flora to the bathroom whenever she claimed to need it, but now that their parents were in charge (and not really paying attention) she could once more walk off as she pleased – and she did, every few days, casually announcing she was going out to play before vanishing for hours at a time. After weeks of this Barry was mad with curiosity, and so at last he followed her, along the road and onto the smaller path towards the Stùc. There he stopped, reluctantly, watching her cross the footbridge and knowing he'd be spotted if he tried to do the same. That night, though, he confronted her, hooking his chin over his bunk's railing as soon as the lights were out.

'Why were you on the Stùc today?'

She rustled beneath him. 'I wasn't.'

'You were so!' He leaned even further over the side of the bed. 'I saw you on the bridge!'

She paused. 'I don't have to tell you if I don't want to.'

'Flora—'

'Leave me alone, Barry!'

In the light from underneath the doorway he could see her duck beneath the covers, hissing that he was horrible and annoying – but she unwillingly showed her face again when he threatened to go to their parents, agreeing to take him with her the next day in exchange for his continued silence.

As soon as they left the house in the morning, though, she seemed to have second thoughts. 'You have to be really quiet when we get there, okay?' She looked at him gravely, stopping in the middle of the path. 'Otherwise we'll get in trouble.'

'I knew it!' said Barry. 'I knew you were doing something bad!'

'It's not bad really,' she told him, starting to walk again. 'You'll see.'

They wound down to the north shore and the bridge to the Stùc, just as when Barry had followed her the day before, but instead of taking the usual path to the school, after they crossed over, Flora led them along the shoreline and onto a rocky trail that ended at a steepish, gorse-covered slope. They clambered up it, using the gnarled branches to steady themselves, and only once they reached the top did Barry realize where they were: behind Bella's orchard. Flora stared pointedly at him, motioning for quiet, and then crept forward to an uneven section of the wall where she climbed up and quickly over. Once on the other side she tiptoed ahead, leading him through the narrow gap between the trees until finally, when the house came into sight, she stopped again, beckoned him closer and sat down on the ground.

As part of her renovations Bella had combined all the rooms along the back of the house into one long space, Barry now saw, and had knocked out large chunks of the outer wall to make way for a continuous line of windows, which filled the studio with plentiful, peaceful daylight, and also put it on display to anyone outside. And there she was, wearing only some running shorts and a stretched-out, threadbare camisole, her chestnut brown hair pulled up in a ponytail. Barry sunk quietly to the ground beside Flora and the two of them began to watch, transfixed – Flora by the woman's arm moving across the canvas, and Barry by the faint shadow of a crease at the base of her shorts. The whole time they sat there she barely moved from her easel, just quietly rocked back and forth on the same spot, and somehow time seemed to do the same thing – until suddenly the sun plunged low enough that its reflection in the window dazzled Barry's eyes, and startled, he looked around him. 'We should get home,' he whispered.

Flora sighed. 'I know.'

They came back the next day, though, and again a few days after that, taking up position beneath two plum trees that soon enough became their own. What else was there to do, that summer? With Trevor not yet one, George and Maureen had not reopened the guesthouse, only the pub, so the children had none of their usual chores – and in fact were encouraged to get out of the house rather than make nuisances of themselves while their parents tended to the day trippers. Usually the children went together, but as July dragged on they occasionally slipped off secretly too, one by one, across the bridge and along the craggy trail, and over that crumbling back wall. When Flora went there, increasingly, it was with the hope that the studio would be empty, so that she could creep closer and peek over the sills; when Barry went, he still just took that shaded spot beneath his tree and sat there, dazed, while a helpless, unconscious love began to sprout. Throughout it all, neither child revealed their lonely stake-outs to the other, and if either one suspected then they never dared to ask – complicit in the silence of those first, seductive secrets.

*

As the summer passed, George started to wonder about the rats himself, if dubiously. He still hadn't seen one, or any other evidence to speak of, and with only the pub to tend to he'd been out and about far more than usual – so it seemed as if he should have noticed *something*, at least if it were really true. But Mr Kilgourie had been grumbling about some mystery animal getting into his pantry – *if it's mice, George, it must be two dozen of them* – and several of the hikers who stopped for a drink before the ferry home had mentioned seeing rats, too, and so at last his incredulity began to falter.

The damning moment came on a Saturday in early August, the same day Bella stormed into the pub wearing nothing but a housecoat and shouting across the bar at George about 'those little fucking monsters!' Around the room the few afternoon drinkers looked up, startled.

'It's like the bloody *Wicker Man*!' she said, slamming both hands down on the bar, and causing a few of the glasses to twitter anxiously while George looked on in dismay. The day trippers in the room began to stand up and shuffle towards the door; the Mannings, in the corner, dipped their heads and pretended not to listen.

'Aye,' shouted Bella, seeing the hikers leaving. 'Get back to the ferry before they start stalking you, too!'

And then, seeing Maureen dash into the pub, George finally found the will to answer. 'Miss Fowkes, *please* calm down. What's happened?'

Maureen was less charitable once she reached the bar. 'Honestly, woman,' she hissed. 'What is the matter with you? Stop your bloody shouting this minute!'

But she would not stop, even as Maureen firmly guided her out of the pub and into the hallway, George following them with a sheepish glance at the Mannings. Bella was still roaring that she had never in her life felt so furious, that she would call the police if this were Glasgow – that she might still call the police here, never mind if it meant waiting hours for the sergeant to tootle over from Mallaig. Only once she started to explain what had actually happened – that she'd been painting in her studio and heard shouting outside, where she'd seen Barry and Flora running from the house – did she finally seem to calm.

'I'm sorry, Miss Fowkes,' said George, at the first break in her tirade. He smiled as he said it, putting on his best publican's charm, and gave Maureen what he hoped was a subtle look to say keep quiet. If the deep red of her neck was anything to go by she'd absorbed most of the anger that Bella had lost these last few minutes, and he doubted her contributions at this particular moment would be much help. 'Obviously this is completely unacceptable,' he went on, 'and I can promise you it won't happen again.'

'Thank you,' she said, fixing the ponytail that had apparently come undone as she'd hurried over from the Stùc. 'I hate to make a scene,' she added, still winding her hair around her fingers, 'but what would you do? I was alone in the house and saw someone watching me outside. They scared me half to death.'

Maureen cut in before George could respond. 'This is really very unlike them, Miss Fowkes.' Her mouth was a thin, grey line. 'To be honest, I can barely believe it.'

'Yes,' said George, and gave her another look. 'And we'd hate for it to sour you on them permanently. Perhaps we could have you to dinner one night, by way of apology. Get everyone back on the right foot again.'

Bella sighed. 'We'll see,' she said. 'For now just make sure they stay away – I've got a big show in the autumn and I don't need these distractions.' Finally her hands fell from her hair and settled in the pockets of her housecoat; her face twitched and she looked down, as if she'd forgotten what she was wearing. She coughed, and tightened the belt a little, blushing. 'I prefer *Ms* Fowkes, by the way.'

'Of course,' said Maureen, and showed her to the door.

Once she was gone, they went upstairs to see if there was anything in the children's version of the story to make it more defensible. George couldn't really believe it had come to this: *spying*, on a half-dressed woman? His children? When he'd been young he'd had the same free reign of the island – all the children had – but he had never done or known of anything so sordid.

If he was finally getting angry, though, he softened again when they opened the children's door and he saw Barry there, trying not to cry. 'It was a rat, Dad,' he said, instantly, his voice cracking. 'It was definitely a rat. That was why she saw us. We were just sitting there and it crawled up onto my leg.' He rolled up his trouser cuff to reveal an angry red gash, already scabbing over. 'When I tried to get it off, it scratched me.'

Flora sniffed and nodded in corroboration, while Maureen gasped and hurried out to fetch the antiseptic – though the bite turned out to be nothing, thankfully, at least as far as Barry was concerned; Dr Nicol prescribed some antibiotics and that was the end of it. More serious was the effect on George, in that instant when he first saw the scar on Barry's leg and could no longer tell himself that the rats were some communal delusion – but also in the months and years to come, when he'd think back to the first day Barry had come to him in the carrot patch, and wonder what might have happened if only he'd believed a little sooner.

3

As autumn descended, and then winter, the rats seemed to retreat – but the reprieve was only temporary. When spring returned the infestation did too, with even greater numbers. Barry and Flora saw the rats almost weekly on their walks to school, and more of the islanders began to find them in their vegetable patches or their feed huts – and the cliffs, covered with nesting seabirds, would periodically erupt with plumes of squawking white as one of the rodents made its way among them. By the summer, the end of Flora's first full year of school, she and Barry would regularly come home to find their parents in a despairing conversation with some neighbour or another, and that September there was an island-wide emergency meeting to come up with a plan of attack. Traps were laid; holes plugged. Fingers crossed.

Meanwhile, the children were busy: with Trevor old enough at last, the guesthouse was open again from April to October, and their days were a frenzy of emptying bins, tidying the kitchen, and hoovering the public rooms at night. In the off months, meanwhile, they still had schoolwork to attend to, and when that was done they were once more given cautious permission to spend their free time out around the island – though to avoid suspicion they mostly stayed away from the Stùc, instead heading for the jetty and along the coast, to a white quartzite beach on the south shore whose sand gleamed in the sunlight and sang in the wind. There they'd watch the puffins and the shearwaters circling overhead as raptly as they'd once sat in the orchard, as if the important part was simply some movement to hold their attention – though occasionally, on the days when their parents were distracted, they might sneak out to their old, hidden spots beneath the plum trees, together or alone.

Another year passed and Trevor grew, sloughing off successive sets of hand-me-downs without his siblings noticing a thing. It was only when he approached three and Barry, himself a few months past ten, recognized a beloved set of old pyjamas at the breakfast table, that suddenly it struck him. In bed that night, he lay with his chin in its now habitual place hooked over the bunk bed's railing, and asked Flora, now seven and a half, if she'd noticed it as well.

She poked her head out from under her covers. 'Yes!' she said. 'And did you hear him at dinner? He said *I want more*!'

'Don't be silly,' Barry replied. 'It was *I want Mum*.'

Flora snorted. '*I want Mum*? Why would he say that? She was right there!'

'It doesn't have to make sense,' said Barry, flopping back onto his pillow. 'He's only two and three-quarters.'

'You're wrong,' she told him, and before he could respond again she'd hidden beneath her blanket.

Soon it was a constant competition between them, seeing who could explain their brother better; every night they argued over what he'd said at dinner, and every afternoon they rushed through their homework, each of them trying to beat the other downstairs and steer Trevor's budding lexicon in their favour. By his third birthday they were vying for nothing less than his complete devotion, and would sit on opposite sides of the room, wooing him with toys and sweets as if the direction of his waddle proved some deeper understanding.

Those were Trevor's first memories, but soon he had amassed more: walking with his family the day a rat jumped at them from the heather; the anxious tingle in his stomach the first time he woke to fog swallowing up the horizon; and a springtime visit from Dr Nicol to administer his shots, the way his bicep had felt as it tensed around the needle. He collected these small, impressionistic flashes painstakingly, reverent, the way an adult might fill a shoebox with old postcards – and with each one the island felt more like it was *his*, somehow. Talking to his brother and sister only confirmed that feeling, because they greeted descriptions of his most vivid memories with confused stares or shaking heads, as if they barely registered the home around them. Not until he was much older did he realize that the events most striking to a three-year-old were a matter of routine to others, and not until he had just turned four did something happen that surprised them all.

It was mid-afternoon on a Wednesday, and Trevor had come downstairs from a post-lunch nap to see if Barry and Flora had returned from school. They had not, but instead, and to his bewilderment, the sitting room was full – with his parents, Mr Kilgourie, and a representative from each of the island's last households, the Pikes and the Thomases and the Mannings. And then, most bizarre: two strangers wearing suits.

When Maureen noticed Trevor in the doorway she waved him off, telling him to go and play with Barry and Flora.

'They aren't home,' he said, not moving. His eyes moved to the strangers. 'Who are you?'

His mother gave a strained smile and answered for them. 'They're friends of ours,' she said, glancing in their direction. 'Now, why don't you go get yourself a snack? Dinner won't be for a while.'

Still hesitant, Trevor did as he was told, but after fetching some oatcakes from the pantry he tiptoed back to the hallway and began to listen beside the open door.

'I'm afraid it's simply unacceptable, Mr McCloud,' said a voice he didn't recognize.

Mr Kilgourie roared. 'Unacceptable! And who are you to tell us what's acceptable and what's not? We're the ones who bloody live here!'

'Calm down, Jack,' said someone else – Mr Thomas, Trevor thought – and there was some scuffling as Mr Kilgourie stalked across the room. Trevor took the opportunity to wedge a few crumbs into his mouth, chewing as softly as he could.

'I'm not sure I see the issue,' said his father.

Another unfamiliar voice responded. 'The field mice on this island are an endangered species, Mr McCloud – that's the issue. Are you familiar with Darwin's finches?'

'Good grief,' muttered Mr Kilgourie, the floor creaking as he began to move around again.

Just then, Trevor felt something brush his elbow and he let out a small gasp, spinning around to see Barry and Flora, at last returned from school. The adults, thankfully, seemed not to hear.

'What's going on?' whispered Flora.

'I don't know,' said Trevor. 'There are strangers here.'

Barry and Flora shared a look, and then all three of them were listening. One of the unfamiliar voices was speaking again. 'The mice here have been isolated on this island for so many years that they've diverged from the mainland species. Now they're unique to Eilean Fìor, and that means you can't go around laying poison all over the place. They need to be protected.'

'I don't think you understand how bad it's become,' their mother said. 'It's not just that they're getting into our homes – they're affecting the whole island. There are fewer plants, fewer birds... I've never seen the shearwaters so thin. I find it hard to believe that's all a coinci—'

'My grazing area is completely ruined too,' Mr Kilgourie interrupted. 'My sheep have nothing to eat and neither do bloody we.'

'These are valid concerns, of course,' said one of the visitors, 'and we're not suggesting that nothing should be done. We're merely telling you that indiscriminately filling the island with rat poison is not an option the Trust is willing to consider.'

Trevor put the last of the oatcakes in his mouth, a little too carelessly, for a few of the pieces went down the wrong way and he began to cough. The two older children turned frantically to shush him, Flora clamping her hand over his mouth and Barry trying to shove them both down the hall and around the corner, but it was too late. The conversation in the sitting room had stopped and footsteps were moving towards the door.

'What are you all doing out here?' said Maureen, stepping out into the hallway, eyes narrowed.

'Nothing, Mum.' Barry shook his head. 'Me and Flora just got home, and—'

'Never mind,' she snapped. 'I don't want to hear it. I taught you better than to eavesdrop on private conversations.'

'But Mum,' began Flora, 'we weren't—'

'I told you, Flora, I'm not interested.' She put her hands on her hips. 'Now go on, all of you. To your rooms. We'll have words later.'

Flora mumbled sorry and the three of them started up the stairs.

Only once they were almost to the top did they hear their mother turn back to the sitting room, making her own apologies and leaving them, bewildered, on the landing.

Soon enough they'd know everything they wanted about the strangers' plans; more, even, once the new year arrived, and the constant stream of consultants from the Trust. In the meantime, however, they found themselves distracted by other things: the end of the school term and a return to Perth for Christmas, and then, on the last night of the winter break, another mysterious conversation.

'You'll go to school alone tomorrow,' Maureen told Barry, as she passed him a plate of seconds. 'Just for one day.'

All three children looked up at this, but Flora, whose dislike of school had inevitably faded over the years, was the first to protest. 'What!' she yelled, her fork clattering against her plate. 'Why?'

'Because,' said George. 'That's what Mr Lewis wanted.'

Flora crossed her arms and announced that it wasn't fair.

'Ach, wheesht,' replied Maureen, and rolled her eyes.

In bed that night, Barry and Flora speculated for an hour as to what this news might mean. 'Maybe he has a secret to tell me,' said Barry, trying not to hope too hard for the return of their former companionship. 'Or maybe he's going to give me some special present.'

Flora was more pessimistic. 'Maybe you're in trouble,' she said, and after that Barry couldn't quite relax. Even at school the next day, when Mr Lewis *did* greet him warmly, that glimmer of their former days only put Barry more on edge.

'So,' the teacher began, leading Barry into the living room. 'I suppose you're wondering why Flora's at home today.'

Barry nodded.

'Well, no need to worry,' he smiled. 'It's nothing sinister. Your parents and I just thought it might be an idea if I talked to you on your own about next year.'

'Next year?'

'The thing is,' said Mr Lewis, nodding, 'unfortunately I'm not qualified to teach beyond primary school – and even if I were there certainly aren't the proper resources here on the island. So...'

'I've to start at boarding school,' Barry said to Flora, explaining it to her in their room later. She'd been waiting for him on the bottom landing when he got home, legs crossed and chewing on a dark tangle of her hair. 'What took you so long?' she'd said, jumping up and smacking him on the arm. 'School finished ages ago.'

He'd stared at his feet and told her he'd gone for a walk, and then they'd hurried upstairs, where he rattled through everything Mr Lewis had said to him: that secondary school would be very different; that being in classes with other children would seem strange at first; and that even though the school where he'd be going, St Fillan's, accepted mainland children, it catered specially to boarders from the islands – so he'd be in very good hands.

They'd heard of St Fillan's before, of course; both their parents had gone there, several years apart, and their father had often told them stories about it. He'd been so homesick his first few weeks, they knew, that one night he'd made an escape rope from his sheets – just like he'd seen in picture books – and broken his leg climbing out the window. For Halloween one year, when the school held its annual guising party, he'd dressed up as the headmaster and been given three weeks' detention, even as the teachers doling out sweets had smirked with ill-disguised amusement. And then there was the girl he'd escorted to the Leavers' Ball in his last year: *she was so nervous*, he'd told them, winking, *she threw up up all over my kilt*.

Their mother was more circumspect in her stories, hewing mainly to a few general observations about the poor quality of the food, and rueing losing touch with several of her friends from those days. But she did also corroborate, when necessary, another of George's adventures: the time he'd returned to St Fillan's, in Maureen's final year, to escort *her* to the Leavers' Ball. *All the other girls were so jealous*, she'd sigh, whenever George mentioned it. *I had a strapping university lad all my own, come to whisk me away.*

To Barry and Flora, though, St Fillan's had never been more than a setting in their parents' past, its role in their own future not quite connecting. So the realization that Barry would soon be disappearing there himself felt like a rude awakening, somehow, a betrayal, never mind all the other things Mr Lewis had told him to expect – a collection of words they barely understood. Cliques. Bullying. Peer pressure. As Barry related each successive detail, Flora's eyes bulged a little more, though in the end he left out the most unsettling thing of all.

'Now,' Mr Lewis had said, frowning very slightly as he leaned back in his armchair. 'St Fillan's is a mixed school, Barry, which means there will be girls there, not just boys.' He paused. 'And so long as Flora's not here today, it seems like as good a time as any to go over some basic sex education. What do you say?'

He'd said nothing, in fact; he'd only nodded again, dumbstruck, and followed Mr Lewis to the classroom, where a few new wall charts were secured to the blackboard with dusty scraps of tape. He'd stayed mostly silent through the lesson, too, but his thoughts had raced away with him. He tried and failed to imagine the few grown-ups on the island engaging in the odd behaviour Mr Lewis was now describing; he thought about the few other girls his age he'd met – children visiting the guesthouse with their parents, mostly – and whether he could picture doing any of it with them. He remembered when Poppy, the Kilgouries' niece, a year or two his senior, had visited the previous summer, and tried to hold his hand as they walked along the beach (he'd given her a look of confusion, and she quickly pulled away).

Mostly, though, he thought about Bella, for the first time with a spark of understanding. That was why he'd been late home, too: after school, in the navy light of the winter's afternoon, he'd doubled back along the path towards her orchard. She was gone for the winter so the studio lights were off, and he could barely see inside – but it didn't matter. He could picture, from so many afternoons watching, exactly what it would look like. What *she* would look like, the way her slender neck rose from her shoulders, and the soft Y at the top of her legs, and how her breastbone always seemed to leave faint shadows beneath her skin. Imagining her now he could see it all and more, his insides churning and a strange, nervous pressure building in his stomach – and that was when, with darkness settling completely and the cold seeping through his coat, he'd turned and hurried home.

It was a few months later, in early spring, when the ratcatchers descended in earnest. By that point the children had grown used to the Trust's occasional, preliminary sorties, but nothing could have prepared them for the crowd that appeared that April, a few weeks before the guesthouse reopened for the season, and a few more again before Flora's ninth birthday.

'What's going on, Mum?' she asked, sneaking in behind the small hallway counter that served as their modest lobby.

'They're here to see about the rats,' Maureen told her, briskly handing out room keys to the dozen or so men trooping past her.

She turned and gave Flora a weary look. 'And for pity's sake, dear, try to stay out of their way.'

That was impossible, though, even for the uncurious, because the visitors were everywhere. They cropped up without warning in the house's nooks and crannies, and all over the island, too, an infestation in their own right. From dawn to dusk they roamed across the village glen or swarmed up and down the surrounding hills, their wheat-coloured trousers and dark-green fleeces a stark contrast against the electric green of the springtime landscape. They crept through the meadows' long grass, and skulked between sheep in the island's modest pastures, and when the children tried to play outside they often found the best spots overrun. Barry, now plagued by self-consciousness about his feelings for Bella, also found himself too afraid to continue sneaking over the orchard wall – he was sure one of the men would see him and report it to his mother.

'They're so annoying, Dad!' Flora whined at dinner one night, as her father ladled out some soup. Maureen was in the pub, seeing to the guests. 'How long are they going to be here?'

'As long as it takes, my love,' he said, handing her a bowl.

'But they're not even doing anything!' She gave her soup a petulant stir. 'All they've caught so far are mice, and they're just keeping *them* in cages in their rooms.'

George gave her a sharp look. 'How do you know that?'

'I – Well…'

'Flora, you're not supposed to snoop in the guest rooms, you know that. Especially not these guests. The less trouble we give them, the sooner they'll be gone.'

'But they're the ones giving us trouble! What are they even doing with all those stupid mice, anyway?'

'They're going to take them to a zoo somewhere and keep them safe.' He sighed. 'That way, when the rats are gone the mice can all come home again.'

She made a sour face. 'Why?'

'It's a long story.' He filled his own bowl and set it down in front of him. 'But it's a very… sensible thing to do. So leave them be.' He shifted in his seat and glanced at Barry and Trevor. 'That goes for both of you, too.'

Barry nodded, silent, while Trevor promised solemnly to behave – though in fact he didn't find the trappers all that troublesome. Now four and a half, he spent his days dreaming up whole sagas for the men while his siblings were at school: one day they were aliens – brain-eating, blood-sucking aliens! – to be avoided at all costs; at other times they were treasure hunters, or cowboys, or army special forces, and he, depending on his mood, their ally or their foe. He would listen to their conversations in the pub each night, and watch them fan out around the village each morning, and sometimes would even follow them, at a distance, as they moved around the island. To him they were a symphony of avatars; a world's worth of souls.

And then, four weeks later, they were gone, just as abruptly as they'd appeared. The older children arrived home from school one day to find the last of them, a middle-aged man with greying temples, standing with their mother in the hallway, his bags at his feet and a rucksack on one shoulder.

'So, Mrs McCloud,' he was saying, 'we're going to spend a few months making sure the mice are good and settled, and then we'll be back to start the rat hunt in earnest.' With a grunt, he slipped his other shoulder through the rucksack's remaining strap. 'We'll confirm closer to the time, but my guess is we'll be back early in the new year.'

'Thank you, Mr Cox,' she said, hands clasped demurely over her waist. 'I hope you won't take it personally when I say I'm not much looking forward to it.'

'Completely understandable.' The two of them shared a quiet smile as Barry and Flora watched – but then Trevor was barrelling down the stairs. 'Barry! Flora! You have to come and see what I found today!'

The ratcatcher started at the noise, as did Maureen, and with her face darkening she turned to Trevor as he reached the ground floor. 'For goodness' sake, calm yourself! We can't have you galloping around shouting your head off all the time – we open next week and our guests occasionally like some peace and quiet!'

Trevor froze. 'But Mum—'

'But Mum nothing. You're old enough to learn some better manners.'

The man cleared his throat. 'Sorry,' he said, as Maureen turned back to him. 'I'm holding you up. Thank you again for your co-operation over the past few weeks. I hope we haven't been too disruptive.'

'No, no,' she said, gazing at him with a strange, sad expression. She took a step backwards. 'Have a safe journey, Mr Cox.'

'And you have a lovely evening, Mrs McCloud.' He picked up his bags and walked to the front door, nodding at the children as he passed. Once he was gone, Maureen turned to them again; Trevor looked about to cry, and Barry and Flora both had their arms around him.

Maureen sighed. 'Your father would have said the same thing.'

Barry and Flora exchanged looks.

'Ach, away with you,' said Maureen, stalking off towards the kitchen and muttering that she needed to start dinner – while Trevor, a few tears sliding down his cheeks, gained yet another memory.

4

THE SUMMER CAME AND WENT in a blur that year. In May, Barry was taken to visit St Fillan's; in June, he turned twelve; and finally, on a Wednesday night in August, the island gathered round to bid him farewell. Maureen had blocked off the date in the reservations book almost a year in advance, so there were no guests upstairs that evening, no customers in the pub – just the islanders, and the heather glowing violet in the summer dusk, and the village, calm and settled.

The Kilgouries arrived first, around seven, a bottle of whisky in his arms and a casserole in hers. Barry greeted them at his mother's instruction – *this is your party*, she'd said, when the doorbell rang, *so be the good host* – and though his adolescent self-consciousness still clung to him as he did so, he also felt a certain pride at being given such an adult job.

'Barry!' said Mr Kilgourie on the doorstep. 'Can't wait to get out, eh? Soon enough, my lad! Soon enough!' He chuckled, mostly to himself.

'Mum's in the kitchen,' Barry told them, 'and Dad's setting up the lounge.' He blushed. 'Can I take that dish from you, Mrs Kilgourie?'

She looked him up and down and seemed to satisfy herself that he could be trusted. 'Aye, Barry,' she said, passing it to him. 'Tell your mother it needs twenty minutes in a hot oven.' Her gaze shifted to Flora, who had quietly appeared just beyond the doorjamb. 'And while he does that, young lady, you can take my coat.'

As Barry disappeared down the hall Flora stepped forward with a dour stare, deliberately taking Mr Kilgourie's coat before his wife's and folding it over her arm as slowly as she could. Then there was another knock at the door, which Flora took great pleasure in answering while Mrs Kilgourie still stood, foot tapping, with her coat in her hands.

'Mr Lewis!' Flora said, as she heaved the door open. 'And...' She gasped, as if waking, suddenly, from a dream.

'Hello, Flora. You remember Bella?' As Mr Lewis stepped into the vestibule he beckoned behind him to where the artist still stood on the front step. Flora nodded dumbly and edged sideways to let them in, before collecting everyone's things and telling them to make their way to the lounge – while she, staggering beneath the heap of coats, started for the closet under the stairs. Glancing back and forth down the hallway, she squeezed inside and quickly shut the door behind her, the smell of must and canker filling her nostrils as she fumbled for the light bulb.

Bella was here. In the house.

Flora's fascination with the woman had changed over the years, perhaps, but never had it wavered; still she made her secret visits to the orchard when the woman was on the island, and just as often recently had started sneaking over even in those months when the place was empty. With Bella gone she could stride up to the windows without fear of discovery or punishment, and study the work left hanging on the walls – and she took full advantage of that freedom, bringing a sketchpad of her own and climbing onto the windowsill to copy the paintings inside. Underneath her mattress she kept a growing sheath of that illicit work: the simple pencil drawings she did in the orchard while light and weather permitted, and studies from memory, in paint or coloured pencil, when the winter was too relentless to go outside. She had almost been disappointed when Bella returned this spring, as it forced her to once more conceal herself among the trees.

In the hallway closet she stared at the woman's coat hanging in front of her. It was flimsy, undyed linen, the colour of baked clay – the sort of thing her mother would have scoffed at. *That'll keep her about as warm as a mothy doily*, she'd say; Flora could hear the words clearly as she reached forward to touch the fabric, to feel its soft stubble against her fingertips, to pull it to her face and breathe…

'What are you doing?'

She dropped the sleeve and turned to the door. Barry had opened it a crack and was peering in.

'Nothing,' she said. 'What are you doing?'

He pulled the door open further. 'I saw the light on. I was going to turn it off.' His eyes moved to Bella's coat, and he stepped all the way into the closet, hunching to fit in beneath the stairs. 'Whose is that?'

Sighing, she told him.

'Bella?' He shut the door. '*Bella?*'

'She came with Mr Lewis.' Flora shifted, trying to move between him and the coat. 'And I was here first, so go away.'

Suddenly the stairs above them creaked. 'Barry!' Their mother sounded irritated. 'Flora! Where have you got to?'

They looked at each other for a moment, and then Barry reluctantly pushed the door open again. 'Sorry, Mum,' he said, stepping out into the hallway. 'We were hanging up the coats.'

'Well, hurry up,' she harrumphed. 'Honestly. Everyone's waiting.'

The atmosphere in the lounge felt thin at first, unnatural. For one thing, there was the vague, lingering animosity between Bella and Maureen – who hadn't expected the woman to turn up, even though Mr Lewis had warned her. By extension there was animosity between Bella and Mrs Kilgourie, too, and since the men – George, Mr Kilgourie and Mr Lewis – seemed almost instantly to fall into their own group in the corner, that awkwardness between the women was all the more pronounced.

But the main problem was the guest of honour. It was Barry's send-off, after all, and so as the other islanders arrived – the Pikes and Thomases with more contributions of food, the Mannings with a hand-knitted scarf as a parting gift – the attention was all on him. Yet he felt like he could barely remember his own name that night, let alone make small talk. The sound of Bella's breathing at his side left him dizzy; the warmth that seemed to radiate from her prickled at his skin. Since his sex education lesson at school that winter, his initial inability to imagine himself – or anyone – in that invasive embrace of Mr Lewis's wall charts had given way quite spectacularly to what felt like hours-long hallucinations: Bella, in such overwhelming nudity and anatomical detail that he would lie awake at night, taking deep breaths as he tried to calm the bursts of adrenalin in his gut, while Flora snored softly in the bunk below him. And now, having her so close, it took all his effort to push those images away again. *Are you excited about St Fillan's, Barry?* someone would ask, and he'd respond in monosyllables, staring at the wisps of hair tucked behind her ears. *Do you know much about your bunkmate?* Her perfume, slowly suffocating him. *What will you miss most about the island?* He felt paralysed by the sensations she seemed to cause in him; terrified by the sudden racing of his pulse and warm sweat beneath his arms.

At last the other guests began to tire of the silence and turn elsewhere, and as the food was brought out, the beer and whisky taking hold, the chatter began to swell. People drifted in and out of Barry's circle, forming and reforming into smaller groups of two or three around the room: Mr Pike and Mr Manning discussed the day's newspaper and a plane crash in Japan, and marvelled at why anyone would ever climb aboard those rickety, airborne death traps; Mr Thomas spoke to George about the summer's superlative weather; and while Maureen bustled to and fro refilling drinks, the other women held hushed summits in the corners, revealing sordid thoughts of leaving for the mainland soon themselves. By the fireplace, Mr Lewis sat with the younger children, Flora monopolizing him the way Barry had the day after Trevor's birth, while Barry himself daydreamed through it all, watching Bella move from huddle to huddle.

'I say,' said Mr Kilgourie loudly, as a post-dinner lull began to settle. A few heads turned to look at him. 'Why don't we give Barry a wee drop of whisky, eh? What better occasion for his first taste?'

'Hardly his first taste,' said George, as more guests fell quiet around the room. 'He had such problems teething we could have opened a distillery.' He laughed. 'Still, it's a fine idea. What do you say, Reenie?'

She shrugged and nodded.

'Splendid!' said Mr Kilgourie, already making his way to the sideboard to examine the malts. After letting his finger float from bottle to bottle for a few seconds, he picked one up by the neck. 'Here we are, my lad – a nice MacAllan. Aged twelve years, just like yourself!'

Barry smiled, anxious. He was still oppressively aware of Bella, a few feet behind him and to the left. She seemed to tug on that whole side of his body, as he watched Mr Kilgourie fill a glass with a generous dram and walk it across the room.

'Now,' said the man, holding out the glass. 'Normally you want to savour a whisky like this, really take your time with it. But I always say your first taste should be one big mouthful, straight down the gullet.' He grinned. 'It might catch you by surprise.'

Everyone was watching as Barry took the tumbler and tilted it from side to side, considering the bronzy liquid. His nose wrinkled at the scent.

'Go on, son,' said Mr Kilgourie. 'Tip it back.'

Mr Lewis stepped forward from his spot at the back of the room, reassuring Barry that he didn't need to gulp it all down at once if he didn't want to, but the boy was already moving the glass to his mouth, its smoothness against his lips, his palate tingling as he inhaled. He took one last deep breath and flung his head back – *Bravo!* – and instantly his throat was screaming from the heat. His fingers still wrapped around the tumbler, he let his arm drop and began to cough.

Mr Kilgourie cackled. 'That's my boy!' he said, patting Barry on the shoulder. 'What a show!' Then he was lifting his own glass again, already refilled, and addressing the room one more time. 'Now let's the rest of us lose a lung – *slainte*.'

After that, the attention began to shift away from Barry again, and Mr Lewis quietly slipped over to ask if he was all right. Barry nodded, eyes watering, then stumbled over to an armchair and slumped into it, surveying the room. His father and Mr Kilgourie were cheersing in the corner, and as he watched them he began once more to feel that strange sense of pride he'd had while greeting guests at the front door. Suddenly, somehow, it seemed as if he'd crossed a threshold, moved one step closer to adulthood. He rubbed his jaw, mimicking his father and feeling for stubble that wasn't there, and glanced at Bella again. With a lopsided grin he stood up, found his glass and crossed the room to pour himself another. This time he took a daintier sip, trying to copy Mr Lewis, who was standing with a glass of his own and talking to Mr Pike.

'Look at this, George!' Mr Kilgourie laughed, when he noticed Barry by the sideboard. 'We'll soon have him writing us tasting notes!'

George glanced over, smiling, and told Barry that ought to be his last, but already the boy was hardly listening, still fixated on Bella as he drained his glass. She was next to the hallway door, and as the other guests parted in front of him, he saw that she was talking to Flora. Room swaying, he wove his way towards them.

'What are you doing?' he blurted out when he was close enough, perhaps a little too loudly.

Flora looked up, scowling. 'I was asking Ms Fowkes if she wanted to see my drawings.'

Barry turned to Bella, for a moment feeling brave enough to meet her gaze. 'Do you?'

She gave them both a polite smile. 'I'm not sure it would be very nice to leave the party like that.'

Just then, however, their mother appeared. 'Bella!' she said. 'Glad to see the three of you have made up!' She was slurring slightly, hanging too long on her vowels. She motioned towards the children. 'I told you they were good 'uns, really.'

Bella nodded, that smile still firmly etched into her face.

'We were asking her if she wanted to come upstairs,' said Barry, quickly adding that it was only so that Flora could show off her drawings.

'What a wonderful idea,' said Maureen, her bleary eyes still scrutinizing Bella. 'Our Flora's quite the artist, you know. Always scribbling away at something.'

Flora blushed, and whined for her mother to stop, but she kept on staring hopefully at Bella – who at last relented, sending the children bounding towards the stairs.

In their room, Flora quickly started pointing out all her favourite things: the shelf where her dolls lived in the cupboard, and the spot by the window where she would sometimes sit and draw, and the pink-and-white beanbag she'd picked out from a catalogue – all by herself! – as a gift for her last birthday. Barry, meanwhile, tuned out his sister's rambling and concentrated entirely on Bella, the walls still swimming behind her. *What if she were naked now?* he thought, as the increasingly familiar feeling of his erection began to press against his underwear; as he imagined her nipples, and her navel, and her thighs, and... Cheeks prickling, he sat down abruptly on Flora's beanbag, just as Bella set her drink on the dresser and sat down at the foot of Flora's bed. 'So,' she said. 'Let's have a look at these drawings.'

Even in his hazy state, Barry registered some surprise as Flora lifted up the corner of her mattress and pulled out a bundle of paper. He'd had no idea she kept anything there; had no idea, either, that she'd done any drawings other than the ones she sometimes showed him.

'These are my really special ones,' she was saying, as she handed them over.

The woman's eyebrows shot up as she looked at the sheet on top of the pile. 'I... This is very good. Especially for someone so young.' She motioned towards one of the corners. 'You have a wonderful sense of perspective here. And it's a nicely muted palette. Very mature.'

Flora beamed back at her.

Yet as Bella set aside each subsequent picture, a frown deepened across her face; her cheeks grew redder, her commentary less substantial. When she reached the last sheet, her jaw now clenched, she handed it back to Flora in silence. Then, hands clasped in her lap, she turned to the girl. 'You've been coming to my studio again, haven't you?'

Across the room, Barry tensed.

'Um…' said Flora. 'Yes. But I didn't think you'd mind. I didn't go inside this time.' Bella opened her mouth to respond, but Flora cut her off. 'And I only did it because I want to be able to paint like you!'

That seemed to briefly disarm the woman, but when she eventually replied her voice was still icy. 'Flattery will get you everywhere,' she said. 'But that doesn't make it okay to spy on people in their homes.' She was standing up now – and so was Barry, yanked back to reality and desperate to calm her down.

'Ms Fowkes,' he said, staggering a little as he got to his feet. 'Wait.'

'Oh ho!' She spun towards him. 'And I suppose you come along for the show as well, do you?'

'No, I—'

'I don't believe this,' she said.

And then she was gone.

'You idiot!' shouted Barry, stalking across the room to where Flora was cowering on the bottom bunk.

'I'm sorry,' she whimpered, beginning to cry, shuffling further back on her mattress. 'I thought it would be okay!'

'How could you think it would be okay? How? You ruined everything!'

He was dashing into the hall now and down the stairs, but the sitting room was a spinning fog of voices and Bella nowhere to be seen. He blinked, tried to focus. Heard Mr Lewis: *I'm sorry. I don't know what's got her so upset*. The room lurched again. *Not to worry,*

Henry – I'd be in a hurry to get her home on her own, too! Shoes were on his feet; the front door opening. *It's not like that, Jack, honestly. We've just had dinner a few times.*

She was already a way down the road.

She was by his side.

'Ms Fowkes,' he managed, just. The air was watery around them, the sky a mauve panel behind the hills.

She stopped and turned. 'Go back inside.'

'Please,' he said. He took another step closer. 'You can't leave.'

Two birds flew overhead, squawking like rubber toys.

'Oh? And why's that?'

He saw the two of them as if through a camera, composed side by side in the darkening valley. The birds overhead were gone. The guesthouse behind him was gone. His family was gone. He lifted his hand and put it, trembling, on her waist.

'*Get. Off me.*' Her lip snarled.

'But—'

She stepped backwards, out of his reach. 'I knew it,' she hissed. 'Oh, they all tried to tell me it wasn't like that, that you didn't mean any harm, that you were too young to understand…'

'No,' he started, 'it wasn't—'

'But get a few drinks in you and the truth comes out, eh?'

This wasn't right. She didn't understand.

'You're a pervy wee peeping Tom,' she said, looking as if she might be about to spit at him, 'and you ought to be ashamed.'

Her lips were red.

He lunged at her, and with a shriek she stepped backwards again and he fell to the ground. The grass tickled his face.

'Barry!' His father was striding over, Mr Lewis a few steps behind him. 'What is going on?'

'I told you,' said Bella, and began to walk away.

Barry clambered to his feet to chase after her, but his father was upon him now, grabbing him by the shoulder and telling him to stay right where he was.

'What happened, Barry?' asked Mr Lewis.

'Nothing,' he said, squirming. He glowered at his father. 'Let go of me.'

George shook his head and started pushing him towards the house. 'I think you need to go inside, young man.'

And at that Barry stopped struggling and looked up, his face whorled with frustration. 'Fine,' he said, shaking free of his father's grip and starting unsteadily towards the house. When the guesthouse door slammed, it sent a muffled echo across the heather.

The next morning, the whole family lined up along the jetty to see Barry off, standing mostly silent as they watched the ferry creep into the harbour. When finally it had docked and a handful of passengers disembarked, Barry and George began to hoist his suitcases on board, still in silence, while Maureen watched, her red-rimmed eyes stinging in the wind.

She'd hardly slept the night before. By the time she and George had seen out the other guests, and found Barry where he'd hidden in one of the upstairs guest rooms, and given him the scolding of his life, it was already past midnight. Worse: her hangover had already kicked in by then, a drone of a headache that surged when she talked, surged when Barry slammed his door, and surged when at last she crawled into bed and George, getting in beside her, made the mattress sink and her head loll sideways.

'Was that really him?' he said, fussing beneath the blanket to get comfortable. 'Our Barry?'

'I suppose so,' she murmured, picturing the quiet rage in her son's face as they'd vituperated him upstairs: how long had he still been going over there, despite them telling him explicitly to leave her be? What possessed him to grab at her, no matter how much whisky? Why did he think it was acceptable to mouth off at his parents and be so rude to his guests and make his sister cry?

Of course, these were the easy questions to ask, the parental ones, the ones borne of Maureen's own frustration at how easily he cast off their control. Now the harder ones began to surface, as she lay there dozing on and off for hours. Why hadn't he told them about his feelings? Did he think they wouldn't understand? And, come to that, *did* they understand? If so, why had they screamed at him for so long? Hadn't they both been young and infatuated once, too?

When at last the edges around the shutters began to flicker with the first signs of northern summer daylight, she gave up on sleep and went downstairs, hopeful that water and tea and cleaning would defeat her tenacious headache; she was sitting in the kitchen staring at the wall when she heard the first stirrings of life upstairs. From the creak on the steps she knew it was Barry – too quick to be George, too heavy for Flora, and Trevor, bless him, could never be roused before eight – but when the boy appeared she still felt a jolt of surprise. Perhaps it was the sudden intrusion of normalcy: she'd expected him to look different, somehow, aged or wizened or tainted from the previous night's scandal, when in fact he was still the same old Barry, coming down for breakfast. He seemed just as startled, too, which reassured her, so she offered him his usual oatmeal, set his place at the table and asked him how he'd slept – as if clinging to the ordinary, repeating it, like a memory on the brink, would keep it from slipping away. To her surprise, after how furious she'd been with him a few hours earlier, she even found herself walking to his seat and hugging him. Squeezing tighter than usual, too.

And at the jetty now she was hugging him again, and whispering in his ear. 'Look after yourself, love.' She leaned back to give him one last, wistful stare. 'And ring us if you need anything. Anything at all.' It was the farewell she'd been imagining for weeks, that she'd rehearsed and tweaked and finally felt was perfect – and yet it felt suddenly callous, as he stared back at her stony-faced and said he would. Because hadn't he needed her last night, too?

George cleared his throat behind her. 'He'll be fine, Reenie, don't worry.' He patted her back. 'Now come on, give everyone else a go.'

So she did. Stepped back. Watched as Flora gave her brother a tentative, unreciprocated goodbye; watched as Trevor gave him his own long, unflappable hug. And then, finally, Barry and George started up the gangplank, disappearing inside and reappearing again on the foredeck a few minutes later, waving, as the engines rumbled to life. On the jetty the rest of them watched as the ship pulled slowly out of the harbour, until Barry was recognizable only by the streak of his black hair in the distance – and after a few more moments, Maureen sniffling and Flora shifting from foot to foot, and Trevor still waving with a giant grin, they turned and started back towards home.

5

A FEW DAYS AFTER BARRY LEFT for St Fillan's, on a beautiful, late summer's morning, Trevor started at primary school himself.

'Well,' Mr Lewis smiled, sitting on the building's front step as the boy skipped up, Flora straggling a few yards behind. 'Isn't this a passing of the torch?' He extended his hand. 'Welcome to Fìor Primary, young man. Here's to many happy years.' Trevor giggled, then reached out and shook on it.

The contrast with Flora's first day was remarkable. Partly it was because Trevor, hopelessly enthusiastic at finally joining his siblings' exclusive club, showed none of the combativeness that had marked his sister's early weeks in the classroom. But mostly it was Flora who once again controlled the mood; she seemed so lifeless, suddenly, that she might as well not have been there, and around that sluggishness the three of them slipped effortlessly into a new routine, Mr Lewis flitting between them at his leisure, always confident that whoever he had his back to would behave.

Really, though, the problem was Barry, his absence conspicuous to Flora and his lack of contact worse. He had called twice since settling at St Fillan's, but his conversations with his sister – with everyone, actually – had been arduous, one-sided, and she'd gleaned little from them other than the very public location of the school's telephone. He'd told her nothing about what the place was like, nothing about the teachers, nothing about the other children... Nothing friendly or conciliatory at all, in fact, confirming in her mind the falling out she already feared they'd had. He hadn't apologized for shouting at her that night with Bella; had barely said another word to her before he'd left. Even when she'd asked if he was okay, when he eventually climbed into the top bunk that night, he'd stayed silent. Had stayed silent at breakfast the next morning, too, even as their mother blathered away at him. And all because of one, honest mistake!

Then again, honest mistake or not, Flora was still brooding about the encounter with Bella, too. She'd been so sure the woman would be thrilled to have an admirer that she'd never considered any other possible reactions – and now what was she supposed to do? This time she really didn't dare return to the studio, not with Bella so angry, and without that source of inspiration she found herself unable to do any drawing of her own. The few ideas she tried felt childish, boring, and thanks to her memory of Bella's furious expression that night, she could barely concentrate when she sat down with her sketchpad anyway.

As the months dragged on, her mood sank even further. The hours after school quickly grew too dark and too cold to spend outside, and in the evenings, with her drawing at a standstill and Trevor in bed a full two hours ahead of her, Flora increasingly found herself slumped in her room with no company but her frustration. A few nights she tried asking her parents to play a game, as they'd often done when Barry was around, but that only gave her another thing to miss about him – and besides, the games usually ended with her mother roping her into some pre-bedtime chore, and even staring vacantly at her bedroom carpet seemed more appealing than that.

At the beginning of November, though, a few weeks past Trevor's fifth birthday, she found herself wandering downstairs, past her mother's clattering in the kitchen and down the hallway to the pub. At that time of year the place was only marginally open – available should some brave camper appear on the ferry, but in practice catering just to Mr Kilgourie – and when she walked in all the lights were off except for a few bulbs around the bar. Most of the seating was packed away, too, turned up on the tables and draped with dust tarps for the winter, the stacks lurking at the edges of the room like giant, spectral jellyfish. Her father was perched on one of the few remaining stools on the customer side of the bar, hunched over a newspaper.

'Hi, Dad,' she said, walking over.

He looked up, surprised. 'Hello, love. Is everything all right?'

She nodded, climbing up onto the stool next to him. 'What are you doing?'

'The crossword,' he said, giving the paper a rueful glance. 'It's not going very well.'

Flora strained to see over his arm, to where a few lone letters had found their way into the grid amidst a cloud of eraser dust. She asked if she could help.

'Why not?' he smiled, and as she shuffled closer to him he launched into an explanation of cryptic crosswords' labyrinthine rules. 'Okay,' he started, tapping his pencil against the page. 'Every clue here is divided into two halves: a cryptic half and a conventional half. The cryptic half shows you how to arrive at the answer through some sort of pun or wordplay, and the conventional half is a more straightforward clue. But the whole thing reads as a complete sentence, and you never know where one half ends and the other begins. Or which comes first.'

Flora stared at him blankly.

'Here,' he said. 'I'll give you an example.' He scanned the page. 'Okay: *shark*. The clue is *Beast told to be quiet on Noah's ship (5)*, so in this case the conventional part is *beast*, which is just another way to describe a shark. Then the cryptic part works like this: if you told someone to be quiet, you'd say *Sh!* and you add that on to Noah's ship, the *ark*. Sh. Ark. Shark! See?'

Flora nodded, her eyes fixed on where she was fidgeting with the hem of her jumper. George sighed and put down his pen. 'I'll tell you what,' he said. 'Let's start with something easier.' He flipped through the paper until he found the normal crossword, and scanned the list of clues. 'Ah. This one you should know: *berg dweller*. Two words.'

Flora's eyes lit up. 'Polar bear!' She'd done a report on the animals at school the year before.

'Well done!' said George. 'Now, let's see what else there is…'

They ended up sitting there for over an hour working on that single puzzle, George coaxing Flora to the answers and stretching it out as long as he could. Eventually, a little after ten, there were footsteps outside the door.

'Have you seen Flora?' said Maureen, looking over her shoulder as she walked in. 'It's past her bedtime and I can't find… Oh.'

Flora looked up at her, beaming. 'We're doing a crossword, Mum!'

'That's lovely, poppet,' she said, with a perfunctory smile. 'But you'll have to come back to it in the morning. It's time for bed.'

George glanced at his watch, then at Maureen. 'Sorry, love. I didn't realize how late it was.' He leaned forward and gave Flora a kiss on the cheek. 'Your mother's right – off you go, and we'll finish it tomorrow. I promise.'

And so they did – and when they were through with that first one they started on another, until on that second night, too,

Maureen had to tear Flora away for bed. It was a strange thing, thought George, as he turned back to his own crossword and listened to Flora clomp up the stairs: she'd never shown any interest in his puzzles before, or any word games, or even English, really; her preference for the visual was always the overarching theme of their parents' evenings with Mr Lewis, right there in the pub. Stranger still, when he thought about it, was that he couldn't remember another time when he and Flora had spent time on their own like this. Barry had always been around, or Trevor, or else they'd all been doing something together as a family. It had never even occurred to him, really, to invite Flora to do something, just the two of them. And in the unexpected pleasure of her company these past two nights, especially after her recent months of sullenness, he realized that he'd missed *her* lately nearly as much as he'd missed Barry. Had missed the old, happy Flora, in any case. Shaking his head as he studied the page in front of him, he marvelled at the difference.

If the mood at home was improving by Barry's winter break, his return seemed instantly to dampen it. He was a different boy than the one they'd sent away, taller, a few mean patches of shadow on his jaw, and with a remoteness none of them remembered – and it quickly became clear that there would be no happy reunion that Christmas, as they'd hoped when they decided to reunite on the island, instead of visiting the relatives in Perth. No possibility of pretending he'd never left.

His arrival that chilly afternoon was like a video played in reverse, as if somebody had flipped a switch after the ferry had vanished over the horizon in August, and sent everything scrambling backwards. The ship reappeared, Maureen and the children took up their positions along the jetty, and finally Barry and his mop of black hair cruised effortlessly back to shore, stepping from the gangplank into a haze of hugs and kisses. Even in those first greetings, though, the change was clear. His broodiness on the morning of his departure seemed warm in comparison.

'Welcome home, dear,' said Maureen, wrapping her arms around him.

He mumbled thanks into her shoulder.

'Hi, Barry!' squealed Trevor, running forward. 'Is it brilliant to be back?'

Flora, watching from a few steps away, gave him a tentative smile – but he only shrugged. 'Yeah. I suppose.'

As they walked towards home, Maureen and George fell into a quiet conversation of their own, while Barry hung back and Flora moved up by his side. It was only three in the afternoon, but the sky was darkening already, the clouds absorbing the night like blotting paper.

'I missed you,' said Flora.

'Uh-huh.'

She pressed on. 'It'll be nice having you home for a bit.'

He made another noise, half-way between a grunt and a laugh.

'Mr Lewis is looking forward to seeing you, too. He said you should go visit him tomorrow, before he leaves for Christmas.' This time Barry didn't react at all, so she reached out and touched his elbow, letting her voice grow softer. 'What's wrong?'

He shook loose. 'Nothing,' he said. 'I'm fine.' And then he started walking faster again, leaving Flora to watch the back of his head bob farther away in silence.

It was like that for the rest of the evening, too, Barry stoic, moodier than Flora had been on even the worst nights in his absence, and the rest of the family trying unsuccessfully to draw him out of it; after a heavy, wordless dinner, he slunk off upstairs.

'He's probably just tired,' said George, hopefully, and when Flora went to bed later she found the lights in their room off and her brother unresponsive, so she assumed their father was right. The next morning, though, it was the same again, Barry disappearing upstairs as soon as breakfast was finished, and re-emerging a few hours later only to shout a gruff goodbye as he hurried out the front door.

Outside he started down the road, and out of force of habit found himself cutting off along the path to the Stùc. After following that for a while, he cut off along an even vaguer trail – a burn, really, after the recent weeks of rainfall – and into a shallow gully. There was a faint drizzle in the air, a fine spray rolling around him, and he sank further into his anorak as he trudged further from the path. A rat scurried past his feet.

Eventually, the right wall of the gully levelled out enough that he could hike up it to a pair of boulders on a small rise, where he looked around briefly to make sure he was alone and out of sight from anyone walking past, and then crouched down and shimmied backwards into the cleft between the rocks. For several minutes he sat there not moving, feeling the damp seep into his trousers and watching a tiny patch of blue-grey sea between the hills in front of him, until he could no longer bear it any more and unzipped his coat to retrieve some cigarettes and a lighter.

He'd tried to follow Mr Lewis's advice about avoiding trouble at the mainland school, but from his very first night he'd somehow managed to bungle it. As soon as George had left after dinner, Barry's bunkmate, an older boy named Tam, had looked him up and down. 'Djou smoke?' he asked, and just as Mr Lewis had told him to, Barry uttered a decisive no; assured the other boy that he'd never even tried.

'Why not?' asked Tam, making a face. 'Are you a saddo or something?'

Barry faltered. 'I… No. They're just bad for you. My teacher told me so.'

'Is that a fact?' Tam was smirking, now, though at what Barry couldn't tell. 'Well, fuck me. Thanks for the tip.'

'You're welcome,' said Barry, still uneasy.

Tam just laughed and swaggered out the door, leaving Barry to sit there on his own for an hour before shutting off the lights and going to bed early. And then, in the playground during lunch the next day, he found himself surrounded.

'This is him,' explained Tam, to a wall of other boys. 'The new school nurse.' The white light from the overcast sky brought out the threatening lines in their faces. Barry noticed a gold stud glinting in one of their ears.

'Anyway, Baz,' said Tam, turning to face him. 'Since you're new, we thought we'd get you a wee welcome gift.' He reached into his pocket and took out the damp, contorted butt of a cigarette. 'Thought maybe since you've never smoked before you'd want to try one.' He held the butt forward. 'Go on, big man. Take a drag.'

Barry stared at him. 'No, thank you,' he said, his voice quavering. 'I… I'm not in the mood.'

There was a roar of laughter from the other boys. 'Not in the mood!' said Tam, his eyebrows shooting up. '*Not in the mood!* Well that's a shame, see, because I've brought it just for you and my feelings'll be hurt if you don't take it.' He took a step closer. 'Don't you know it's rude to refuse a gift?'

Barry edged backwards. His body felt like a shell, and he a tiny, diminishing light inside. Not because of Tam, or not entirely, anyway, but because of all the other indignities of the past few days: Bella's angry rejection, and his parents' subsequent recriminations, and his stupid tiff with Flora. He didn't know what he'd done to deserve any of it, really, but especially not this. The predatory speed with which Tam had turned on him seemed entirely unprovoked. Instinctively he hugged his arms around his body as he continued to inch away – but by now the throng had seen enough, and pounced, pinning him to the ground. Tam knelt down beside him.

'We were only trying to be friendly,' he said, reaching forward and prying Barry's jaw open with a look of horrifying concentration on his face, and shoving the cigarette butt inside. The taste of mildew and smoky ash filled Barry's mouth. 'Now swallow it.'

Barry's eyes bulged; he tried not to wretch.

'I said fucking swallow it!'

So Barry did as he was told, a few tears finally working their way down the sides of his face, the wet streaks on his skin prickling in the breeze. The filter stuck in his throat on its way down, and as he stuck out his tongue to prove the butt was gone, he felt a gagging wave of nausea that he desperately gulped back. With a satisfied nod, Tam released him and stood up, the other boys following suit, and finally, as Barry tried to sit up, his nausea surged again – and this time he couldn't hold it. Leaning quickly to one side he threw up onto the asphalt, a few drops of bile splattering on his hand as the cigarette butt bounced once and came to a rest at the edge of the puddle. Still heaving, he wiped his mouth against his sleeve.

'Dearie me,' said Tam, shaking his head. 'It looks like you were right, Barry – they really are bad for you.' And then he and the rest of his cronies were walking away laughing.

Once they were gone, Barry struggled to his feet. Recalling Mr Lewis's brief lesson on bullying he ran to the first teacher he could find, a short woman with a grey bun and half-moon spectacles, who looked as if she'd stand for no nonsense. When she took him to the headmaster's office, though, Tam was already waiting outside, and when Barry pointed at him and tried to explain what had happened, the other boy just innocently shook his head.

'It's not true, Miss. I never touched him. We were trying to start a game of tig and he kicked me and ran away.' He rolled up his trouser leg to reveal a smug, purple bruise.

'No,' mewled Barry, but the teacher was already nodding, dismissing Tam and ushering Barry into the office, where she explained the situation to the headmaster without Barry getting a word in. The man leaned back in his chair with an acid smile on his face. 'I know you're new, young man, so I'll let you off this time. But we don't tolerate troublemakers here at St Fillan's – one more incident like this and I'll be calling your parents.'

Barry nodded, dazed, and left the office.

If it had been a simple case of bullying, perhaps things would have been different; perhaps Barry would have found the strength to resist the abuse, and the pranks, and the braying taunts to try telling on them again. But having to return to the room he shared with Tam each evening, and lie awake with the slats of the other boy's bunk bulging ominously above him: it broke him down. He lived in constant dread of whatever new cruelty might be in store; his nerves were worn into brittle, twisted strands. It was only a few more weeks before he asked the question from the bottom bunk one night, his voice quiet but with every ounce of will behind making it sound firm.

'Can I join your gang?' he asked. It was self-preservation, nothing more.

In the darkness he heard Tam shift above him, and for a brief, sad moment, he thought of Flora in their bunks at home. 'Can you *what*?'

'I want to join your gang,' he repeated. 'What do I have to do?' What else could he do? If he told his parents they'd just talk to the headmaster, who'd tell them about the bruise on Tam's leg and Barry's alleged part in it – and what if he couldn't convince them that it was a lie? He could imagine his mother's voice cracking with disappointment: *Barry McCloud! Starting fights! You ought to know better!* At least this way he could leave his family out of it.

Tam responded to Barry's request enthusiastically, no doubt for the fresh opportunities for torment it presented – but if he'd been expecting Barry's resolve to crumble he wound up proven wrong. Whatever obstacles and initiations they threw in his way – stealing other kids' belongings, vandalizing the boys' toilets, spying in the girls' – Barry did it all with grim determination, and emerged still asking flatly to be admitted to the fold.

Sitting in his crook on the hillside now, the damp beginning to soak through his coat, he finally put a cigarette between his lips and lit it. The smoke warmed him instantly.

The cigarettes had been another of Tam's mandated misdemeanours, but one Barry assumed would be just another front – something he'd do at school and then easily put aside during visits home. He hadn't even packed any cigarettes for the break. By the end of the short train ride to Mallaig, though, the cravings had already sunk their claws in, and after he'd greeted his dad at the train station he made up some excuse about wanting a snack and ran off to the Co-op on the high street. He must have seemed particularly pathetic, out of breath and tears welling, because the cashier didn't even ask for proof of age – just shook her head and handed them over, whispering to her next customer as he hurried out the door. A few minutes later, crouching behind a boat ramp and hidden from the road, he'd desperately sucked in the nicotine, hands shaking, and then rummaged through his bag for deodorant and chewing gum to mask the smell. That much, at least, he'd learnt to do at school.

'Where did you get to for so long?' George had asked, when Barry finally jogged up beside him at the jetty. 'I was beginning to think you'd hopped a train back!' He'd smiled and patted his son on the shoulder, and Barry's heart had crumpled.

The rain and wind were picking up now, and even in his little shelter between the rocks Barry was struggling to keep his cigarette lit. Sighing, he stubbed it out on the ground beside him.

His victory, if that was the right word, had come on Halloween. The students had spent all day making costumes in class, and at night began roaming up and down the corridors, knocking on teachers' doors and doing tricks in exchange for sweets. When Barry left his room to join the fun, in the ghost outfit he'd so carefully prepared, Tam – dressed as a vampire – yanked him aside and led them instead to the playground, beneath the windows of the darkened staffroom. He handed Barry a rock.

'Throw this through the window,' he said, 'and you're in.'

Barry weighed the rock in his hand, not flinching even slightly at the command. The pangs of conscience he'd felt during Tam's first few challenges had grown easier and easier to ignore, even as the challenges themselves had grown more transgressive. It wasn't that Barry was any less repulsed by the things he found himself agreeing to; he was simply in too deep. What would be the point in refusing now, when his reward – his relief – was so tantalizingly close? He paused for only a few seconds before he closed his eyes and hefted the rock into the air.

'Fucking hell!' hissed Tam, as the window shattered above them, and then they ran, stopping only when they'd reached the junior common room and slipped into the crowd of other ghouls. 'You're a mad cunt, McCloud,' Tam had said, it seemed with a glimmer of respect creeping into his voice. 'I didn't think you had it in you.' For the first time in weeks, Barry fell asleep easily that night.

He stood up from his nook now and kicked some dirt over the butt of his cigarette, starting on some chewing gum as he made his way back to the path and on towards the beach.

Since Halloween he and Tam had settled into an uneasy truce. The situation had improved, he had no doubt: he was sleeping better and finding it easier to concentrate on his homework, and was even being spared from rule-breaking as often, with the impetus to prove himself removed. Every now and then, though, his old terror would return, Tam's mischievous smirk producing some Pavlovian response and convincing Barry that the gang was about to turn on him once more. He doubted he would ever shake that feeling completely.

When he reached the shore at the end of the path he stopped and stared out across the retreating tide, towards the Stùc. He avoided looking at Bella's house, farther back on the islet and fainter in the mist. He'd often thought about her over the past few months, but his fantasies had mostly been replaced by his humiliating memory of that last night, new details returning to him each time he recalled it: the disgust on her face, the feeling of her coat slipping through his fingers. Instead, lips numbing, he focused on the schoolhouse now, where a few wisps of smoke were escaping from the chimney. He pictured Mr Lewis inside, packing by himself. Glancing out of the window every now and then, maybe, and wondering whether Barry would show up.

He wished he could. Wished he could run over the bridge and tell Mr Lewis everything, and turn to the man for help and comfort as he'd done so many times before: the rats, and Trevor's birth, and Flora's too, not to mention the countless bad dreams that his parents – too busy dealing with breakfasts for guests – had failed to address. Even that night with Bella, Mr Lewis had been the only one to look concerned instead of furious. But that was precisely why Barry couldn't confess to him – not after the man had tried so hard to prepare him for St Fillan's, after he'd explicitly warned Barry against everything that he'd gone and done anyway. Barry couldn't bear admitting he'd been such a failure.

Finally, spitting a tarry glob into the sand, he turned and started home. At least, he thought, he had a few weeks away from Tam.

6

Barry was due to return to St Fillan's a week after Hogmanay, and though no one in the house would admit it, they were counting down the days. His moodiness from that first evening had lasted his entire visit, and though there had been a few signs of the old Barry reappearing – he'd gone for a walk with Flora and his father one morning, and spent the whole of Christmas Day downstairs – those victories, so hard-earned, had never seemed to stick. Their decision to stay on the island that year seemed more foolish with each passing day.

Worse, it was a bitter winter, the wind monstrous and the rain icy. When the sky finally flickered to life late each morning, fuzzy blotches of frost bloomed across the meadows, and the water in the island's inlets lay frozen and opaque. And around ten on Barry's last morning at home, after Trevor and Flora had already left for their first day back at school, a brutal storm descended – a diluvial howl of rain, sleet and gales, rattling the guesthouse windows so violently that Maureen, her face pressed against one to peer outside, wondered if the glass might break.

'It's a bloody monsoon out there!' she said, turning to where George sat at the kitchen table, the previous day's paper in front of him. She had to shout to be heard over the rain's incessant drone. 'I'm not sure you'll find much left of your veggie patch in the morning.'

He frowned. 'Aye, it does sound nasty.' He held up the paper, still open at his not quite finished crossword, and tapped the page with the back of his hand. 'They didn't mention anything like it in the forecast – just said rain and a bit of wind.'

She snorted. 'The Met Office's usual mastery of understatement.'

'I suppose this means we won't be seeing the ferry today,' said George. 'Is there anything we're running short on?'

Maureen shook her head, already returning to her vigil at the window.

The storm blew on all morning, the noise outside not relenting until they sat down with Barry for lunch.

'Maybe you should go get them,' said Maureen, as she cleared the plates, looking first to the window and then to George. 'Now that it's died down a bit.'

'Oh, don't be silly Reenie.' He dabbed at his mouth with his napkin. 'I'm sure if Henry thinks they need to come home early, he'll bring them back himself.'

Maureen had been trying to tell herself the same thing, but hearing it from her husband didn't make it any more convincing; it seemed just as likely that Mr Lewis was waiting for them. They couldn't call to find out, either, because the school didn't have a phone. Nowhere on the island did, except the guesthouse, which had two: a private one for the business, and one in the pub for everyone else. Even after the telecom company had appeared in the fifties, when the mainland economy was booming while the island's withered, and installed an exchange on Fìor big enough to accommodate every household, no one had really seen the point. The only people most of the islanders ever talked to were a few minutes' walk away, and the guesthouse phone was always there if anyone needed to call the mainland. It had added an extra poignancy for George and Maureen to the recent years of emigration from the island – they always knew when someone was considering a move, from the sudden hours they'd start spending in the pub.

Maureen cleared her throat. 'George,' she said. 'We don't know what Henry might be thinking, and it's not fair to force the decision on him anyway. I want you to go over there and collect them. Who knows how bad it might get again later?'

'But Reenie—'

'I'll go,' said Barry.

Maureen swivelled on her chair. 'Absolutely not. I don't want another of you out in this.'

'I'll be fine, Mum,' he said, pushing back from the table. 'It's died down, you said so yourself. And I haven't seen Mr Lewis the whole time I've been home. If I don't go now I won't have another chance.'

George nodded earnestly. 'Yes, why not let Barry go?'

Maureen clenched her jaw and turned back to him. 'Stop it, George.'

'What? He's young and spry – he'll probably get over there faster than me anyway.'

'Yeah,' said Barry, already heading for the door. 'I can be there and back in less than an hour. Honest.'

Maureen felt her shoulders tense. 'Fine,' she said. 'But get going. The sooner you're all back here the better.' She glared at George as Barry left the room; he just shrugged, and stood up to start the dishes.

A few minutes after four, Maureen was back at the kitchen window, the remains of an anxious afternoon snack strewn behind her on the table. By two o'clock, an hour since Barry had left, there had still been no sign of him; by three, darkness had started to fall. And now, past even the normal time when Flora and Trevor should have been home, the sky was black and all three of them were missing. Outside, the hail had intensified, hammering against the window in marble-sized chunks. There was a lone flash, somewhere far over the sea, and a single, echoing thunderclap. Every time the wind gusted, Maureen could hear the walls creak.

Suddenly she slammed her palm against the edge of the sink and sent a bar of soap flying towards the drain, where it came to rest beside a piece of decomposing lettuce. Taking a deep breath and trying to hold onto some composure, she left the room and walked towards the lounge. George, sitting in his armchair reading, looked up as she entered.

'Still no sign?'

'Of course there's still no bloody sign!' she snapped. 'Look at it out there!' She threw up her arm towards the window, stalking towards it. 'Look at it!'

Quietly, he closed his book.

'It's after four, George. They should be back by now. They should have been back hours ago.'

He stood up and joined her by the window. 'Henry never would have let them out in this, Reenie. They're fine. He's just keeping them there with him 'til it's safe.' He tried to put a hand on her shoulder, but she wriggled loose.

'And what about Barry? We don't even know if he made it there in the first place. Anything could have happened to him.'

George hesitated, wetting the inside of his mouth. 'It was still calm when he left. I'm sure he got there safely.' He tilted his head in sympathy. 'It's not as if he's some clueless tourist, Reenie. He knows how to handle himself out there.'

'He's only twelve, George! He doesn't know anything!' Her voice was shaking. 'You should have gone yourself. You know you should have.'

He pursed his lips. 'You're right,' he said. 'I should have. I just – it looked like it was clearing up, and it was so nice to see him enthusiastic about something…' He reached for her shoulder again, more firmly this time, and pulled her around to look at him. 'I'm sorry. I am.'

'Well,' she muttered. 'Apologies aren't what we need right now, are they?'

He gave her a withering look. 'You don't still expect me to go over there, do you? Even if I get across in one piece, then what am I supposed to do? It's far too dangerous for any of them to be out in it.'

'I just need to know if he's okay, George. And as you very astutely pointed out, this is all your bloody fault – the least you can do is get out there and fix it.'

'Reenie…' They stared at each other for a few seconds. 'Fine,' he said, at last, shaking his head. 'I'll go now.'

Bundling up against the weather took another fifteen minutes, though, and it was twenty more again before he reached the path to the Stùc, unable to even see his feet without the torch pointed straight at them. He tramped down to the beach, coughing and wiping water from his face, and at last made it to the messy slop of sand almost forty-five minutes after leaving the house. He stopped to catch his breath, and shone his light towards the bridge.

It wasn't there.

He swung the torch from side to side, certain he must be looking in the wrong place, and took a few panicked steps forwards. Rain was pooling in his philtrum, forming thick clumps in his eyelashes and trickling down the back of his neck – and then, finally, he spotted it. In the wind it had been wrenched free of its steps to the main island, and now, the boardwalk half-ripped away, it was writhing in the swell like some giant, dying insect – still tethered, just, to its foundation on the Stùc.

For several minutes – he wasn't sure quite how long – he simply stood there staring, the beam from his flashlight still pointed straight ahead, as he struggled to think of some other way to get across. He tried not to wonder what had become of Barry. The boy must have made it over safely, he told himself; after all, if the bridge had been gone already when he reached the shore, he would have turned around and come home. And what were the chances it could have broken in those short moments that Barry was crossing? Tiny, surely.

Then again, he thought, what if Barry *had* made it across, and the bridge had given way as all three of them were crossing back?

Teeth chattering, he snapped himself out of it. The chances of that were also tiny, he told himself – and standing here with the wind peeling his skin off wasn't going to make things any different. Starting for the path again, he pulled his hat tighter around his face and wondered how he was going to explain all this to Reenie.

In the end, he opted for straightforward. 'The bridge is gone,' he said, as he closed the front door behind him.

'Gone?' she repeated, staring at him from beyond the vestibule. 'What do you mean, gone?'

'I mean it's gone,' he said. 'Not there. Blown away.' He tossed his soaking hat to the ground.

'My God.' Her face had turned grey. 'So what are we going to do?'

He grimaced, shaking the water from his sleeves. 'Nothing.'

'Nothing! How can we do nothing?'

He pulled off one boot, and with the other still on his foot he looked up at her, lopsided. 'How can we do *anything*, Reenie?

The bridge is gone. We're stuck here. We have to wait 'til it dies down.'

There was a crackle of hail against the transom, as if to emphasize the point, and Maureen, groaning, turned and left George standing by the door.

At first she returned to her pacing by the sitting room window, dreaming up worst-case scenarios and listening to George skulk around upstairs before he eventually retreated to the pub. After an hour of that, desperate for some distraction, she stomped to the kitchen, glaring at the light around the pub door as she passed it, and began to cook – anything she could think of, just stirring and chopping and frying and baking in a helpless, mechanical frenzy. Before long, two different soups simmered on the stove, and the flapjacks cooling on the table filled the whole ground floor with the smell of oats and toffee. She stood in the centre of the room for a few moments, surveying it all, her gaze finally coming to rest on the door to the hallway. George still hadn't emerged from hiding.

Against her better judgement, she started towards the pub.

'I'm just here to get a drink,' she said, as she barged in.

He nodded at the empty glasses beside him. 'Why do you think I've been here all night?'

She didn't answer – just bustled behind the bar, where she poured a liberal slug of gin into a tumbler and, after a few seconds scanning the bottles arranged on the shelf, a splash of vermouth. During their courtship she'd hated martinis but had choked them down to appear sophisticated; over time they'd become her nip of choice. She turned and looked beneath the counter. 'Where are the olives?'

'We're out,' he said, still frowning at his crossword. 'I wasn't going to reorder 'til we opened.'

Letting out an irritated sigh, she set the tumbler down on the bar and stirred it with her finger.

'Olives!' George exclaimed. He scribbled something on the crossword. '*Oil supplier turned evil in the bones once.*'

Rolling her eyes, she asked him how he could be doing a crossword at a time like this; he crossed out the successfully cracked clue and looked up, raising an eyebrow. 'How can you be cooking?'

She took a sip of her drink and swished it around her mouth for a few moments before swallowing. 'Fair enough.' She sighed. 'I'm sorry. I know you're upset too.' She slipped out from behind the bar and took a seat next to him. 'I'm just at my wit's end.'

He put down his paper and shuffled sideways on his stool to put an arm around her. 'I know, Reenie. I am too.' He pulled her closer. 'But I'm sure they're fine.'

They sat like that for some time, eyes closed and saying nothing, beating back the day's tension. He stroked her hair; she squeezed his knee. The windows kept on crackling in the rain. Finally, she lifted her head slightly and turned to stare at him for what felt like the fiftieth time that day – and then, to her surprise, they kissed. Not the usual goodnight kiss they exchanged in the evenings, or even the more protracted sort they sometimes allowed themselves on Hogmanay. Not even the sort they shared on the rare occasions when they had sex, which these days felt largely ceremonial. No, this was something else, borne of the high emotions of the past few hours; more like the closer, deeper-felt kisses of their earliest years. It seemed almost alien to her after so long, the pressing and prodding of his stubble against her chin, and his tongue swishing over hers. To her embarrassment, she found herself reminded of her last trip to the dentist.

Yet it was comforting, too, she realized, as her hand found his. It must have been years since they'd sought each other out like this, and much longer still since those winter mornings when they would lie in bed for hours, giggling as George's parents clomped around pointedly outside the door. That such fondness had reappeared, suddenly, seemed like proof that they had made at least one good decision in the past, no matter what had happened since or might today – and it was that thought, at last, that forced out Maureen's memories of the dentist, and her visions of the bridge and of her children, and pushed her focus instead towards the increasingly natural feeling of kissing her husband, and their gradual undressing, and their slow, silent sinking to the pub's cool floor.

It was later, perhaps another hour or two, when the phone began to ring, and by then Maureen was back in the kitchen, spooning cooled soup into storage tubs. She looked up at the sound, instinctively fearing the worst – even as, dropping her ladle and running to answer, she struggled to think of any way the call could be about the children.

'Maureen?' The voice on the line was faint. 'It's Henry Lewis.'

'Henry!' She gripped the handset tighter. Had they been airlifted to the mainland, somehow? In this weather? 'How are you calling? Where are you?'

'I'm at Bella's,' the tinny voice replied. 'I should have known she'd keep a working phone year round.'

Maureen shut her eyes tight. 'Is everyone okay? Is Barry with you?'

Down the hall, George emerged from the pub.

'Everyone's fine,' said Mr Lewis, hesitant. 'Barry's here.'

She felt her knees go weak. 'Thank God.'

'I'm worried about him, though.' Lowering his voice, he explained what had happened that afternoon: how Barry had appeared at the school's door, babbling about the bridge coming apart behind him;

how he'd seemed to relax as the hours passed, chatting to Mr Lewis while Flora and Trevor worked at their desks; how Trevor had told Barry, over dinner, how nice it was to see him happy again. But then, too, how they'd moved to the sofa to read aloud together; how the generator had died, plunging them into darkness; how, as Mr Lewis had bundled them up and taken them instead to Bella's empty house, Barry had lagged behind, his good mood just as suddenly evaporating. 'And then he just broke down, Maureen.' A sheepish pause. 'Bella and I have been seeing each other, and when he realized he started screaming at me. Completely lost the plot. Said I'd betrayed him, or something like that.' His voice dropped even further. 'I couldn't really follow him, to be honest – it was all very emotional and incoherent and teenagerish. Goodness knows what must have been going on at St Fillan's the past few months.'

Maureen wrapped her cardigan more tightly around her. 'He hasn't been himself,' she murmured.

'Anyway,' Mr Lewis said. 'I've put him to bed, but maybe we should sit him down tomorrow and find out what's bothering him.'

Maureen grimaced, predicting – correctly, it would turn out – that they'd get no further than the few attempts she'd already made; that Barry would simply clam up and tell them he liked St Fillan's fine. But out loud she told Mr Lewis it was a good idea, and then thanked him before finally hanging up. She turned to George, who had moved up beside her, and smiled. 'They're okay,' she said. 'Barry's okay.'

He smiled back, and hugged her.

On the Stùc, however, Barry was not okay; he had just listened to Mr Lewis's side of the whole conversation, crouched outside the box room where Bella kept her upstairs telephone, and was seething. He'd already been seething, in fact, when he'd heard Mr Lewis begin to talk and had crept out of bed. Had already been seething, even, when Mr Lewis had dragged him to bed in the first place and wrestled him under the covers, pleading with him to calm down and patiently enduring Barry's alternating silence and profanity.

But now he could barely think straight for his fury, not only at Mr Lewis's blithe papering over of his tryst with Bella, but at how cannily he'd summarized the day. Barry *had* relaxed that afternoon, *had* found being back with his old teacher soothing, infinitely more so than his past weeks at home; had even begun to contemplate confiding in Mr Lewis after all. And it was true, too, that Barry's mood had soured again as soon as the man produced his spare key for Bella's front door. It simply hadn't squared with Barry's social map of the island, no matter how he'd tried to convince himself there was some more innocent explanation. And when they stepped into her entryway – into the house he'd so long dreamt of – and immediately Barry had spotted one of Mr Lewis's scarves hanging on the coat rack, well, that was it. He'd exploded, unable to believe the man could even fathom pursuing Bella when Barry had already made his own feelings so spectacularly clear. Had let months of frustration pour out against his teacher while his siblings edged backwards, agog.

And though years later he would remember this night and be forced to admit that Mr Lewis was right to call Barry's reaction emotional and incoherent and teenagerish, hearing it described that way, with his wounds so fresh, only enraged him further. So when Mr Lewis put down the phone and stood up, Barry turned and ran, not stopping for even a second when the man entered the hallway behind him and called for him to wait. He leapt down the stairs two at a time, sprinting through the kitchen and into Bella's studio, and hurried to the corner of the room and through a small back door into the orchard. Ran until he reached his old hiding spot beneath one of the trees, then looked back towards the windows to see the light click on and Mr Lewis's mouth moving as he called out Barry's name. Only then did he let his head fall back against the tree, defeated. Mr Lewis would catch him soon enough and march him back upstairs, he knew that, and resisting would only get him wetter.

But he also knew he wouldn't budge, wouldn't tell the man any more than he'd told his parents, no matter how earnest a chat he tried to sit him down for. He wouldn't grant that fucking traitor one more piece of his trust. And he told himself, too – screamed it in his head – that he was finished with the island. That he wouldn't come back, couldn't, not permanently, not after this and his past few miserable weeks at home. Because what else was left for him now, really? What would he *do* here, other than face his painful memories daily?

He asked himself that question again as Mr Lewis finally found him, teeth chattering beneath the tree, and led him back inside. Asked it again as he peeled off his sodden clothes, and again as he lay in Bella's guest bed, listening to the softening patter of rain against the windows and watching the shadows make patterns on the ceiling. Each time he found himself at a loss for an answer – and his last thoughts before he fell asleep, sometime past midnight, were of his family growing old without him, and all the places he could live instead, and a desperate plan to escape as soon as possible.

1995

7

MAY, AND THE START of another tourist season. As if in preparation, the weather had been warm and dry that spring, and an unusually large flock of puffins had returned, swooping overhead from nest to sea and back, their beaks luminous even silhouetted against the sky. And though it was probably mere fancy, it sounded to the few remaining islanders – George and Maureen, and Flora, and Bella and no one else – as if there were an extra liveliness to the puffins' cries this year, a feeling of triumph at the reclamation of their home.

Flora had been back on the island for almost a year now, after finishing her final term at St Fillan's. In the face of so many other islanders departing, her homecoming had felt like a milestone, of sorts – especially since Barry had never returned – but it had passed without much fanfare, at least on her part: she simply stepped from the ferry that afternoon with a reserved smile, no more than if this were just another visit. Each summer since she'd left for St Fillan's, she'd hauled her bulging trunk home with her father; each summer her spirits had leapt at the first glimpse of the village; and each summer she'd practically skipped around her room the morning after her arrival, replacing belongings in the gaps on her shelves with a haphazard kind of joy.

But it was precisely during her unpacking this time when she'd had the first, hazy realization that she wouldn't be disappearing again in August. That she had no idea, actually, when she might ever disappear anywhere again. And suddenly her room felt as if it were shrinking around her, the worn pink beanbag she'd picked out for her birthday years ago creeping ominously in her direction, the bunk beds she'd once shared with Barry towering in the corner. Dropping the jumper she was holding, she hurried downstairs to see if her mother needed help in the kitchen.

After breakfast the feeling weakened, thankfully, and once she was thrown into her duties at the guesthouse it seemed to pass altogether, tidied up or forgotten in the bustle of the everyday. Occasionally she even enjoyed being back, taking a nostalgic pleasure in her daily chores, pouring pints with the same precision as her father, or fluffing the guest room pillows with the ferocity she'd always seen in her mother. When the season finished that first summer she'd started to discover the other perks of adult life on the island, too. Compared to her final year at St Fillan's, a whirlwind of straight As and prefecture and the hockey squad and art club, the calm of the off-season was luxurious. She slept late and spent as many hours as she liked hunched over her sketchbook, and took lazy walks almost every afternoon – either around the hills with her father or on her own, to the Stùc and a visit with Bella.

Bella's coolness following Barry's going-away party had given way a year or so later to after-school art lessons, arranged by Mr Lewis – much to Flora's surprise. (Until then, she had remained convinced that the woman hated her just as much as Barry still seemed to.) Though initially they met for just an hour every Wednesday, Bella had quickly warmed to her and their time expanded to two hours twice a week; by the time Flora left for St Fillan's the art lessons were more like joint studio sessions, the two of them chatting while they painted and Bella offering pointers only occasionally, if at all. While Flora was away at school, or Bella on the mainland for the winter, they kept up a healthy correspondence, Flora sending photographs of her recent work and Bella replying with her critique – and before long other details also began to seep into their letters: worries about exams and other teenage dramas from Flora, and news of professional success and a deepening love with Mr Lewis from Bella (whose eventual wedding, naturally, Flora had attended). And even with Mr Lewis reassigned to Edinburgh nowadays, and his new wife spending less and less time on the island, she and Flora remained fast friends, regularly meeting for afternoon tea whenever Bella was around.

Flora's visits with Bella were the only thing that let her forget her fears about the future, even though she was doing her best to transform the guesthouse into someplace she could picture living in again, long term and contented. She made small changes at first: two of the preset stations on the sitting room radio were quietly retuned; her ratty beanbag was covered tactfully with a throw. But as the months passed, larger differences also started to accumulate, her stacks of old books and drawings packed away in a closet, a small CD player purchased for her bedside table, and her home improvements encroaching beyond the confines of her bedroom. She hung a few of her pictures in the hallway, and put her desk lamp from St Fillan's on the downstairs telephone table, and after Christmas – spent on the island, as had become their custom since Barry left for St Fillan's, despite that year's disasters – she arranged for a subscription to the *Guardian*, a hipper newspaper to supplement her father's stodgy *Scotsman*. (They tried one of its crosswords one night, but George couldn't get his head around the different style of the other paper's clues.)

The biggest change – the biggest drama – came at the start of spring, when Flora suggested they replace the bunk beds. To her the issue seemed relatively innocuous, and so she broached it flippantly over breakfast one day: *Why don't we finally chuck the bunks, eh?* But her parents were so aggrieved by the suggestion, her mother in particular, that it took weeks of smoothing things over before she could bring it up again. Even then she'd had to propose a compromise: detaching the top bunk and moving it to one of the single rooms upstairs. She sold the idea mainly as an extra bed to offer when the season started – *but of course*, she'd added, though she found it somewhat ridiculous, *whenever Barry wants to come back we can always move it down again*. As if he ever would; it had been almost two years since they'd even *heard* from him and three since he'd last visited – and five, already, since he'd left for the job on the oil rig. Before that he'd shown no desire to spend any more time on the island than absolutely necessary, and Flora, at least, had given up on him ever coming back. Frankly, after his alternating apathy and mean-spiritedness during his last few years at home, she didn't particularly want him to, and couldn't quite understand why her parents did. Only when Trevor returned for the Easter holidays and was livid to find his brother's bed moved – *you can't just go around changing things like that!* – did she wonder if perhaps she'd been a little heartless.

In any case, as the season started again for her first full summer back home, her new life on the island – or rather, her old life, made over – had started to take shape. And while that suffocating feeling of the first few days still found her from time to time, she ignored it as best she could. Because she couldn't leave now, she knew that. Couldn't even consider it. Her parents were both approaching sixty, and it was increasingly difficult for them to run the guesthouse on their own: her mother's hands, riddled with arthritic knots, made her former chores impossible, and her father's legs would ache and swell whenever he manned the bar too long. Hiring help was also out of the question; George laughed the one time Flora suggested it and told her they were barely making a profit as it was. *Besides, what are we supposed to do?* he'd added. *Put a notice in the local paper?*

So with Trevor still at school and Barry long since vanished, the filial duty clearly fell on Flora. She had to be the one to stay, the one to make the sacrifice – and with the same studiousness she'd shown at school she threw herself into it, wilfully forgetting how effusive the careers officer at St Fillan's had been as he'd looked over her exam results, wilfully forgetting the awards her artwork had won at local competitions in Fort William, and the certificates of achievement now packed away in her bedroom closet. Wilfully forgetting, at least for the time being, her thoughts of anything else.

The season's first week felt brisk, as it always did. Flora was constantly rushing from the guest rooms to the kitchen, from the laundry to the pub, from the house to the jetty, even with only four guests out of a possible eight, and at night she would slump into bed and exhale deeply, every muscle like lead, staring at the ceiling for half an hour until the day's buzz subsided and she gradually fell asleep.

But as it always did, too, that perpetual weariness soon began to feel normal, and by the end of the second week it no longer even felt like weariness. Instead it became just another layer in her life's daily rhythm, and one she could easily gloss over while she focused on the things she found more pleasant. In particular she started to enjoy her shifts in the pub, and more and more found herself unwinding there as the evening tapered away, doodling absent-minded caricatures of customers on her waiter's pad, or fiddling with new cocktail recipes, or simply listening, moony and enchanted, to the stories people told about life elsewhere.

She was even amused by the clumsy flirting she drew from middle-aged husbands on vacation with their wives, and flattered on the few occasions when it happened with the men closer to her age – usually campers who wanted a nightcap before bundling up for the evening. But she was never tempted to reciprocate; such encounters were only a game, she firmly told herself, another harmless way to pass the time. Any sign of real attraction would only create another shortcoming that the island couldn't possibly resolve.

And then, in August, he appeared.

It was a golden summer evening, the sun well above the horizon even at seven o'clock, and casting long, inviting shadows as the week's guests, two couples, looked over their menus. When he walked in she was mixing aperitifs at the bar, and she looked up, startled, at the creak of the door; her mother had checked him in that morning and he'd been out walking all day, so this was the first time she'd set eyes on him.

He seemed an unusual sort to be staying, she thought, as he surveyed the room's tables and made his way to one by the window. His crisp, cropped hair, for a start, and his equally crisp shirt – he looked more like a businessman than the salt-of-the-earth vacationers who usually took rooms. He was younger, too, the sort of age when most visitors would rough it in tents; she wondered what had inspired him to stay in a stuffy old B&B like this. Then again, she mused, maybe the crisp shirt answered that question.

'Nice night,' she said, walking over to him with a menu. He turned from the window and looked at her, dumbstruck, as if he'd forgotten for a moment that he was sitting in a pub. She straightened her shirt in the awkward silence. 'Can I get you something?'

'Um, yes,' he said, seeming to snap out of his trance. 'I'll have a pint.'

'Of…?'

This flummoxed him again. 'I don't know. Something local. Some good Scottish beer.'

With a cynical laugh she told him she'd see what she could do, and returned to the bar. She was mostly quiet as she went about the rest of the evening, though, disconcerted by the way he'd stared at her so intently, and delivering his food with a minimum of small talk. He lingered, though, 'til long past eight, the other customers gone and the kitchen closed for the night, and as she returned to take his last, empty glass, he did it again: gave her that searching look. Smiled.

'That was delicious,' he said.

She muttered thanks and hurried back to the bar. To her dismay, he followed.

'I'm Michael,' he said, taking a seat on one of the stools. The sun had dropped below the hills, finally, but the sky in the windows behind him was still smeared with pastel pinks and blues. She let out a small, resigned sigh.

'Flora.'

There wasn't any difference, she tried to reassure herself, between him and the other young men who usually took an interest in her. If anything he had less appeal: he lacked the athletic physique of the hikers and the ruggedness of the campers, and on careful scrutiny wasn't any more than moderately attractive, his hairline in the first stages of receding and his nose a little crooked. And yet there was still that something, tightening up her stomach. A feeling normally not there.

She picked up a fresh pint glass and tipped it towards him; he nodded and asked for another of whatever he'd had with dinner, and she nodded back, glad to have something else to focus on. As she poured the beer she frowned in concentration, making tiny adjustments to the glass's tilt as a line of thin bubbles began to bloom across the surface. When she was done she pulled it away from the tap and set it down on the counter with a flourish, announcing the price; he smiled and glanced down to where he'd already put the money in front of her. She blushed.

'So,' he said, as she gathered up the coins. 'You live here?'

'Aye,' she replied. 'Always have done.'

He raised an eyebrow. 'You've never left?'

'Don't be daft,' she said. She picked up a cloth from next to the glass-washing sink and began to wipe down the bar. 'I went to boarding school near Fort William.'

He leaned backwards, still perched on his stool. 'But you haven't been to Glasgow, even? Or Edinburgh?'

She shook her head and asked him where he was from. London, he told her; he worked at an investment bank.

'And what brings you here?' She dropped the cloth in the sink and began searching for some other task to fill her hands.

'I'd never been to Scotland,' he shrugged. 'And I had a long weekend so I thought I'd give it a look. I felt like a holiday.'

She laughed. 'You felt like a holiday and you came to *Scotland*?'

He smiled sheepishly. 'I read about this place a few years ago – when you were having your rat problems. I've been curious ever since. Is that strange?'

Flora shook her head. 'Happens all the time. I'm not sure what it is about vermin, but they're a real crowd pleaser.' She motioned for him to look above the bar, where her father had blown up and framed a series of news clippings about the infestation. 'I hope you're not too disappointed that we're rid of them these days.'

'Oh no,' he said. 'It's so beautiful up here. And I can't tell you how amazing it is to get out of the city. This is exactly what I needed.'

She laughed again and told him he was a funny one, and after that she began to feel a little less on guard. He told her about his childhood in a village in southern England – *not too different from this one*, he said, winking, *though we had one or two more people* – and she told him about the history of the guesthouse, and the island, and, unwittingly, about its slow, unwavering decline. He asked her about her time on the mainland, and whether she ever considered going back, and when she hesitated, he quickly changed the subject. Instead he began to talk about what he'd done that day, how he'd walked to the bluffs on the island's north coast and seen another, smaller islet a short way off; how he'd seen buildings on it and yet no obvious way to get across.

'I spent fifteen minutes staring at it,' he told her, 'trying to work it out. There's no bridge, no dock – nothing! I'm still completely baffled.'

'Oh, it's easy,' she said, glad to know the answer. Inexplicably glad.

'Well then,' he said, banging his hand against the counter with a laugh. 'Put me out of my misery!'

Before she could, though, the door to the pub swung open and George strolled in. 'Evening, love,' he said to Flora. 'Evening, Mr… Talbot, is it?'

'Michael,' he said. 'Please.'

'Michael, then.' George leaned sideways against the bar. 'I hate to ask, but a couple of people over walking for the day have managed to miss the last ferry – thought it left at seven, not six.' He rolled his eyes. 'They've been waiting at the jetty for the last two hours wondering what was taking so long.'

Michael nodded. 'Is there no schedule down there?'

'I… Well… No.' He shook his head. 'Anyway, if it wouldn't be too much trouble I was hoping we could move you to another room so that we can squeeze them in for the evening. We'll offer you a discount, of course.'

Waving him off, Michael insisted that wasn't necessary – he'd be happy to move.

'Splendid.' George turned to his daughter. 'And if you don't mind, love, they'd like some supper. Could you whip something up for them?'

She glared at him, about to ask why her mother couldn't do it, but his expression told her not to bother; probably Maureen was already in bed. 'Ach, fine,' she said, glancing wistfully at Michael, who had drained his glass and was standing up.

'You'll have to tell me later,' he said, smiling, and then he and George went to move his things – leaving Flora alone in the pub, her mind racing.

'Sounds like you fancy him,' Bella told her two days later, both of them sipping tea in her studio. Flora was describing what she'd done the day before: how she'd woken early and dragged Michael down to the beach; how she'd waltzed him across the wet sand of the land bridge, barely recognizing herself, leaping and bobbing between puddles and rust-coloured seaweed; and how she'd taken him to the chilly, bluish bareness of the abandoned schoolhouse. In the classroom, the blackboard had been wiped clean into chalky circles, and an old projector sat next to it on the floor, the power cord wrapped around its neck as if it had strangled itself in desperation; several bundles of jotters were stacked in one corner, collecting dust. And though that desolation seemed sad as she explained it to Bella now, in the moment she'd been too distracted by telling Michael all the island's stories, and by the stories about London that he told her in return: the deafening march of City commuters on the Tube each morning; early evening pub crawls home, through grand-sounding places like Threadneedle Street and Bishopsgate and Hoxton; and his frantic report-writing marathons until three in the morning, leaving time only for a few hours' sleep beneath his desk while the sun rose over the Thames. Mostly, though, she loved how captivated he was by the island itself, and how his interest seemed to imbue new value in her life there. How he made it feel like something she could be proud of. After their visit to the school they'd walked back to the guesthouse together, and that evening spent several more hours in the pub – and then Flora had been late getting to the Stùc today, too, because she'd lost track of time while talking to him over lunch.

But sitting in the studio that day, she assured Bella that romance was the last thing on her mind.

'I don't see why you're so opposed to the idea,' she replied, stirring her tea. 'You're nineteen. Occasionally nineteen-year-olds are attracted to the opposite sex.'

'I'm not opposed to the idea, it's just—'

'You're stuck wasting away on this island and don't want to get too attached to anyone?' She leaned back with a smug look.

Bella's bluntness had ceased to surprise Flora, after so many years of being at its mercy; from their earliest art lessons the woman had hardly shied from candour. *Don't be so derivative*, she'd said of an ambitious watercolour of a sunset; *twee*, she'd dismissed a sketch of Trevor sleeping. *Monet might have got away with it, but Monet could do convincing foreshortening*. Such comments had often sent Flora home in tears, but that had only made her try twice as hard the next time. And part of the reason the barbs hurt so much was that most of the time they tapped doubts she'd already had herself.

Bella was wrong about Michael, though, Flora thought now, taking a bite of scone. It wasn't that simple. Yes, okay, she was stuck on the island for the time being, and yes, she was often conscious of that when rebuffing other advances in the pub. But she still doubted she had any serious interest in Michael, because never, not once, not in a year of charming customers or nearly five at school, had she ever, as Bella put it, 'fancied' anyone. And why, of all people, would this stiff English twit have changed that?

St Fillan's had given her plenty of experience with the mechanics of lust, of course, thanks mainly to the irresistible concupiscence of her friend Maisie. On Flora's very first night, after George had left for the ferry, Maisie had somehow engineered a game of spin the bottle with a gaggle of other first years, and those early, curious kisses had developed over the years into countless fumbling embraces after school dances, and stolen moments in dark corners of the playground. In a pleasing sort of symmetry, Maisie had also engineered, after the Leavers' Ball on their last night, a very compromising situation between Flora and a member of the school rugby team. But all of it, the slobbery kissing and the awkward mutual undressing, and the repeated attempts to guide hands beneath waistbands – it ultimately struck her as rather pointless. Even the poor rugby player she sent away after barely twenty minutes.

It wasn't that she failed to grasp the potential for excitement in such things, and certainly she was no more interested in other girls, despite the sweatiest requests and fantasies of the boys' dorm over the years. She simply failed to actually find that excitement with anyone who cared to try. Not since the incident with Tam.

It had started in the dining hall one lunchtime, a few weeks after the start of term: she'd been sitting with her bunkmate, Judith, and Maisie, two tables over from Barry and the rest of his posse, when she'd heard her name and looked over to see several of the boys laughing. *Don't look!* Maisie had hissed, but despite Flora's best, self-conscious efforts to ignore them, she couldn't help but steal a few more glances – and the boys had continued to whoop and holler about something for the rest of lunch. Finally, as they were standing up and leaving, Tam had looked right at her, and winked.

'*Did you see that?*' Maisie whispered, nudging Flora as soon as they were out of earshot. 'Tam McLaren just winked at you!'

Judith leaned in. 'Do you know him, or something?'

Flora assured them she did not.

'It must be because he's friends with your brother,' said Maisie, relishing the speculation. 'He probably put in a good word for you.'

Flora doubted it, and told her friends as much – she and Barry hadn't been on good enough terms to do each other any favours since he'd started at St Fillan's, never mind the screaming match they'd had the night before she'd started, a few weeks earlier. But they wouldn't listen.

'You should definitely ask him out,' said Maisie, nodding. 'I bet he'd well do it.'

'But he's a fifth year!' shrieked Judith. 'Fifth years don't go out with first years!'

'This is different,' said Maisie. 'He knows her brother. Besides,' she narrowed her eyes and added, in a conspiratorial whisper, 'I hear he has a massive willy.'

Looking back, Flora couldn't quite tell if her attraction to Tam had started then or later, or when exactly she'd realized what it was – but somewhere between that wink and her friends' encouragement, it took hold. When she saw him in the corridor or the playground her palms would sweat and tingle, her insides spiralling around themselves; at night she'd lie awake and imagine being with him on her own, replaying the few kisses she'd had on that first night of spin the bottle, with Tam in the place of the spotty, nervous first years – and then imagining doing all the other things Maisie always described in such gleeful, lurid detail. He took her over, engulfed her, and when a few weeks later she was by herself in the library and abruptly he appeared at her side, she couldn't do anything except stare up at him.

'How'd you like to take a wee walk?' he said.

Nodding helplessly, she followed. 'Are we going to your room?' she asked, struggling to keep up as he strode out of the library and ahead of her down the hallway.

He grinned down at her. 'You'll see.'

But suddenly there had been a commotion behind them; a shout, and the frantic clap-clap of footsteps on stone floor.

'Lay one more fucking finger on her, Tam, and you're dead!'

Flora turned and saw Barry running towards them, two of his other friends in pursuit. Tam saw it too, and grabbing Flora by the hand he tried to run himself – but still she couldn't keep up, and Barry was drawing ever nearer.

'Barry!' she'd screamed at him over her shoulder. 'What are you *doing*? Leave us alone!'

Tam skipped to a stop at that and turned around. 'Hear that, Baz? She wants you to leave us alone!' He was still squeezing her hand. 'Looks like she knows what she's doing after all, eh?'

And then it was all over: Barry, still hurtling forward, reached where they were standing, and with one last shout of *You're fucking dead!* he smashed his forehead into Tam's face. The boy's grip on Flora loosened instantly, and as the brawl intensified she slipped away, the cries of approaching teachers echoing behind her.

Furious, she returned to her room, where Judith quickly summoned Maisie and the three of them picked the incident apart. Judith told her that she might still have a chance with Tam; Maisie theorized at some length as to what combinations of protuberance and orifice might have occurred without Barry's interruption. Before long, however, there was a frantic knock at the door, and Barry, blood caked on his shirt, was pushing his way in. Tam had claimed that Flora lured him to the hallway deliberately, Barry told them, for an ambush, and the headmaster was already threatening both of them with expulsion – but Flora would be fine, he assured her, looking pointedly at each of the three girls, if they did exactly what he said. *Just tell them she's been here all afternoon.*

Still angry, Flora had screamed at him to get out; probably she would have stewed all evening had the deputy headmistress not shown up twenty minutes later and asked exactly the same questions Barry said she would. At that she numbly acquiesced, lying stony-faced about where she'd spent the afternoon, her longing for Tam evaporating – too shocked that someone would deceive her like that, unprovoked, to muster any other response. It was little wonder, really, that romance had since failed to interest her.

Out of embarrassment she'd never confided any of this to Bella, however, and now she simply said that Michael wasn't anything special. 'He's clumsy,' she said, 'and he's balding and… he's *gauche*. I'd rather have that enthusiastic groper from the rugby team.'

'Ha!' Bella set her teacup down. '*Gauche*, is he? Glad to see you've spent some time with the thesaurus since you've been home.'

'I—'

'And if he's so unremarkable, why do you seem congenitally unable to stop talking about him?'

Flora set her own cup down, and crossed her arms. 'You asked.'

'Anyway,' said Bella, clearing her throat. 'If you can bear to change the subject I have something else I want to talk about.' She leaned back in her chair. 'I'd like you to have my studio.'

Flora gawked at her.

'I mean, I'm not giving it to you for good – I'll still want to use it from time to time, and one of these days I might even try and sell it again. But now that Henry and I are living in marital bliss there's not much point in me spending six months a year on my own here, not when I have perfectly good studio space in Edinburgh. And meanwhile it seems a shame to have you struggling away in that cramped bedroom of yours. Besides,' she smirked, never passing up a chance to tease Flora about her childhood spying, 'I know how much you enjoy lurking around this place.'

'I don't know what to say,' said Flora, at last.

'Say thank you,' Bella replied. 'And then have some fantastic work to show for it the next time I'm here.'

Flora took a deep breath. 'Okay,' she said. 'Thank you.'

'You're more than welcome.' She looked at her watch and smirked again. 'Now, you'd best be making your way home – the tide'll be in soon and you wouldn't want to get stuck over here on Prince Charming's last night.'

Glancing at her own watch, Flora was surprised at how late it was – so she did as Bella had suggested and hurried out, all the while insisting that Michael had nothing to do with it. Indeed, determined to prove Bella wrong, she told her father she had a splitting headache when she got home and begged off her pub shift for the night, instead spending the evening locked up in her room, not seeking Michael out or even going downstairs for dinner lest she accidentally run into him. Not that she needed to avoid him, she reminded herself, because he *was* awkward and he was a little plain, and whatever she might have thought she felt, it was just a passing madness – a side-effect of spending so much time with him the past few days – and nothing else.

But as Maisie had done with Tam years earlier, Bella's hand in the situation had changed things, somehow, her suggestion of attraction carving relief into Flora's unspoken feelings. Even as she continued with her hopeless rationalizations, she was already hatching a plan for the next morning: she would talk her way out of serving and instead help her mother in the kitchen, so that when it came time to meet the ferry for the morning delivery she could innocently volunteer – and make her way to the jetty as Michael did too. *What a coincidence!* she'd say, pulling on her shoes at the bottom landing while he clomped down behind her with his backpack and gaudy bright-red anorak. They would make the walk together, and then, at the jetty, with the ferry ready to depart, they would look at each other, and she would step forward, and finally she would kiss him, still telling herself, probably, that it meant nothing – and hoping as she did so that it would purge any trace of her infatuation, unload it onto him, and that once the ferry glided away she would never have to think of him again.

Which was how it happened, mostly, up until the final moment. But for some reason, instead of kissing him, all she could bring herself to do was grip him in a hug. 'It's been really nice getting to know you,' she said, pulling away, shouting over the roar of the ferry's engine.

He fished his ticket from his pocket. 'You too, Flora,' he said, and turned to make his way up the gangplank. The bitter smell of petrol rushed to fill the space where he'd been standing, and without even a single, remorseful look behind him, he was gone.

8

Towards the end of that October, George sat working on a crossword in the pub, the house quiet and empty around him: Flora was on the Stùc again (she never seemed to be anywhere else, these days), and Maureen had gone to the mainland to visit Trevor, for his half-term break and birthday.

Flora had suggested that George go along for the trip too, but he'd demurred. Even now, with the season weeks past, the phone still rang frequently with enquiries, which often turned into bookings for the next year – and precisely because Flora was on the Stùc so much recently he felt he couldn't leave the place unmanned. *Somebody* had to worry about the business.

He frowned at the clue in front of him: *Annoyed expressions a cow might make? (5)*.

It wasn't really fair to say the women didn't care about the business, he knew that, but they often seemed to shuffle through their guesthouse duties with little more than a stoic sense of obligation. In spite of all the years they'd given to the place, and all his efforts to make them care, they never seemed that invested in whether the place flopped or flourished. It stung, sometimes.

Or perhaps, alone in the house again, as lately he increasingly was, he simply felt sorry for himself.

Annoyed expressions a cow might make? Was *might make* a clue for an anagram, he wondered? He tried rearranging *a cow* in his head a few times – *ocaw? cwao? awoc?* – but he was too distracted to picture the letters dancing around as he normally did. He looked up at the clock above the bar. Where was Flora, anyway?

When she'd first told them that Bella was giving her free rein of the studio, he hadn't known what to think. Hadn't known what to think, either, that Flora was so thrilled by the idea. Of course, she'd always been fond of her drawing and painting, and she'd always been fascinated with Bella and the old manor, too – but it had caught him quite off guard the way she'd latched onto the place, growing more and more excited with each passing day before the handover, and wasting not a single second when the end of summer arrived and Bella finally left. Flora had skipped back and forth across the isthmus as much as the tide allowed that day, carrying armfuls of her things – sketchpads, paintbrushes, old jumpers, books – and that night she'd even slept there, as if suddenly she had no need for home at all.

Waco? Wacos? Could that be an annoyed expression? Some reference to that bust-up in Texas a few years back? He'd followed the siege closely in the paper at the time, fascinated not by the gruesome voyeurism but by the fact that even in a country as big as America, people couldn't seem to live without getting in each other's way. He'd always supposed that all the conflict on the island in his lifetime – the clashes between the crofters and entrepreneurs in his childhood, and between him and the Trust as he'd grown older, and of course between Maureen and Bella – had been down to the tininess of the place. But reading about Waco made him wonder if such territorial disagreements were simply a part of life. Without a doubt that was why Reenie had been livid when she'd learnt about the studio – even if, sensing that a more objective tack might have more luck, she'd dressed up her objections as something else. *You know I get nervous about the Stùc now that the bridge is gone*, she'd said. *I won't have you over there a second more than necessary – what if you get stranded in a storm again?* Flora hadn't bought it, though, pointing out all the reasons why the studio was actually an excellent idea – no more paint stains on her room's carpet, no more of Reenie's kitchen implements going missing for still lifes. Besides, she'd reminded them, it wasn't any safer being stranded in the guesthouse during a storm. She'd stared at her mother, then, as if willing her to bring up Bella, but Reenie had reluctantly backed down.

He stared at the crossword some more. It probably wasn't an anagram after all, he told himself. *Annoyed expressions: frowns? Growls?*

Maybe, he supposed, he was wrong about Reenie's motives – or at least was oversimplifying. Yes, she and Bella had a history, and no, the line about storms hadn't been terribly convincing. But perhaps his wife was upset simply because Flora had taken the studio without even consulting them. Maybe she was upset because yet another child was drifting away from her. Indeed, with Barry vanished into the North Sea and Trevor still at school, to have Flora suddenly decamp felt like a particularly cruel desertion. Even he'd been hurt.

Scowls? That had *cow* in it, at least – but it was too many letters.

Once he might have tried to talk to Reenie, to find out exactly what was bothering her, but now it hardly seemed worth the effort. The past few years she'd ceased discussing much of anything with him other than the dull, day-to-day matters around the guesthouse. When they'd been young she had always been so expressive, too, he thought, faintly shaking his head. Right from their very first conversation, her openness had startled him.

She had been sixteen at the time, and he twenty, spending the last weeks of summer on the island before returning for his final year at Glasgow. He hadn't expected to be at home at all that year; in fact, he'd planned a pilgrim's progress around Europe to mark his final summer as a student. But then his older brother, James, had died while on deployment in Cyprus, and after seeing his mother's awful state at the funeral he hadn't been able to leave her alone. So he'd cancelled his trip and returned home instead, and had been strolling down to the jetty that morning to fetch the messages when, out of nowhere, Maureen had appeared next to him as if blooming from the gorse.

'George McCloud,' she'd said, and he'd turned with a start.

'Oh.' He squinted at her. 'Hello. It's Maureen, isn't it?' They'd overlapped for a few years at the primary school, so he was vaguely aware of her existence, but other than that they'd never had much to do with each other. Her parents were fishers, and the fishers spurned anyone who catered to the island's tourists; respectable jobs involved hard labour, as far as they were concerned, not hawking souvenirs or entertaining rich Englishmen or selling up the island's secret spots. (No doubt the Calvinist homilies delivered by the island's pastor each week only further confirmed that prejudice.)

'My friends call me Reenie,' she said, beginning to skip alongside him. 'You can too, if you like.'

He swallowed. 'Well, how can I help you today, Reenie?'

And that was when, quite matter-of-factly, she'd replied she was going to marry him.

'Marry me?' he said, laughing off the suggestion. 'But I'm going back to uni next month! And once I'm finished there my uncle's arranging an internship for me with *The Scotsman*. In Edinburgh.'

'I'll come with you,' she said, without blinking. 'It won't matter where you go if I'm your wife.' She smiled coyly. 'Anyway, Edinburgh doesn't sound so bad.'

He'd laughed again, more uneasily this time. 'Aye, well. We'll have to wait and see.' He cleared his throat. 'Now go on, away with you. I'm not your babysitter.'

'Whatever you say, George McCloud,' she'd replied, and bounded away down the hill, as naturally as if they'd been discussing the weather.

He'd put her out of his head after that, returning to Glasgow without seeing her again; by the time he visited at Christmas he had mostly forgotten about her. But there she was, still, now seventeen, and unofficially permitted in the pub – where she turned up every evening to try and snatch a few minutes of his time. He pretended to find it awkward, assuring his curious parents he had no idea why she kept hanging about, and yet something about her determination stoked his ego; this time when he returned to Glasgow he didn't as successfully forget about her, and as his Easter break drew near he began to wonder if she'd be waiting for him again. Hoping that she would be, even. To his surprise he found he liked the notion of a willing woman standing by for his return – and return he would, he knew that. Going off to Edinburgh for a few years was a fine thing for a young man to do, but he couldn't stay forever, not with James gone. He was the only son left now; it was up to him to take over from his parents when they could no longer manage on their own. And if he had a prospective wife there, with hardly any effort, well, so much the better.

Maureen always was waiting for him, too, and if the gossip his parents picked up was accurate she had rejected several other suitors from among the island's young men. After that he unabashedly began to miss her, to count the days until his brief visits home, and during those weeks he savoured every moment. In the evenings they'd sit in the lounge well past midnight, Reenie giggling at his jokes or stroking his arm in admiration, and in the afternoons they went on walks along the beach, to steal passionate embraces in a small cove near the Stùc. And, of course, he'd returned to St Fillan's in her final year to take her to the Leavers' Ball.

He never suggested she visit him, though, in Glasgow or in Edinburgh. After all, he told himself, the whole point of his time on the mainland was to go out and experience the world, to be a carefree young man, not to start a family with the girl from back home. Besides – and this is what he told her when she asked – he was staying at his uncle's house in Edinburgh; bringing her along would have been too much of an imposition. She'd tried not to show her disappointment.

Instead they'd exchanged letters for the years he was abroad, and after that, at twenty-four, he'd returned to the island ready to settle down. They were engaged within weeks and married within months, an extremely modest ceremony in the chapel (George borrowing a kilt for the occasion) and an equally modest reception afterwards at the pub. *Let's save our money for the honeymoon*, Maureen had said, though in the end that had been modest, too: a weekend at a fancy hotel in St Andrews, where they'd been mostly trapped inside by stormy weather. Everything back then seemed so effortlessly like the right decision, though – and for several years it seemed that neither of them could be happier.

Annoyed expressions… That could mean complaints, too, he thought. *Jeers? Boos? Beefs?*

Beefs!

He scribbled the word into the grid and read it over again with a satisfied nod. From the hallway he heard the front door open, and the thump-thump of Flora kicking off her boots.

Their first few years of marriage, Reenie had agitated often for them to move away again – they were both still young, she constantly reminded him, and his parents in good enough nick to manage without them a little longer. He'd entertained the possibility, too, he really had; he even called an old uni friend for advice about where they might go. At the same time, though, he assumed they'd be having kids before too long, and he didn't want to be away from home for that. And what would either of them *do* anywhere else? He had little taste for further work in the newspaper business, and other than a minor role in the Glasgow student government he'd never held another job; had never even considered another job, really, with the guesthouse always waiting on the horizon. So month after month, year after year, he'd put off their alleged move, and all of a sudden he was thirty – his parents almost sixty, and increasingly frail – and it no longer seemed an option.

Children, though, had still not been forthcoming. Reenie was assiduous in her birth control and insistent that they wait, and whenever he brought it up she just asked him what the rush was. *We've got our whole lives for children, George – why start so early?* The truth was, it didn't feel early to him; as he slowly assumed more of the guesthouse duties, he was growing impatient to fully take on his role as head of the household. He yearned for a child – and not just to quiet his mother's constant pestering about grandkids.

But he never pressed Reenie, not at first, sensing that her leisurely attitude was a cover for some underlying ambivalence whose depths he dared not plumb. He understood why she might be afraid of childbirth, of course, given how her own mother had died, but then, after Barry was finally conceived, she acted so uninterested, so unmoved – so in denial, almost – that he asked her outright: *Do you even want children?* Immediately she'd waved him off. Told him he was being ridiculous, that she was thrilled to be having a child with him, and that if she ever acted otherwise it was only down to first pregnancy jitters. And when Barry was born she'd taken to motherhood with such an amazed, devoted sort of glow that George was soon wondering what he'd ever been worried about.

Before long, however, Reenie had slipped into a new, more sombre mood. Or maybe sombre was the wrong word: listless? Defeated? Even years later he couldn't quite decide. He could only remember the way she'd spend days at a time in an apathetic fog, staring blankly at the walls, or peeling dozens more vegetables than they needed because she'd lost track of time – and then to have conceived a second child, with the first barely two, and after so many years of carefully planned nothing! Something had to have changed. Something had to be wrong.

Once again, she told him he was being ridiculous. 'Honestly, George,' she said, fishing a box of maternity clothes from the back of their bedroom closet. 'We've got one child already, that's all – what difference does another make? We're a family now.'

He smiled, not quite believing her. 'I've started, so I'll finish?'

She held up a tiny knitted hat and laughed. 'Something like that, aye.'

Flora poked her head through the door, now. 'I'm home, Dad.' She walked over to where he was hunched on his stool and glanced down at the crossword. '*Beefs* is wrong.'

He gave her a warm glare. 'And what makes you so sure?'

'Because,' she said, patting him on the back. 'Six down is *armour*, so that one has to start with an *M*.'

He looked down at the grid again, and at the clue for six down, and blinked. She was right, of course – she always was. 'Fine,' he said, erasing *beefs* and wiping away the dust with the side of his pinkie. 'Do you fancy bangers and mash for tea? We've got those nice sausages that still need eating.'

'Fine by me,' she said, leaning forward and kissing him on the cheek. 'I'll go get started.'

'I'll be through in a minute,' he told her. 'I just have to get this answer, first.'

'I know you do.' She winked from the doorway. 'Don't be too long.'

With Reenie so steadfast in her reassurances while she was pregnant with Flora, he'd once more put his concerns out of his head. He had plenty of other things to focus on at the time, anyway: the day-to-day business at the guesthouse, and the continuing diaspora, and without warning his parents' passing away, shortly before Flora's birth and within a few weeks of each other – as if tethered, somehow, even after death. And then there was baby Barry, too. Beyond George's abstract desire to start a family, it turned out he enjoyed fatherhood immensely, and would spend hours with the boy in the sitting room, amazed at what he'd helped create.

After Flora was born, Reenie's mood had worsened again, her retreat accelerating; during her pregnancy with Trevor she seemed to shut him out altogether. Oonagh had more to do with her those nine months than he did, and although the excitement at Trevor's arrival had provided a brief reprieve from the gloom, once life returned to normal again it began to feel as if their marriage were a matter of course, and little else. He fell more deeply into his crosswords, and she, likewise, into her cooking, and though they both continued to muddle through their days with apparent love and tenderness it began to seem strangely automatic, secondary to some other feeling they were unable to identify and unwilling to discuss.

Moues, he thought, taking one last look at the grid. *Annoyed expressions a cow might make*. He groaned and filled in the answer, then stood up to make his way to the kitchen, his back protesting after so long on the stool.

Dinner was much as it had been since Maureen had been away: comfortably silent, he and Flora trading occasional comments, and bringing up the absent family members only when something sparked a memory (the time Trevor, for instance, had run from the table in tears, having expected the bangers in bangers and mash to be literal firecrackers). Towards the end of the meal, however, Flora departed from the usual script. 'I've been meaning to tell you,' she said, casually, mopping up the last of her gravy with a heap of potatoes. 'There's a gallery in Fort William that wants to show a painting of mine.'

George set down his fork. 'Oh?' He wasn't quite sure how to respond. 'So that's, er… good news, is it?' He hadn't intended to come across as deadpanning, but Flora seemed to take it that way.

'Of course it is, you daft old bugger!' she laughed. 'It's fantastic news!'

'Well then,' he said with a smile. 'Congratulations. Tell me about it.'

It was the same gallery that had run the competition she'd won at school, she explained, the Western Eye in Fort William, who were now organizing an exhibit of rising local stars. 'Rising stars!' she repeated, with a squeal. Oh, it was small fry, she knew that really, the 'gallery' not much more than a largish function room in a local hotel, and the exhibit itself a money-making scheme for them rather than a genuine career opportunity for her. But still, that thrill of recognition! Now she could legitimately call herself an artist, she told him – and though she didn't finish the sentence he could work out from her general demeanour the unspoken second half: *and not just the boss's daughter at some pokey guesthouse.*

'That's why I've been over at the studio so much,' she said, standing and starting to clear the dishes. 'The show's at the end of next month, and I've been trying to come up with something really special for it.'

He coughed. 'That's wonderful.'

She stopped next to him as she reached for his plate. 'You don't seem very excited.'

'What?' He blinked. 'No, of course I am.' He forced a smile. 'It's hard to see your little girl grow up, that's all.'

She sighed and made for the sink. 'Don't worry,' she said. 'I'll still be here to do your dishes for many more years.'

'That's not what I meant,' he said, shifting in his seat. 'It's just—'

'I'm joking, Dad. Calm yourself.'

To his relief, the phone rang then, and he hurried from the room. In the hall he paused by the telephone table and took a deep breath. 'Fìor Guesthouse,' he said, switching to his most booming, professional tone as he picked up. 'How can I help you?'

'Ah, Mr McCloud, good evening.' The line was crackly, the voice distant. 'My name's Michael Talbot. I wonder if you might remember me – I was a customer of yours a few months ago. The end of August.'

George cleared his throat and furrowed his brow, trying to remember a face. 'Ah,' he began. 'I'm not quite sure…'

'Well,' said the voice. 'No matter. You must get far too many guests to remember us all.'

A faint memory clicked into place. 'Mr Talbot!' he exclaimed. 'We had to move you to a different room because of those idiots who missed the ferry!' The details were already filtering back to him. An Englishman, some sort of finance type. Had clung to Flora a bit. Told them they needed a timetable at the jetty.

There was a laugh at the other end of the line. 'That was me, yes.'

'Well, Mr Talbot – what can I do for you today?'

He took a deep breath. 'I was wondering,' he said, speaking carefully, 'if there was any time in the next month or so when I would be able to come and see you.'

Turning through the weekly calendar they kept by the phone, looking for the next year's pages, George slipped immediately into his ordinary patter about the season being over.

'Actually,' the other man interrupted, 'I'm not really coming for a holiday. I was hoping to discuss a business proposal.'

George hesitated. 'A business proposal?'

'Yes – though I was hoping you could still put me up for one night. I'll happily pay, but I'm not much of a camper.'

'A business proposal,' George repeated, as in the kitchen the sound of rushing water grew louder. He told himself he had to tread carefully, here – these big city types always thought they knew best. Then again, he thought, the timetable had been a good idea, hadn't it?

'Mr McCloud?'

'I… what kind of business proposal?'

There was a pause on the other end of the line. 'I'd rather leave the particulars until we can speak face-to-face. The phone is so impersonal.'

'Surely you don't expect me to agree to a meeting without knowing what it's about, Mr Talbot.'

The man sighed. 'I'll cut to the chase, then. I'd like to move in.'

'I beg your pardon?'

'Not into the guesthouse itself, of course,' he added, 'and not full-time – I could live in one of the village houses, maybe six or seven months a year. But I want to be there for a long enough stretch that I can get a proper feel for the place, and then start acting as a kind of… consultant, I suppose. To help you build your business, and improve it, and make sure your wonderful little guesthouse survives for future generations to enjoy.'

George let out a choked sort of laugh. 'Is that so?' Despite how obviously the speech had been rehearsed, he was curious, now, his defences dropping. 'And what makes you think we need your help?'

'It's not that I think you have a poor operation there, let me be clear.' He seemed to be gaining confidence. 'But even in the few days I was visiting I saw several things that could be made more efficient – not to mention a few needlessly empty beds losing you money.' He took a deep breath. 'So you're right, you don't need my help. But that doesn't mean you can't benefit from it.'

'And what do you stand to gain from it, Mr Talbot?' He looked down the hall towards the front door, imagining the empty village beyond it. 'Don't tell me you're coming for the social scene.'

'I'm twenty-five, Mr McCloud, and I've been working at the same awful job for too long already. I see the old-timers here and they're no different than the trainees – it's still all money money money, more more more. Even once they retire they can't stay away. I just don't think I want that. I want to be able to look back and feel like I did something more with my life. And there's something about your island, and your guesthouse… I don't know. It's so wonderful up there. I want to help you share it with more people.'

George hesitated for a few seconds, digesting it all. 'Okay,' he said, finally. 'I'm intrigued.' More than intrigued, really. Optimistic. Finally, here was someone to ease the burden on the rest of them. He ran his finger along the days in the calendar. 'Would you be able to come the weekend of November twenty-fifth?' That would give him enough time to prepare Reenie for the idea. He wasn't sure how she'd react to more outside meddling – ever since the ratcatchers, she'd scowled every time the Trust was mentioned.

'Whatever's most convenient for you, Mr McCloud. Thank you.'

The water in the kitchen shut off.

'Don't thank me yet,' said George. 'I'm not making any guarantees.' He heard Flora push the chairs under the table in the kitchen, and began hurrying the man off the phone; he was hanging up just as Flora stepped into the hallway. She gave him a quizzical look and asked who he'd been blathering away with for so long.

Even in bed that night, he wouldn't be able to articulate quite what had suddenly possessed him to lie to her; it was one of those decisions that his mind seemed to make without any conscious deliberation. Perhaps with her news about the art show still fresh in his mind, and his nagging worries lately about her losing interest in the guesthouse, he hadn't wanted to give her any reason that might make it seem easier to leave; perhaps he didn't want to risk Reenie finding out before he'd told her himself. Or perhaps he didn't want to say anything yet in case the other man changed his mind – came to his senses, more like – and George ended up looking like a fool for believing him in the first place.

Whatever the reason, though, when Flora asked he just shrugged and shook his head. 'Some deaf biddy from the Borders asking about a room. I had to tell her everything three times.' He grinned. 'And she didn't even bloody book anything, either!'

Flora laughed. 'Better you than me, then.' She nodded towards the pub and asked if he'd like to take another crack at the crossword with her.

'Aye,' he said. 'Why not?' And putting his arm around her, he guided them down the hallway – wondering, as they walked, what might suddenly be possible.

9

The Wednesday night before Flora's show she took the ferry to the mainland; though the opening wasn't until Saturday, she needed to get her piece there a few days early for the set-up, so she thought she'd make a vacation of it (the hotel was putting her up for nothing, anyway). In the end she'd submitted a simple pastel landscape, nothing too ambitious – the sorts of people who bought paintings at a Highland hotel probably weren't looking for avant-garde – but after weeks of tinkering she was pleased with the result, and more pleased still when the manager at the hotel lifted it up and cooed that it was *splendid, Miss McCloud!* Miss McCloud! That alone made her giddy.

It was a pleasant change, as well, to have some time away from home, where the atmosphere the last few weeks had been particularly tense. Her parents' apparent lack of pride or even interest in the exhibition was bad enough; after her father's flat reaction the night she told him, her mother was downright dismissive, as if Flora were little more than a child completing her first jigsaw puzzle. But far worse was the bitter discovery that they weren't even coming to the opening. When she'd asked, her father's face had turned bright red. 'Oh no,' he said. 'Your opening is that weekend?' Flora gave him a sharp look. 'Yes, Dad – I told you last week. You circled it on the calendar.'

That was when, stuttering slightly and apologizing nearly every other word, George told her that, no, the date was circled on the calendar for something else. That he'd arranged a business meeting for that day. Then it was Maureen's turn to give him a sharp look, and ask what kind of meeting – and his response was the other reason why home had been so uncomfortable lately: he wouldn't tell them. He claimed it was because he wasn't quite sure himself, yet, that some former guest had approached him with a business proposal – probably some retiree who'd discovered he hated his wife and wanted a way out of the house, thought Flora. But her father wanted them to hear this mysterious man out together, instead of saying anything himself to get them too excited.

'Oh, yes,' crowed Maureen, 'surprise visitors are always a real bloody excitement. Were you ever planning to mention this, or was it going to be a rabbit out of the hat sort of thing?'

George assured them he had just been waiting for the right time, and continued to apologize, but still he wouldn't give them anything else – insisting it would just be speculation. 'And I'm sorry about your opening, love,' he added, giving Flora an imploring stare. 'I promise we'll make it over later in the month.'

That was some comfort, she supposed. But after the charm of her arrival in Fort William had worn off; after she spent two hours alone in her hotel room on Saturday afternoon, trying on outfits that all seemed impossibly frumpy or outdated; after she spent most of the opening skulking in the corner, her stomach cramping from having skipped both lunch and dinner through anxiety; and after the early train back to Mallaig in the morning, hungover from too much free champagne: she wished there'd been a friendly face to keep her company. For the first time in her life she felt that there were some things her *family* simply couldn't do for her.

The weather in Mallaig that morning was typical for November, a gloomy swirl of mist and a choking wind, and the crossing was a rough one. Flora hardly noticed, though, staring from the canteen windows in a trance; even once they'd docked at Fìor she took a minute or two to snap back to reality, gathering her things and slipping to the loo only when the crew came through to clear the cabin before the return passengers boarded, and when she finally hurried down the gangplank it was with only a minute or two to spare before departure. As she reached the jetty she thought she caught a whiff of some familiar scent, one she couldn't quite place – until she looked up at the ship and glimpsed a flash of a familiar red coat in one of the windows.

No, she'd told herself, remembering the way that coat had rustled in her arms all those months earlier. *It couldn't be.*

The exhibition, despite Flora's nervousness, was an undeniable success. A red dot adorned her piece's frame by the end of the week, and the sole picture accompanying the show's coverage in the local paper was of her, a nervous grin on her face, left arm drawn protectively across her body and gripping her right elbow. But it wasn't until April, and Bella's return to the island for the summer, that the pull of her artwork became impossible to ignore.

It was still a few weeks before the guesthouse opened for the season, and Flora had escaped to the Stùc for the day to help Bella settle in. At first, as they unpacked her supplies and reorganized the studio to her liking, they chatted away as usual – but then, halfway through tacking a sketch to the wall, Bella abruptly changed the subject.

'You need to apply to art college.' She pushed the paper's last corner to the wall with her thumb. 'This year, ideally, to capitalize on your momentum from that sale in the winter.' She took a step back and cocked her head, checking the sketch was straight, and finally turned to Flora. 'If this...' she motioned to the far corner, where a few of Flora's drawings were yet to be taken down, 'is really what you want to do with your life, it's time you started pursuing it more seriously.'

Flora objected that she pursued it as seriously as she could, given her other commitments, but Bella waved her off, not listening. 'You don't have other commitments, dear, you have guilt, and that's only because your mother actively cultivates it.'

'Oh, she does no—'

'There's no reason you have to stay here, Flora, other than that you think your parents can't manage without you. But your brother will finish school in a year or two, and until then I'm sure they can get by.' There was that well-practised smirk again. 'Besides, what about Prince Charming? When's he arriving?'

Mumbling, Flora told her it was the next day, annoyed at the reminder; she was far more ambivalent about Michael's return than either Bella or her father. She had spent the months since finding out, in fact, alternately dreading and fantasizing about it. Sometimes those fantasies were the predictable lovelorn stuff – long kisses, frantic undressings, that sort of thing – but more often lately she'd found herself imagining the guesthouse growing so successful, with Michael's help, that she was able to leave it and him behind altogether, and retain an agent for her artwork, and never have to worry about her parents growing old again. And the dread, maybe, came from the same place.

Of course, it didn't help that the intent behind Michael's return remained maddeningly vague. The few times she'd answered the phone to him over the past few months, her father had rushed her off the line before she could get in more than a few words, and she didn't dare call him herself. So all she knew, still, was that he would be there *for a few months to get a feel for things*, as her father had explained it; she had no idea if it were just for this year or for several, no idea how closely he'd linger, and no idea, worst of all, where she figured in any of it. Because there had been something between them when he'd visited the previous summer, hadn't there? Surely she hadn't imagined it. Surely it had at least crossed his mind when he was drawing up his plan.

'It's not as easy as that,' she added now, after a long pause. 'Mum and Dad are barely scraping by as it is, Michael or no Michael. I can't just leave them in the lurch.'

Bella waved her off again and reached for another sketch. 'Look, I'm no business expert. But it's their business, Flora, not yours. You shouldn't be forced to stay here if it isn't what you want.' There were a few more moments of silence as, on her tiptoes, she pressed the drawing to the wall – and when she turned again Flora thought she saw, briefly, a glimmer of sympathy, or compassion, or *something* beyond that cool exterior for a change.

'At least think about it,' said Bella. 'Please?'

'Fine,' Flora harrumphed. 'I will.'

And of course she did, at length, reading and rereading the prospectus Bella had pushed on her as she was leaving, until she could recite each of its exciting claims from memory. With only a few years' study she would be able to *Innovate! Synthesize! Explore her individual style!* She would work with *renowned international artists*, and receive *complementary lectures in literature and philosophy*! It all sounded utterly wonderful – but that only got her more annoyed at Bella for making her consider it. Because her parents couldn't get by without her, no matter what Bella thought. And even once Trevor returned from school, even if Michael stayed long term, could she really in good conscience swan off to Edinburgh and leave the two of them as trapped here as she was now?

Besides, once Michael actually arrived, she quickly wrote off his potential as a helper around the guesthouse. If anything, he made her work there harder, following her around with a spiral-bound black-and-red notebook, the sight of which she quickly came to loathe, and practically demanding that she explain every aspect of her duties, no matter how piddling. *Why do you have a separate grocery order each day? Why do you do laundry so often? What do you do with food scraps when you're clearing meals?*

When he wasn't badgering her he was eating up her parents' spare time, insisting on endless meetings about suppliers and room rates and marketing, and a whole heap of other issues they weren't accustomed to considering – never mind justifying. And although he promised he would start to lend a hand once he properly understood how everything worked, that mythical moment remained always just over the horizon, even as the guesthouse leeched more and more from Flora's life. In the entire month of May, she managed to eke out only two afternoons to sit alone with her sketchbook, and the prospect of devoting any serious time to her work seemed less feasible than ever.

As if the dashing of that dream wasn't bad enough, none of her imagined passions with Michael materialized, either. Her previous reservations about falling for him, too fast or at all, had evaporated the moment she'd seen him again, a few specks of grey in his stubble and his eyes the colour of black tea. His first week on the island she appeared almost every night at the front door of the old Leslie house, where he'd moved in, and assumed that before long they would fall into each other's arms. But then the cold shower: he greeted her with a polite professionalism each time, as if the Michael who'd visited the island as a tourist were some embarrassing past self to be forgotten.

Logically, Flora told herself she should welcome being spurned, trying to recall all her past hang-ups about her interest in him. But his remoteness instead woke her instinctive stubbornness – reinforced by Bella, who assured Flora he was only playing hard to get – and even as the season moved into full swing she pursued him with ever more brazen tactics, visiting him with bottles of wine, and offering him massages, and pouting with exaggerated disappointment whenever he tried to send her on her way. When at last she did elicit a response, it wasn't the one she wanted. It was June, and she'd announced, after another evening in his living room, that she was too tired to go home and would rather stay at his. *Oh, for God's sake, Flora!* he snapped, and told her very firmly that nothing was going to happen between them. That her parents would throw him out in a second if they suspected he was *corrupting their only daughter*, and that it was better, surely, to have his platonic company than nothing at all.

She asked him if he really believed they didn't already suspect something – a foolish move, in hindsight, as it only strengthened his resolve – but later his comment gave her pause. Not that she thought her parents would care that much; her mother had only been a year or two older when she'd married, and if Flora had to get involved with anyone she was sure they'd prefer Michael to a man living full-time on the mainland. But it had at least opened her mind to other possibilities with him, beyond romance or nothing at all. *His platonic company*, he'd called it; would that really be so bad? She'd been enjoying the extra person to spend time with, after all, especially one closer to her age than her parents or Bella, and the idea of a *friend*, she realized, was every bit as appealing as the idea of... what? A lover? A boyfriend? Not that it made any difference for the next few months, as in the wake of their confrontation the few encounters they did have, usually in the pub, were more awkward than anything else.

Once the summer was over, though – once the bustle of customers had died down, once Flora's days had opened up again and she had time to sit and think – she gradually resumed her evening visits. And now, though he was still impeccably professional, he greeted her more warmly; after so many stiff conversations at the guesthouse, they both seemed to exhale – as if the whole, self-conscious summer they'd been saving up stories, knowing that eventually they'd drop the pretence. Which was a relief, for Flora, though it did little to resolve the same old, niggling questions. What did he really want from her? What, come to that, did she really want from him?

Adding to her frustration as the autumn spooled away were the long afternoons she spent working on the Stùc, reclaimed again from Bella. The work itself was a joy, as usual, but that only served to underscore her passion for it, and how inadequately she could pursue it here. Some days she got so happily absorbed that she forgot the time and ended up stranded by the high tide, forced to sheepishly call her parents and tell them to eat without her.

And at last, caught again and again by the unforgiving one-two of her fantasies of art school and her ambiguous feelings for Michael, Flora cracked. Decided she had to get out, or at least explore the possibility. So one night, a few weeks before Trevor returned for Christmas – only one before Michael was due to leave for the winter – she announced to her parents at the end of dinner that she wanted to talk to them about something.

'Can't it wait?' asked Maureen, as if the thought of postponing her evening cleaning by even a few minutes left her physically in pain.

'No, Mum,' said Flora, steeling herself. 'It can't.'

'Fine,' she huffed, glancing at the clock above the door. 'What is it?'

'Well...' Flora looked to her father, hoping for a supportive smile, but he seemed as anxious as she felt. 'Before I say anything,' she started again, 'please remember this is only an idea. I haven't made any decisions, and even if I did I would make sure it didn't affect you or the business. You know I'd never dream of abandoning you.'

Her mother shifted in her chair, and Flora recalled, suddenly, the night that Barry had announced he was leaving, right in this very room and at this very table and at this very time of the evening, to her and her mother and Trevor. She remembered the way her own fingers had seemed to ice up, and how her throat had tightened at the prospect of his departure. She cursed herself for not thinking of it sooner – because if she was remembering that scene right now, she was sure her mother must be too.

'You know how much I love my work, though,' she pressed on, determined not to lose her momentum. 'I've been drawing and painting for as long as I can remember, and I'm getting – I think I'm getting – pretty good at it.' She swallowed. Her mother's face was darkening; her father's was still plastered with an uneasy smile. 'And to be honest, it's something I can see myself taking further. As a career. That piece in Fort William sold in three days.' As she'd rehearsed this speech in her head earlier she'd debated leaving that part out, because despite their promises her parents had never visited the exhibition – a sore point between them that the intervening seasons hadn't completely healed. In the end, though, she could hardly make the argument without it, could she?

'The thing is,' she continued, 'there's only so much more I can do on my own, especially with everything I have to do around here. Bella thinks I need to take some time off and go to art school if I want to get any further, and I – I think maybe I want to. I think maybe I should.' She sat back in her chair. 'So... Yeah.'

'Well,' her mother said, her cheeks flushed red and her voice as quiet and distant as if she'd been in another room, '*I* think that's entirely out of the question.'

Flora gritted her teeth. 'Can't we at least discuss it?'

'Yes, Reenie,' said George, slowly, his eyes still fixed on Flora. 'Maybe we should—'

'Oh, be quiet, George.' She turned to him, her eyes bulging, her voice growing louder. 'That woman putting these ridiculous ideas in her head is bad enough – don't you bloody start.' She looked at Flora again, her face almost purple now, her breathing heavy. 'Real people don't get to run off and be artists whenever they please, Flora!' She wiped her hand across her forehead, where a few beads of sweat were starting to form. 'The sooner you accept that, the better.'

'Mum, this isn't about running off to be an artist, it's about developing a talent! About making a living doing something that I'm good at and enjoy! What's so wrong with that?'

'Oh, get your head out of the bloody clouds!' She was struggling to talk now, her breathing laboured.

'Fine,' said Flora. 'Forget I said anything. I'll just go back upstairs and await your orders.' She pushed away from the table, sending her chair clattering to the floor, and started for the hallway as her father called for her to wait, standing up to follow her.

But then there was that haunting sound behind them, the sound Flora would never quite forget: her mother gasping, her chair sliding against the floor as she tried to stand up, and the deep *thunk* as she fell against the table for support. Flora and her father spun around in time to see her slump to the floor on her hands and knees, sweat beading across her face like condensation on a glass. 'I can't breathe,' she croaked, tugging desperately at the collar of her cardigan, and without thinking Flora was running to the phone with a frantic prayer that her mother not die because of *this*. Which she didn't, of course. Didn't even come close. When Dr Nicol arrived from Rum an hour later, and the helicopter paramedics from the mainland a few minutes after that, Maureen seemed already to have recovered. *Probably a panic attack*, the doctor told them, once he'd examined her and sent her to bed. *Good thing, too*, he added, his voice dropping, *if it really had been her heart, we never would have arrived in time.*

Michael, who had come running from his house at the sound of the helicopter, nodded gravely at that assessment, clearly aghast at how suddenly death could stalk the island, and asked if it would be worth buying a defibrillator for the guesthouse, just in case. The doctor laughed. *Not unless one of you wants to learn how to use one!* he said, and that seemed to be the end of it. George went upstairs to check on Maureen; the helicopter buzzed away; and the doctor, with one of his customary wistful remarks about how empty the island seemed these days, said his goodbyes and set off, leaving Flora and Michael alone in the vestibule.

They looked at each other. 'Are you all right?' he asked, putting a hand on her arm.

'I don't know,' she said, at last. 'That was… unexpected.' She shook off his hand from where it still rested at her elbow, and started down the hallway. 'Drink?' she said, over her shoulder.

Shrugging, he followed her.

'I only wanted to suggest it,' she told him, once she'd explained what had happened. She was standing behind the bar, drinking one of the more recent elaborate cocktails she'd invented, while he sat in front of it sipping the same beer he'd had his first night there. 'Test the waters, you know? See how they'd react.' She snorted. 'I suppose we answered that question.'

Michael tried to convince her that things might not be as bad as they seemed; told her it was unlikely a full-blown panic attack could be caused by something as harmless as a discussion about art school. 'Maybe she's worried about something else right now,' he said. 'If she was already on edge, this might just have been the last straw, you know?'

'The last straw!' She laughed bitterly. 'And what was the first bloody straw, eh? Or the second or the third? It's not exactly one of your high-pressure investment banks around here.'

Michael gazed down at his drink, in that lost puppy sort of way she found so infuriatingly charming. 'I just mean,' he said, 'that there might be something on her mind that you don't know about.'

Again, Flora pooh-poohed him. There weren't many ways to keep a secret around here, she said – if anything stressful enough to send her mother into a fit like that were going on, they'd know about it. As soon as she'd said it, though, she began to wonder. Never mind that night; her mother's behaviour the whole year – ever since Flora had returned from St Fillan's, actually, if she thought about it – had been so inexplicably different from what she remembered growing up, so dour and pessimistic and solitary, that maybe Michael was right. Otherwise, the only explanation seemed to be that her mother had simply become meaner and more selfish, and despite all the skirmishes they'd had since Flora moved home, she didn't quite believe that was possible.

In any case, her mother's panic attack, whatever the cause, had rattled Flora enough that she was ready to give up on the art school idea, just like that. As she sipped at her drink behind the bar, she imagined the coming years, her time on the Stùc growing shorter and shorter as her parents grew older and more infirm. Imagined Bella giving up on her. Imagined her pictures fading on the studio walls, and finally imagined herself in her room, withering away alone.

And then she looked at Michael again.

'At least I still have you,' she murmured, and reached across the bar. Her fingers brushed against the top of his hand, and she felt the faint thud of his pulse beneath the skin. His eyes dropped, his expression inscrutable – but he didn't pull away. At least, not at first. But after a few more moments he raised his head and met her eyes, and gently withdrew his hand.

'I should go,' he said, taking one more sip of beer and setting the glass down, still half full. She fancied she saw his fingers shaking a little. 'Goodnight, Flora.'

Her shoulders slumped, and she whispered goodnight back as she watched him stand and leave; heard the creak of the hallway floorboards as he stepped into his shoes. Once the front door had clicked shut, she reached under the counter and dimmed the pub lights, until she could see the faint glow of his torch through the windows – bobbing away down the path, and eventually disappearing altogether.

10

IT WAS A QUIET CHRISTMAS that year, the atmosphere awkward, acrimonious. Maureen had no desire to revisit the embarrassment of her panic attack, and Flora none to dwell on the veto of art school, and in the extensive detours necessary to avoid talking about either they mostly talked about nothing at all. Even with George trying valiantly to bridge the long silences between them, their hours together – at meals, and around the tree, and on their habitual Christmas Day constitutional – ended up feeling more like time with their demons.

Trevor also tried his best to right the situation during his few weeks at home, suggesting cards or a board game after dinner, the way they'd always done before Barry left – or, when that didn't work, pulling out old photo albums of holidays past, as if to jolt everyone into remembering how happy they could be. None of it worked, though, and the rest of them, George included, were glad when Trevor returned to school. With him gone and the holidays over, they could drop any pretence of familial harmony and retreat without guilt – without as much guilt, anyway – to their own private corners: Flora to her bedroom or the Stùc, Maureen to the kitchen, and George to the pub and his crosswords.

With the McClouds the only ones left on the island, of course, their silent feuding couldn't last long; some deeper urge for company and conversation forced them, after a few more months, to swallow their misgivings and seek each other out. Flora began to rejoin George in the pub at nights, and she and Maureen began to warm to each other during their dinnertime conversations – and when one evening in March Maureen suggested a game of rummy, George and Flora both agreed without any hesitation.

Sometimes, though, it seemed to George as if that meagre progress had come too late. In the months since Christmas, Flora's routine had absorbed more hours on the Stùc than ever before – she regularly stayed the night there now, stranded or not – and the idea of art school was clearly still on her mind. On a sunny morning in April she brought it up again, this time with George on his own as they carried home the shopping together. She asked him if it was really that unreasonable. Asked him if *he* thought it was ridiculous.

For an uncomfortably long time he'd said nothing, listening to the faint shearwater calls over the wind as he tried to come up with a suitably diplomatic answer. But in the end all he could manage was, 'Oh, I don't know, Flora. It's complicated.'

He'd entertained some feeble hope that the vague response would satisfy her, but he was quickly disappointed; she responded without waiting a single beat. 'So you don't think it's entirely impossible?'

He turned to look at her more closely, and replied carefully. 'No. I suppose I don't. But do you really want to put this on the table again? After what happened last time? You know your mother has to be a part of this discussion.'

'But that's just it, Dad!' she said, her voice rising. 'She won't even have the discussion! It's only such an issue because she makes it one.' He could see the tendons in her neck tensing as she carried on. 'What's wrong with wanting to get out and see the world beyond this bloody island and this bloody guesthouse, anyway?' At that, she paused. 'Sorry,' she said. 'I didn't mean for it to come out that way.'

'It's okay.' He shook his head. 'And I don't think there's anything wrong with wanting to get out and see the world, and I won't stop you if you bring it up again.' He readjusted his grip on the shopping bag. 'But I wish you wouldn't. For my sake, if not hers.'

In fact, she didn't bring it up again – but that wasn't the end of it, either.

It was a few days later, and George had gone out for another morning walk, this time on his own, to try and clear his head. Since Flora's outburst he'd been able to think of little else, not because he'd been upset by it but because, to his surprise, he had never considered art college the way she'd put it to him then, as a window to life outside the island – even though his own time at university had been the same thing, really, hadn't it? So how had it never occurred to him that his daughter might have that same itch to see the world?

There were a few threads of cloud overhead as he wandered off the road and into the heather, and in front of him the hillside was a rich palette of colour: bright-green grass and deep-brown soil, and the yellow and purple dots of spring flowers. Every few minutes he heard rabbits scurrying away in the brush at his approach, but other than that and the occasional breeze, the air was still and quiet. It was days like this, he thought, that reminded him why he loved the place so much. Even when he'd visited Edinburgh's nicest parks – when the crocuses and daffodils pushed through the ground each spring, or the trees in Princes Street Gardens turned golden each autumn – he'd always felt sure the island could have conjured something prettier.

And that, he supposed, was his biggest reservation about Flora leaving: the suspicion that she didn't feel the same way. More and more since returning from St Fillan's she'd seemed to outgrow the island, to cultivate sophistication beyond what the place could possibly sustain, and he doubted that if she left she'd ever come back. She was seduced by the glamour and charm of the mainland, it was clear, and by its apparently limitless potential. She craved the freedom it promised – or the illusion of freedom, anyway. He was disappointed, just as when Barry had moved away, that he'd been unable to give the island a similar allure. Every walk he'd dragged the children on, every story he'd told, every encouragement to explore as they pleased – in the end, it seemed, it had all been futile.

It was Trevor, actually, to whom George had given the least attention, who was the most attached to home. When he was younger he had constantly collected things from around the island: bird feathers, and strange-shaped pebbles, and flowers that George would find later, pressed between the pages of his ledgers. And George's old photos, when Trevor discovered them, had left him especially smitten. The little scamp had actually pinched a few, thinking no one would notice – so when his next birthday came around they'd splashed out and bought him his own instamatic. He'd spent hours with it out around the village, taking so many rolls of film they'd had to enforce limits on the number he was allowed; it was costing too much to keep sending it to the mainland for development.

George chuckled to himself as he reached the crest of the hill he'd been climbing, and stopped for a moment to sit on a mound of rocks in the brush. He'd always thought *develop film* sounded like crosswordese, and he often tried to write it into clues in his head. *Develop film with no Scots to irritate (7). Most of film developed before drug tale becomes biopic (4, 5).* Occasionally he would try out some of them on Flora, who of course saw right through them, leaving him to wonder whether he should be embarrassed for himself or proud for her.

That pretty well captured how he felt about Flora in general these days. Her frequent flashes of brilliance only served as proof that all the other things she did to bewilder him – and there were lots – were simply beyond his grasp. The cocktails, for instance. She was constantly soliciting interesting new ingredients from visitors to the bar, usually some tropical juice or liquor, and when one of them struck her fancy she'd add a bottle to the bar order and spend hours trying it out in new recipes. Then, each month, she'd sit down at the old Remington in George's office and type out a fresh set of drink menus filled with silly-named concoctions: the *Perestroika*, for example, a martini made with lime juice and white rum, or the *Culloden*, a mixture of chartreuse and single malt. No one ever ordered the bloody things, naturally, but despite the cost he could never bring himself to put his foot down. It was one of the few things she still genuinely seemed to like about the pub – and anyway, on the rare nights when she persuaded him to try one, it was usually very good.

Worse than the cocktails were the books: she read mountains of them, and not the mysteries and romances Reenie ordered from the supermarket. No, Flora read books that intimidated him, books he remembered seeing in the libraries of his mainland relatives; books those same relatives had lukewarmly recommended to his younger self, with a disdain suggesting they doubted he'd get much out of it. And perhaps, because of that, he didn't. He'd never finished *Pride and Prejudice* or *Oliver Twist*, never even started *Madame Bovary*, and certainly never came close to enjoying any of the books his daughter now regularly tore through.

Worst by far, though, was her art. It was actually fitting, he thought, sitting there with the sun warming his neck and the sea glinting all around him, that it was her art now most strongly pulling her away – because it was her art that had made him realize, finally, how much he'd already lost her. It had been a year earlier, the middle of spring, and she had gone to the mainland for the weekend; he needed a new part for the generator, and she'd volunteered to collect it so she could visit with an old school friend. The morning after she left he'd gone out for his usual stroll, and ended up – perhaps not quite by accident – on the beach across from the Stùc. And because he still felt guilty about missing her exhibition, and because her eagerness to leave that weekend had made him worry, even then, that she was slipping away, he'd hurried over the land bridge and towards the old laird's manor – desperate for some way to claw her back.

The door was locked, bizarrely, and he wished now he'd taken that as a sign his conscience was right, that he ought to turn home. Instead, though, he walked to the rear of the building, where he tried to peer over the orchard wall and through the studio windows. Still he couldn't see much, so over the protests of his ageing arms and legs he climbed the wall and carefully lowered himself to the ground on the other side. A rotting plum squelched beneath his foot as he landed.

Almost instantly he regretted it. What he saw on the walls weren't the modest landscapes and still lifes that Flora sometimes showed him and Reenie, the ones he had always suspected were chosen for being unremarkable and unlikely to elicit a strong reaction. This was stranger stuff: ink-slashed monochromes of household objects, and giant, sweating eyes that took up entire canvases, and familiar island views sliced up with abstract blocks of colour. And nudes. A great number of nudes, striking charcoal figure sketches, their wild hatching smeared and redrawn again and again so that the bodies in them seemed to stretch and limber. They were mostly faceless, and yet every one of them, without a doubt, was his daughter. Blushing, he'd hoisted himself back over the wall and jogged home.

He'd never told Flora about that day. Didn't know what he could say about it to make his behaviour seem acceptable. Didn't know what he could say, either, that would accomplish the one thing he'd set out to do that day, and breathe new life into their relationship. So instead he resigned himself to that intangible sense of her drifting away, and to relishing, still, as if a consolation prize, those few moments they sometimes shared: their conversations in the pub, and her help with his crosswords, and those heart-melting smiles when she came downstairs for breakfast. At least, he thought, he still had that. At least she was still here.

But now even that was unravelling; when he got home from his walk that morning, still pondering their recent conversation about art school, the phone was ringing.

'Reenie?' he called out, as he unlaced his shoes.

She appeared in the sitting room doorway. 'What?'

'Were you going to answer that?'

'It's just that bloody Fowkes woman.' She shrugged. 'She's already called three times since you've been gone.'

Frowning, he asked what she wanted.

'No idea. Said she needed to talk to Flora. Apparently she's not answering at the Stùc.'

They both stared at the still ringing phone.

'I'm not getting it,' said Maureen, with another shrug, and retreated to the sitting room – leaving George to mull it over for a few seconds longer, and finally to dash down the hall and snatch up the receiver.

Bella seemed to start half-way through the conversation. 'Look,' she began, 'I know we haven't always seen eye to eye, but can you please put that aside for today? I need to talk to Flora. I wouldn't be calling if it weren't urgent.'

George cleared his throat. There was a pause at the other end of the line, and he could almost hear her reassessing the situation. 'Mr McCloud.'

'Hello, Ms Fowkes. What can I help you with?'

'I need to get in touch with your daughter.' She took a deep breath. 'I've managed to get her a place at Edinburgh for this autumn.'

The words settled like a damp cloak on his shoulders as Bella explained the details: she'd shown her colleagues at the art school some photographs of Flora's work and they'd been wildly impressed – and though it was far too late to apply through normal channels they could guarantee her a clearing place as long as she filed the paperwork within a week.

'This is a fantastic opportunity for her, Mr McCloud, but she needs to go to the mainland to get the forms first thing tomorrow. First thing yesterday, really.' She left a delicate pause. 'I know you and your wife have mixed feelings about this, and about me. But I'm trusting you to do the right thing.'

George nodded slowly. 'I will,' he said, letting the numbers on the telephone go blurry in his vision. 'I will.'

That same morning Flora had woken in a foul mood. This would be her eighth day straight rising early to cross to the studio, where she'd been desperately trying to put the last touches on an oil figure study before they opened the guesthouse the following week. The stupid thing was already taking far longer than she'd expected, a fact she blamed mostly on her parents' incessant piling on of chores – even if in the back of her mind she suspected it had more to do with her loneliness in Michael's months-long absence, and worse, the spectre of the approaching season. Because if she couldn't make progress on her work now, how would she ever manage when they opened?

As she shrugged on her coat that morning she was getting ready to give herself a typically morose answer, when she opened the front door and came face to face with Michael. 'Oh!' Her bag slid from her shoulder. 'Hello. How long have you been back?'

He smiled. 'Just since last night. I was coming over to make sure you hadn't all abandoned the place.'

Flora tried to return the smile, though in her current mood it felt more like a grimace. 'Nope – still here.'

'And back to the drawing board, it looks like.' He motioned to her bag with a wink that she supposed was meant to look rakish. 'Excuse the pun.'

'Groan.'

Rubbing absent-mindedly at a razor nick on his jaw, he asked if he would finally be allowed to see the studio this year. She narrowed her eyes. In more ways than she usually cared to admit, she'd become a lot like Bella, and that was especially true of her sense of privacy about the studio. No one had ever been invited to see it, not even Michael, not even when he'd badgered her repeatedly the previous year. Not even when she'd been desperate to seduce him.

'We'll see,' was all she said now, moving past him to leave.

'Oh, go on.' He took a step to the side to block her way.

She kept pushing past. 'Sorry.'

He called after her. 'No exceptions? Not even for a clueless old Sassenach like me?' She stopped, sighing, and thought back to the only other time they'd been on the Stùc together, in the school, that first summer he'd visited. How exhilarated she had felt. She wondered if he was thinking of the same thing; if he ever thought of it, as fondly and as often as she did.

'Fine,' she said, turning to face him. 'What are you doing this afternoon?'

His eyes lit up. 'Sounds like I'm visiting you! How's three o'clock?'

She shrugged. 'Tide should be out again by then.'

'Fantastic,' he said, and disappeared inside.

It might actually be quite nice having him over, she told herself, dew soaking into her shoes as she trudged towards the beach. Even their short conversation just now had lifted her mood more quickly than anything else that month, and after his winter away it would be nice to catch up. Besides, wasn't she always wishing more people could see her work? If she wasn't going to art school any time soon she might as well start bringing people to her.

By the time she got to the Stùc, though, she was already regretting the invitation. The prospect of his arrival left her too jittery to concentrate, and certainly too jittery to strip naked and sit in front of the full-length mirror as her current painting required. She'd been uncomfortable enough lounging around undressed to begin with, after Bella had insisted that no one would take her seriously if she couldn't paint a decent nude, but with the thought of Michael walking in on her – even though they'd agreed a specific time, even though the tide was in, even though she'd double- and triple-checked the front door was locked – it was positively unbearable. Instead she sat fully clothed, chipping away at superficial details on the portrait's face, and when her watch passed two she gave up altogether, covering the canvas with a cloth and turning to a book until he arrived, promptly, at three.

Once he'd taken off his shoes – Bella's rule, not hers – she led him to the kitchen, ignoring his eager stares towards the studio and insisting they ought to sit down for tea first. He made some comment about being able to get tea at home, as if he thought she were stalling – but now that she'd admitted someone to her private space, she simply wanted to do it right. She was already planning out the full tour she would give him: the living room, and the sofa where she sat by the fire on the nights she didn't go home; the spot in the orchard where she'd hidden as a child; and the guest bedroom upstairs that she'd now made hers, with a heavy feather pillow from home, and a few books lined up on the nightstand. She would even take him to Bella's room, where she'd lain awake all those years ago, Trevor by her side, listening to the storm outside the windows and Barry's shouting outside the door, and imagining what it would be like to live there all the time.

'So,' Michael said, taking a seat at the kitchen table as she fetched tea makings from the cupboard. 'This is your secret hideaway.'

She laughed. 'I don't know that I'd call it secret.' The kettle was beginning to rattle as the water heated up inside. 'It's not much of a hideaway, either, since Mum and Dad realized the phone was still connected.'

As if on cue, the hall telephone began to ring, but she made no move to answer it; when he asked if she was going to she told him she didn't usually, that it was Bella's line, and that she'd already ignored it a few times that day – and that if it were her parents calling they'd be more persistent. Also on cue, the ringing stopped. 'See?' she said. 'Not even a minute. Mum lets it ring for ten sometimes.'

They chatted for a while longer, but Michael was clearly antsy to get on with it, his leg bouncing up and down under the table and his gaze wandering every minute or two from Flora to the wall clock to the door – so they picked up their mostly full mugs and carried them around the house as she led him from room to room. He seemed pleasantly surprised that he was being shown more than just the studio, nodding intently as she pointed out each of her private landmarks. And just as in the schoolhouse on his first visit, she was in turn pleasantly surprised that he found it all so interesting.

As they made their way downstairs and towards the studio at last, the phone began to ring again. 'You really don't find that annoying?' he asked, shaking his head. She looked up from her place a few steps below him and shrugged. 'They'll give up eventually.'

In the studio itself Flora stood quietly by the door while Michael looked around, remembering Bella's advice before Fort William that she should let her work speak for itself. But Michael's progress from piece to piece was torturously slow, and with each pause, each frown, each silence, her stomach tensed – until she couldn't bear it any longer.

'For God's sake!' she blurted out. 'It's not a bloody museum!'

He glanced at her from the corner of his eye and grinned. 'I know,' he said. 'If it were, there'd be some plaques on the wall to tell me what I'm supposed to think.'

She laughed nervously.

'It's all very good.' He turned to face her now. 'Honest. I'm genuinely impressed.' He nodded towards a messy pastel still life a few feet away. 'I especially like that one. I may have to commission you.'

Her spirits soared at that – and then, when he asked if she was still thinking about art college, plummeted again.

'No,' she said, walking to the window. A few rain clouds were rolling in from the north-west. 'And don't you start.' What was it about these bloody mainlanders that made them think she could just up and disappear?

She felt the floorboards shift as he came towards her. Felt his hand rest on her arm. 'What's wrong?' he asked.

'Nothing,' she said, folding her arms. 'I would love to go to art college, but I can't – and I wish people would stop asking about it.'

'Sorry.' His hand lingered on her shoulder. 'I thought maybe with your brother coming back next year—'

'Forget it,' she sighed. 'It's fine.' He still hadn't moved his hand, and before he could she turned towards him and rested her head on his shoulder.

'You know,' he said, finally. 'I'm here, too. I'm sure we could cope without you.'

'I told you, forget it. It's like my mum said – a pipe dream.' The phone rang again, for longer this time. They waited for it to stop.

'If it's any consolation,' he said. 'I'm glad you'll be sticking around.'

She nuzzled her head against his neck. 'Are you?'

There was a faint rumble of thunder in the distance.

'Of course I am.' He slid his arm all the way around her; still she didn't move.

'I thought you were only interested in the business,' she whispered, her fingers tingling. 'I was too young, you said. The boss's daughter.'

With her ear still to his neck, his reply sounded strangely amplified. 'I don't know.' His hand tensed against her. 'Maybe I was kidding myself.'

She raised her head now and stared at him. 'What?'

'Never mind,' he said. 'Nothing.'

'Michael.' She turned so that they were face to face, with only a few centimetres between them. She could smell the faint, grassy aroma of tea on his breath; the powdery scent of laundry on his shirt.

'Flora, I—'

She kissed him before he could finish, straining forwards on her tiptoes, then stumbled backwards as his hands pushed at her waist. Ended up pressed against the window.

The phone rang again.

'Oh, for fuck's sake.' She pulled away from him, slipped out from beneath his arms and ran into the hallway. Her fingers were still tingling, and the palms of her hands, and her arms, all the way up to her shoulders. She picked up the receiver and growled hello.

'Flora?' It was her father. 'I... your mother and I think you should make your way home for the evening.'

She groaned. 'Why, Dad? What is it?'

There was a long, sad silence.

'Dad?'

'There's a big storm on its way,' he said at last. 'We're worried about you.'

A creamy shade of white began to spread beneath Flora's fingernails as she gripped the edge of the telephone table. 'I'm fine, Dad. I'll leave soon.'

'Flora, please.'

Michael had come into the hallway, and stood listening as she gave in, exasperated. Once she'd hung up, he shook his head. 'Maybe it's a sign.'

She pouted. 'It's a sign I should take this bloody thing off the hook.'

'No.' He walked over to her. 'You might not mind staying over here for the night, but it would look pretty bad if I did.'

She hung her arms around his neck. 'They might not notice.'

'Flora.'

'Oh, fine.' She let her hands drop and pushed past him to turn off the studio lights.

They made the walk across the isthmus in silence, dark seeping down the sides of the sky and their footsteps in the spring grass the only sound between them; their goodbye outside the guesthouse was just as quiet, fumbling, a handshake becoming a pat on the arm becoming a kiss on the cheek, but stopping there, clouds of breath dissolving all around them and the air the colour of blue eyes. Inside, she took off her shoes, and had climbed half-way up the stairs, a faint smile on her face and the small of her back still humming from where it had pushed up against the window, when her father appeared in the shadows on the landing.

'We left some soup on the stove if you're hungry.'

She shook her head and mumbled that she wasn't, and after mechanically giving him a hug she started towards her room. It was only once she'd flopped down on her bed, that smile still on her face, and lain for almost a minute with the lights off, staring out of her window at the streak of the Milky Way, that she finally heard her father's study door click shut.

11

Flora often imagined, in the following weeks, what sort of leisurely romance she and Michael might have enjoyed if the circumstances had been different. She pictured months of secret meetings on the Stùc and brief encounters, before they told her parents, under the cover of night by the guesthouse back door; she pictured mornings wrapped up in the bedsheets at his cottage, afternoons spent reading each other their favourite books, and evenings drinking wine on the studio floor, watching the sunset through the giant windows. After a few months of that – once he'd conquered his silly fear of being banished forever – they'd have finally come clean, and entered a pleasant, gradual descent into domesticity and marriage and children, taking over the guesthouse the way her father had always hoped one of the children would.

It might have been nice, she'd think to herself – and then she would shudder, relieved, and be thankful things had taken another turn.

The morning after she had left Michael on the doorstep, she'd started awake in her clothes a little before six-thirty, light pouring in through her still open shutters. Rather than leaving for the Stùc she busied herself downstairs with the week's accumulated chores, assuming it would be only a few hours until he returned to sweep her off her feet – but the whole day there was no sign of him. She waited right through until the stars were out again, forgoing any time at the studio and her languishing figure painting, and by the time she sat down for dinner she was scolding herself for wasting an entire day. She debated seeking him out at his cottage that evening, but each hour she'd sat waiting her confidence from the night before had dripped away, as if a dream, until she was convinced he wasn't coming over because he regretted what had happened.

So doing the washing up that night she was in a bleak mood, standing in silence while her mother passed her dishes to dry and her father retreated with his crossword as usual. Or not quite as usual: gone was any suggestion that she join him. Anxious that he, too, had somehow lost interest in her, she started towards the pub as soon as the kitchen was clean, wiping her hands against her jeans, but as she passed the phone it began to ring and she stopped to answer it, picking up to Bella's voice just as she heard the almighty clatter in the pub, her father practically falling through the door. He stood there watching, a panicked look in his eyes as her confusion quickly gave way to anger, and once she'd thanked Bella and reassured her that yes, it certainly *was* worth considering, and yes, she'd be on the first ferry the next morning, she slammed down the phone and stalked towards George, still cowering in the pub doorway.

'What were you thinking?' she screamed, spittle flying from her mouth. 'I thought you were on my side!'

'I was going to tell you,' he stammered, looking at the floor. 'I was. I promise.'

But she didn't listen, couldn't listen, just spun and pushed past her mother – summoned from the kitchen by the commotion – and stormed upstairs, wedging a chair beneath her room's door handle and ignoring his every entreaty to come out. The next morning she woke with the first light again, this time on purpose, and was out of the house and on the road to the jetty before either of her parents could intercept her. She waited there for three hours, shivering in the damp morning air and watching alternately for the ferry on the horizon and her father coming towards her down the road. He didn't, which somehow infuriated her more.

On the mainland she climbed on the first train south and made her way straight to St Fillan's, where the delighted career officer supplied her with a university application and talked her through completing it. That done, she dashed straight out again, not pausing until the form was safely in the post at Fort William. Only then did she exhale, and only once she was back at the dock in Mallaig, her mind slowly unwinding, did she realize that she hadn't thought to stop and visit Trevor. And more startling still, she had spent the entire day – and the entire restless night before it – without thinking once of Michael. She felt an odd sort of guilt that she'd forgotten him so easily – but when he finally turned up to see her that night it was clear she needn't have. He hadn't even known she'd left.

'I'm sorry I didn't come sooner,' he said, sitting down next to her in the sitting room. (She was pointedly avoiding both the pub and her father that night, after a cursory, mostly silent family dinner.) 'The truth is, I didn't really know what I was going to say.' He'd been talking to the floor until now, but here he looked up. 'I've had some time to think things through the last few days, though, and... I think – I mean, I'd like—'

She didn't let him finish; by now she felt so sure in her decision, so serene, there seemed little point in dragging things out.

'I'm leaving,' she said.

He stopped, confused. 'You're what?'

'I'm leaving,' she repeated. 'At the end of the summer. I'm going to Edinburgh.'

'But…' He shook his head as she continued to stare calmly at him. 'But what about your parents? What about all the work you need to do here?' His face flushed. 'What about me?'

'I'm sure my parents can work out a way to cope,' she told him. 'You said so yourself.' She cocked her head. 'And what about you, anyway? It took you three days to decide what you wanted. Is that supposed to make me feel hopeful?' She thought back again to that moment in the studio those few days earlier, the one that had left her so electrified, but still she didn't waver – because now she thought back, too, to the night of the Leavers' Dinner at St Fillan's, and the subsequent drunken groping; to the first boy she'd properly, privately kissed, at Maisie's behest, after the lads had raided the lassies' dormitory one night; to her distant, youthful fantasies about Tam. And she asked herself what the difference was between all of it, really, as long as she got out now.

He was looking at the floor again. 'I just thought…' He swallowed. 'I thought we had something.' He shut his eyes tightly for a moment, and then looked up at her. 'And I don't mean what happened the other day, I mean everything. Even the first time I came here there was something – wasn't there?'

That confirmation, finally, that she'd correctly guessed his feelings all along, almost made her crack – or at least made her consider leaning forward and kissing him again. But she knew that would be the wrong decision, for both of them, so instead she stared back, trying to compose an expression that looked both sympathetic and firm, and took a deep breath. Reminded herself of all the justifications she'd already cooked up for herself: that she wasn't abandoning anyone this way, wasn't *choosing* to apply to art school, wasn't putting anyone second. She was only taking advantage of an opportunity that had presented itself, and if she got to Edinburgh and suddenly had a change of heart – realized she had to drop everything and run home and fall into Michael's arms – well, she could still do that. But it didn't seem very likely.

'I'm sorry,' she said, reaching over to squeeze his hand. He squeezed back, but the room stayed glum, and silent.

Compared to Flora's many departures for St Fillan's over the years, her send-off to Edinburgh that autumn was subdued. She hadn't, of course, been expecting a party; the feelings at home were still too raw to yield even to feigned optimism. But over the months since her decision, the necessities of living closely knit had as usual dulled any initial animosity, and she had at least expected everybody to turn up.

Her mother announced she was staying at home that afternoon, though, clucking that somebody had to watch the guests, and Michael, to Flora's dismay, wouldn't even answer her last, desperate knocks on his door. And though Trevor and her father were at the ferry to say goodbye, neither of them helped drag her trunk on board; neither of them offered words of reassurance. Her father merely pleaded that she stay in touch, and Trevor begrudged her a single, limp hug – and then she was watching the island pull away, and scanning the hills for any sign of Michael.

That tepid farewell left her brooding, through the ferry crossing and the restless night at her Mallaig B&B, and for the entire trip to Edinburgh the next morning, too. From the time her train pulled out of the station at six o'clock, all the way down through the glens and lochs and barren hills of the west coast, she wondered why they were finding it so hard to be happy for her. Wondered why she was the only one to whom this didn't seem like a disaster and a betrayal. It was only when the train emerged from the tunnel below Princes

Street, when she saw the black spire of the Scott Monument ahead of her and the castle towering to her right, that her worries drained away. She stepped onto the platform at Waverley, inhaling the musty smoke in the air, and it was as if she had been reset. For those next months she was too busy starting her course – and meeting new people, and exploring Edinburgh – to think of anything else.

When she returned home for Christmas, Michael had already left for his habitual months in England, and while she wished he'd been there to reassure her that he still, at least, considered her a friend, she told herself his absence was for the best; she was glad to be able to focus on her family. There was something this Christmas that seemed different from her trips home from St Fillan's, something more joyful, in spite – or maybe because – of all the conflict earlier that year.

In any case, it wasn't until her Easter break that she next overlapped with Michael on the island, and to her relief he seemed pleased to see her. It was almost as if his failure to say goodbye that previous summer had never happened; he invited her to his cottage for a nightcap her first evening back, and they chatted happily for hours. He told her how nice it was to see her again, and how much he'd missed her, and about the pet projects he'd started in order to pass the time: a reference book about British films he'd always dreamed of writing; a small vegetable patch to supplement George's. Mostly, though, he complained about his lack of progress at the guesthouse, and her parents' intractable resistance to his proposed improvements.

She'd already heard the other side of his complaints from her parents themselves, who'd grown equally frustrated with Michael: *sometimes it's as if he's changing things just to give him something to do!* her mother had grumbled over Christmas dinner, and though her father was as usual more measured in his reaction, he still clearly disapproved. *It's not that they're not good ideas*, he'd said – *I'm just not sure they're right for us. What do we need a computer for, anyway?*

In her parents' retelling much of it *had* sounded unnecessary, and she'd shared their knee-jerk suspicions, but the way Michael put it now it all seemed eminently reasonable. The computer, he said, his cheeks turning pink, would reduce their costs in the long term, not to mention saving countless hours of labour – and the new laundry schedule he'd proposed could hardly be any less efficient than the haphazard 'system' they'd had before.

'And the bloody bacon!' he added, rolling his eyes. 'I swear they don't want me to save them any money.' (He'd switched the guesthouse's supplier to a wholesaler on the mainland, who gave them a better deal on the cost of distribution. It was, in fact, exactly the same bacon from exactly the same farmer George had always dealt with, but he and Maureen insisted it tasted odd, and had asked Michael repeatedly to change it back. *There's just... something*, George had said, gravely.)

As they opened their second bottle of wine that night she promised she'd try to soften them up a little, and he laughed and wished her luck. 'But look at me being rude,' he said, shaking his head. 'You don't want to talk about this boring business stuff – what have you been up to all year?'

So she told him: regaled him with stories of her tiny room in Bella's Marchmont flat, and the double-decker buses that swooped by on the city streets and left her breathless; about her sunset strolls up Arthur's Seat, and her studio space at the art college, and the intoxicating bustle of people that had greeted her at every turn. The only thing she didn't tell him about – not at first, anyway – was Oliver, the handsome, irrepressible boy from the Borders with whom she'd fallen hopelessly in love. They'd met during her first month in town at some freshers' event: he had long black hair and a thin face, the way she imagined Barry might look these days, and he had stunned her into an odd sort of silence. At nineteen he was several years her junior, and yet somehow seemed more worldly than anyone she'd met before, with his designer clothes and wicked sense of humour and stories from his gap year in Malaysia – and she'd been enchanted. Her thoughts of him replaced all her lingering *what ifs* about Michael, and a week after the start of term she'd followed him, puppy-like, from class to the pub to his flat in Tollcross, where they'd fallen into bed together and hardly left since.

Her plan had been not to divulge any of this to Michael, for some murky reason she couldn't quite identify – but while she succeeded for a while he soon forced her hand. Around two in the morning, the third bottle of wine half-empty at their feet, he leaned forward and tried to kiss her. She pulled away, inhaling sharply. 'Michael.'

He pulled away, too, and looked immediately, as always, to the floor. His hair had grown into a messy, side-parted shag while she'd been away, and she thought to herself, as she stared at him staring at the floor, that it suited him; matched his personality better than the professional crop he'd always had before. A little more youthful; a little harder to predict.

'I'm sorry,' he said, quietly.

'Don't be.' She shuffled closer to him and put her hand on his arm. 'I wish I could. I mean, I'm flattered. But—'

'It doesn't matter,' he said. 'You don't need to explain yourself.'

She squeezed his arm tighter. 'I have a boyfriend now. It wouldn't be right.'

He sat there, nodding, still silent.

'I should probably leave,' she said, wobbling to her feet.

'You don't have to.' He sniffed. 'I'm not angry or anything. Not at you. I'm glad you're happy.'

She thanked him and left in a hurry, too charmed by that answer to be sure she could resist much longer. For that same reason she avoided him for the rest of the trip, and he seemed to get the message. While nothing had happened, though, the mere act of considering Michael again made her feel so guilty that when she returned to Edinburgh she flung herself, out of some twisted sense of atonement, into ever larger commitments with Oliver. Soon they were living together, and she spent the following Christmas with his family instead of hers, and increasingly she wriggled out of spending any time on the island at all, except for the occasional weekend when she knew Michael would be away. She missed the place, of course. Missed the silence of the studio and the long sunsets in July, and most of all, despite everything, missed her evenings with her father in the pub.

Each day she spent in Edinburgh, though, each new friend made and each success at school, convinced her more and more that her future lay beyond the island's shores – and pushed her family into the final stages of the slow, inexorable decline that had started, one spring, almost an entire decade earlier.

1988

12

It was April, and Maureen was alone in the house: George was taking Flora for her introductory visit to St Fillan's, and Trevor had gone to the jetty to see them off. Under other circumstances she might have gone with them, or at least waved from the window as they disappeared down the road, but the trip had become such a point of contention over the past few days that she'd only stood, arms crossed, as they pulled on their shoes in the hallway – and as soon as the door slammed she bustled off to the kitchen. *Stubborn old sod didn't even say goodbye.*

It had started the previous week, when he came upstairs to bed one night. Maureen had been lying beneath their quilt for almost an hour already, planning what to say while she half-read a tattered Poirot, and when he walked in and began to undress, she looked up, swallowing. 'I've been thinking,' she said, softly. 'Maybe I could take Flora to St Fillan's next week.'

He climbed under the covers next to her. 'Why?'

'I don't know,' she said, as casually as she'd been practising it in her head. 'I thought it might be nice to go to Glasgow afterwards and do some shopping.' A pause – also well rehearsed. 'A few of the bedspreads upstairs could do with replacing.'

George grunted, trying to find a comfortable spot on the

pillow. 'Why do you need to go all the way to Glasgow to get bedspreads?'

Sighing, she set her book down on the bedside table, next to her old, brass alarm clock. 'I don't.' She'd been prepared for this, too, even if she'd hoped she was being pessimistic. 'But there's a public lecture at the university next week I'd like to go to. A history professor who's just back from Morocco.'

'Well, I've got banking to do next week,' he said, reaching across her to turn out the bedside lamp and planting his usual goodnight kiss on her cheek. 'And we can't leave Trevor on his own – so I think you'll have to miss it, this time.'

Calmly, resigned, she'd turned towards him, though in the dark she couldn't see anything except the light's lingering neon afterimage. 'I could take Trevor with me. Or do the banking for you.'

'Let's talk about it in the morning,' he yawned. 'I'm shattered.'

She felt her jaw clench. 'Fine,' she said. 'Goodnight.'

But predictably, they didn't talk about it in the morning; she wouldn't bring it up, waiting with equal parts hope and bitterness to see if he'd do it himself, and he, of course, had already made up his mind. Her, doing the banking? What a ridiculous suggestion! It was completely bloody typical: he was so particular about the guesthouse errands that he never let anybody else take over. Or never let *her* take over, anyway. His monopoly over mainland visits was so absolute it had been years since she'd been anywhere other than her cousins' house in Perth, or the pub in Mallaig for Sunday lunch – and though in the past she'd sometimes visited Glasgow on days out with the other island women, Mrs Kilgourie was the only one of them left now, and lately she didn't have much appetite for travel.

Whenever she broached the issue with George, however, he always gave the same, silly excuse: *you've not spent as much time on the mainland as I have, Reenie. You don't know how to handle yourself.* What cheek! And whose fault was that, anyway? One of these days she should just go without telling him – spend a week living large and then waltz back and see what he said! Except the fear always nagged that maybe he was right – that if she disappeared by herself she *would* end up in a gutter somewhere, and with no one back home having the slightest idea where to look for her. When she was fifteen she'd stowed away to Mallaig, thinking she would travel the world, but she'd had no real plan, no money, and when she'd arrived she only stood there on the dock, paralysed – until one of the ferrymen recognized her and asked if she needed any help, and she burst into tears and asked to be taken home. And despite her many years of experience since, she'd always wondered if, faced once more with the prospect of self-reliance on the mainland, she'd freeze just as she had then.

Still, in bed again the night before George and Flora were due to leave, she'd made one last attempt to change his mind, asking if she might take Flora after all – and one last time, he instantly dismissed her. Frustrated, she tried to take a firmer stand, but he just snapped at her to let it be, and they started to argue, and only stopped when Trevor appeared at the door to ask if everything was all right.

In the kitchen, now, she sighed, walking to a shelf above the sink and pulling down a recipe book. She would put her foot down next time, she told herself, settling into a chair at the table to decide on dinner – even as, in the back of her mind, she suspected that probably she wouldn't.

At the jetty, George and the children found Mr Kilgourie also waiting for the ferry. 'My my,' said the man, with his usual chuckle, when he noticed Flora's overnight bag. 'It seems like only yesterday we were saying farewell to Barry.'

'She's not leaving yet,' mumbled Trevor, fidgeting with the life preserver hanging next to him on the sea wall. 'It's just a visit.'

George patted Trevor on the head, and smiled at Mr Kilgourie. 'And what brings you over today?'

He laughed. 'Oh, nothing much. A few bits of business.'

Trevor saw his father raise an eyebrow at that, saw his forehead wrinkle as he asked what sort of business, but then he returned to staring at the life preserver, uninterested in the conversation and too upset at Flora's departure to talk to her. Even as they hugged goodbye, Trevor's gaze stayed wilfully on some vague point behind her, and it wasn't until the rest of them had climbed aboard and the ship was reversing into the sound that he let himself look up. Flora, smiling, waved at him from the foredeck; he gave a reluctant half-wave back, and then watched as she turned and disappeared inside.

Spring had come early that year, on the heels of a mild winter. Already the island was dotted with primrose and coltsfoot, plus a few shearwaters that had returned early for the summer, and instead of walking home Trevor took advantage of the mild weather and turned off the road from the jetty, skirting the island's shoreline in the breeze off the water. A way down the beach he passed one of the intrepid shearwaters, perched alone on a rock; it gave him an inquisitive caw.

Mr Lewis had told Trevor once that when the Vikings visited the Hebrides they had been so terrified by the birds' calls, a ghostly, roaring wail, that they'd assumed the islands were full of trolls. Trevor snorted at the thought as he studied the bird now, its head a downy grey and its beak a gleaming stick of charcoal, and wondered how anyone could ever find the things scary. As if to prove his fearlessness he picked up a pebble and pitched it towards the shearwater's perch, but the throw landed short and the bird, unfazed, only stared back.

In the distance the ferry's foghorn sounded, a long, bassoon lament, and Trevor felt a few tears sting his eyes. There had been talk of Flora leaving for months, of course, but until his sister started to pack the night before Trevor had remained impervious to even the slightest unease; it was only with the ferry disappearing that the truth completely struck him: soon, he'd be on his own. The island's final child. He pictured Flora's room back at the house – the heaps of clothes draped over every chair and bedpost, the creeping mess of toys and coloured pencils – and imagined it getting gradually tidied away over the coming months, after Flora's departure proper. Imagined it emptied out completely.

If he'd been older than seven and a half, he might not have cried – might have tried to keep the tears in, or to pretend they were down to the cool wind blowing in his face. If he'd been older, too, he might have been better able to rationalize, to tell himself that he didn't see Flora much these days anyway, between her art lessons with Bella and her evenings in the pub with dad and their mysterious little word games – and that after a day or two he'd barely notice her absence. But all he could do now was think of their walks to school, and of listening to her hum as she dressed each morning, and of all their rainy-day projects together since Barry had left for St Fillan's. Just a month ago they'd written a book, concocting a story in the cave of Flora's bottom bunk and transferring it to paper, page by page, illustrations by her and smudged, wobbly lettering by him. Who would he do that with now? Who would he talk to while his parents worked?

Angry, he kicked at a lone dandelion that had strayed into the sand from the grass bordering the beach, and plopped to the ground to tear at its leaves. After a few minutes of that he just sat drawing spirals on the ground until eventually, light fading, he started back towards home.

His mother greeted him in the hallway, hands on hips and expression stern. 'Where have you been?' she clucked. 'The ferry left two hours ago.'

'Sorry.' He looked at his feet. 'I was at the beach.'

'Well, come along, no more dawdling – I need your help with dinner.'

He followed her obediently to the kitchen, where three giant pots bubbled on the stove and a mess of cookbooks, cutting blocks and vegetables covered the table. In the past she'd often tried to get him and Flora to help with the cooking, but they were so good at distracting each other with side games – peeling designs into potato skins, making up songs to go along with their chores – that usually she ended up excusing them. So was *this* what was in store for him, he wondered, with Flora leaving? Endless evenings spent actually helping his mother, bored and on his own? He felt himself tearing up again and quickly shut his eyes, letting the room's humid, fragrant air wash against his face.

'Now what?' she asked. When he opened his eyes she was staring at him and tightening her apron, a few new reddish stains down its front. 'Come on, we haven't got all night.'

This military cooking regime of hers was a recent development, one that Trevor had watched with curiosity. Though his mother had always been in charge of food at the guesthouse, both for customers and for the family, in the past year or so her planning and freezer restocking had become increasingly elaborate. Where once she'd used the off-season to pursue other projects – mending clothes, reading books, spending evenings with the children – now she seemed to see that extra time as the principal front in some ongoing campaign against famine. Each week her grocery orders swelled as she experimented with exotic new recipes, and each week the pantry shelves would fill with cooling jams and pickles and preserves, their jars dark-coloured and full of shadows – like the shelves, Trevor imagined, of some mad scientist's laboratory.

A few months earlier she had completely filled the chest freezer, for the first time ever, and after many nights of squabbling had convinced George to buy a second for the overflow. The thing had finally floated across on the ferry just a few weeks ago, and had taken most of the day to get home because the dolly they normally used to shift heavy supplies wasn't big enough. Instead George, Mr Kilgourie and Mr Lewis had taken turns carrying it in pairs, sweat freckling across their backs as the sun burnt off the morning mist and Trevor, giving occasional shouts of encouragement, cleared the path ahead of them. By early afternoon, when at last they'd reached the hillcrest overlooking the village, Mr Lewis had burst into giddy laughter at the task's absurdity, quickly setting the rest of them off, and amidst their guffaws they decided it was time for a break; they sent Trevor home to fetch some sandwiches, and when he returned he found them using the freezer as a bench, still giggling to each other and squeezing sweat from the hair behind their ears. When at last they deposited the monolith at the guesthouse's front door, the sun had almost set, and they immediately stumbled to the pub – where George set a line of pints along the bar and told the other two to drink up.

'What should I do?' Trevor asked now, flopping into a seat at the table.

'Stand up again, for a start,' his mother replied, dragging her finger down a recipe and leaving a faint, glistening trail on the page.

'Keep an eye on that stew on the front burner for me. It needs stirring, and I've carrots to chop.'

Without a word, Trevor got up and pulled his chair over to the stove.

'And once that comes off the heat,' she continued, still peering at her cookbook, 'you can clear the table and set out some plates.'

He managed a quiet *Yes, Mum*, and climbed onto the chair, staring into the muddy, mahogany goop in the pot. Behind him, a knife began to clack-clack against one of the cutting boards, and with a sigh he began to stir.

Later, at the dinner table, they ate in silence; even with the others gone they had taken their normal seats out of habit, Maureen at the head of the table and Trevor two places down and perpendicular to her. That odd configuration made conversation seem unnatural somehow, stilted, and after a few half-hearted questions and answers about Trevor's homework they simply gave up, listening instead to a clock tick in the next room and the creak of the table as they mopped their plates with bread.

As they cleared the dishes afterwards, Trevor asked hopefully if they could play a board game, desperate not to go upstairs to the empty family rooms – and to his surprise, his mother quickly agreed. When they moved to the sitting room and dug through the toy cabinet, though, they realized that almost everything they owned required four players.

'We could try Monopoly,' Trevor said, starting to pull it from the stack.

Maureen shook her head and told him it would take too long. Instead she reached into the back of the cupboard and dislodged a dog-eared deck of cards wrapped in a brittle rubber band. 'Why don't I teach you rummy?' she said, waving the cards from side to side. 'Your father and I used to play that all the time before Barry was born.'

They returned to the kitchen to sit at the table, this time huddled together at the corner nearest the sink. Maureen explained the rules as she dealt the first hand, and though she faltered over several of the finer details Trevor was a natural, falling into the rhythm of the game almost immediately and thoroughly trouncing his mother, six hands in a row, until she announced it was time for bed. He couldn't stop chattering about it as they marched upstairs – *I was good, wasn't I, Mum? Do you think Dad'll be impressed, Mum?* – and even as he brushed his teeth on tiptoes at the sink, he kept mumbling through the minty foam: *can we play again tomorrow?* It was only after she'd tucked him in and he was lying alone in his darkened room, his excitement wearing off, that he realized she hadn't given him a kiss before turning off the light.

Suddenly he found himself missing Flora again, wishing she were there so he could sneak across the hallway, as he'd often done before, and ask her what she thought that meant. With a muffled cry he lifted his arms and slammed them into the mattress beside him, whispering angrily to himself about how much he hated that stupid mainland school. He spent another hour, almost, lying there clenching and unclenching his fists in frustration, his quiet tears returning and warming the pillow against his face, until finally, sometime past eleven, he drifted off to sleep.

In the kitchen, for different reasons, Maureen was also upset. Or not upset, exactly; unsettled. Distracted. Every few minutes she would blink and find herself staring at a ribbon of carrot skin on the floor, or lost in the woodgrain of the countertop, her mind miles away and her brow sore from frowning.

It was the rummy. Years had passed since she'd last seen those cards, the peeling gloss at their corners and the kitschy photographs on their versos, and finding them again had reminded her of the day she and George had bought them. It was during a rare trip to Edinburgh, long before the children were born, for the wedding of some wealthy cousin of his to which they nearly hadn't gone; George ignored the invitation when it came, and only after Maureen discovered it, while emptying the bins just days before the RSVP was due, had he reluctantly agreed to go. *It will be so nice!* she'd said, stroking his collarbone underneath their sheets that night. *We can see the castle, and go to the National Museum… And you can show me where you used to work!* And maybe, she thought to herself, she could vicariously live the grand wedding she'd never had herself. Oh, it had seemed like a wonderful idea – until they got there. The ceremony in the old vaulted hall at St Giles was nice enough, but the reception afterwards in the City Chambers was an unmitigated embarrassment: she'd worn her best formal dress, a navy-blue one made of heavy draped wool, and he a second-hand taupe suit with flared trousers that he'd bought in Fort William on their way down. Both seemed to moulder, in the Chambers' warm yellow light, among the rich blacks and reds of so many carefully tailored gowns – and they'd spent an hour huddled in a corner while packs of Edinburgh's well-to-do sneered in their direction. When they at last gave up and said their goodbyes, the bride and groom smiled kindly and expressed disappointment, but Maureen was convinced she saw a look of relief in their eyes.

On the way back to their hotel, they'd passed a clutch of gaudy souvenir stores on the Royal Mile, and George, with a laugh, steered them inside, insisting they get something to preserve their treasured memories of Edinburgh. They tried on scratchy T-shirts and flimsy tam o'shanters, played with plush Loch Ness monsters and googly-eyed haggises, and eventually they settled on the playing cards, with their ridiculous photographs on the back: a bagpiper in full tartan regalia, standing in front of a castle on a loch. (It had no relation to the city at all, which was perhaps why they liked it so much.) They snickered all the way back to the hotel and, lucky enough to snag a table on the train north, gleefully tore open the box and played rummy the whole way. They played it once they were home, too, and other games with George's parents – whist, bridge – until, as she'd told Trevor earlier, Barry was born and their nights at the card table came to a quiet end.

She snapped out of her reverie again, this time to her own reflection in the darkened kitchen window, and turned to the stove, where one of the pots from earlier was full of now-cold stew. With a ladle she transferred the stuff to two large storage tubs, which she lidded and labelled and stacked on the counter before making her way towards the back door. Like the pantry, it opened off a small alcove in the corner of the room and onto their modest, walled-in garden, which was suddenly illuminated, as she stepped outside, by a motion-sensitive floodlight above the door. She trudged across the grass to where a rotting wood gate sagged in a gap in the stonework, and propped it open with a rock before returning to the kitchen to fetch the stew.

When George and Mr Kilgourie had tried to move the new freezer inside, they'd caught on an unexpected snag: they couldn't get it through the pantry door. It wasn't an issue of width, which George had measured three times before parting with any cash, but the angles of rotation required through the alcove from the kitchen; they spent an hour trying to manoeuvre it around the corner, and two days drawing diagrams in search of a solution – and in the meantime the thing just sprawled there in the kitchen, wedged beside the alcove door, until eventually Maureen, frustrated, told them to give up. *And do what with it, Reenie?* George had snapped back. *You're not the one who carried it all the way down here!*

That was when she'd suggested putting it in one of the old village houses – she only wanted it for extra storage, she said, so she wouldn't need to get at it that often. And while George had initially scoffed, dismayed by the prospect of carrying it another few hundred feet down the road, by the end of the day he was tinkering with the generator at the old Braithwaite house – he'd had enough of Mr Kilgourie's attempts at geometry lessons.

With the garden door propped open, Maureen fetched a camping headlamp from the drawer beside the sink and slipped it over her head, fiddling with the strap as she moved towards the counter and the waiting stew. Once she'd switched on the bulb she took a deep breath and picked up the two tubs, and finally hobbled from the kitchen and into the garden.

At the gate she turned onto a small path that ran behind the village buildings, an old byway for the locals from the days when boatloads of tourists would clog the main road. The guesthouse floodlight clicked off and slowly dimmed behind her as she shuffled along, the brush on either side darkening until the halo from her headlamp was all that lit the ground at her feet.

When she finally reached the Braithwaite house, shoulders aching, she carefully bent her knees and set the containers down by the back door, leaning against the wall for a minute as she caught her breath. In the distance she could still make out the dark silhouette of the guesthouse, and was glad to see no light coming from Trevor's window; he'd been so worked up after their game tonight she'd been afraid he might not sleep.

Shaking out her arms, she turned to the cottage door and pushed it open. The new freezer was right there, just beyond the threshold, an enormous white coffin sitting in the middle of what had once been the Braithwaites' kitchen – where Maureen had sat herself, more times than she could remember, chatting with Gillian and looking through mail-order catalogues. She hated that the freezer had been plonked there so carelessly, not even flush against a wall – but when George had carried it over with Mr Kilgourie, shirt drenched in sweat again, he'd refused to move it any farther than the door, and she hadn't been able to come up with a good reason why he should. It just made the place feel less like anything that had once been a home, somehow; seemed to seal the building's fate as derelict.

The Braithwaites had left years earlier, when Barry was only a few years old, but in fact Maureen had been here much more recently: when the ratcatchers had reappeared two Januaries ago to start their cull, there had been too many of them, with too much equipment, to accommodate the whole lot at the guesthouse, so instead they'd camped out in several of the old village homes. The Braithwaites', the closest to the guesthouse, became their unofficial headquarters, and Maureen stopped by almost daily with news and mail from the mainland. Out of good manners she always tried not to linger, but David, the team leader, a tallish man with silver hair at his temples and large oblong glasses, would often stand and chat with her on the doorstep – about the weather, or the team's progress, or whatever else happened to occur to him.

The men were there for months, toiling away at their gruesome task, and if they'd seemed a nuisance on their first visit then on their return they were out-and-out invasive. Their giant metal traps cluttered the island from edge to edge, laid out every few yards as if some strange new weed had taken root, and whenever

Maureen walked to the Stùc to collect the children – a necessity, with the bridge blown away – she would hear the things snapping shut around her, chunks of bloody carcass flying out of the grass. At the peak of the cull, when the clean-up crew was struggling to keep up, she would smell the rotting flesh almost everywhere she went.

What struck the islanders more, though, before long, was the constant presence of the trappers in the pub: they were like a whole new set of regulars, appearing every evening for the home-cooked dinners Maureen provided or, when they opted instead for instant noodles by their sleeping bags, for a post-meal drink to soothe the aches and pains of work. *It's nice to have the place full again*, Peter Manning whispered to her one night, and Mr Kilgourie, eavesdropping from the next stool, nodded vigorously in agreement. So did Maureen; though the crowd was clearly smaller than it often could be on busy summer weekends, this felt more like a community than those streams of day-tripping tourists, and it was nice to have people to talk to beyond the Kilgouries and the Mannings and the Pikes. (The Thomases, the only other hangers-on, had moved to Dundee a few weeks after Christmas.)

That May, near the notional start of the season, and after a full three weeks of empty traps, David had appeared in the pub one night and declared the cull complete. *Rejoice!* cried George, who was so relieved they'd be able to open on time that he announced free drinks for all, and sent Trevor and Flora to fetch the other islanders. Soon the room was churning with bodies and roaring with cheer, and the party carried on for hours, through a whole keg and a late summer sunset – until eventually, sometime past midnight, the guests began to trickle away. Maureen was at the front door seeing off the Pikes when she heard the commotion. Hurrying back to the pub, she found that one of the trappers, a little too merry, had thrown up in the middle of the room. David was kneeling beside the man and apologizing repeatedly to George, who meanwhile was standing feckless behind the bar – so with a brusque step forward Maureen took charge, waking Flora from where she'd dozed off in the corner and commanding her to fetch the mop, and snapping at George to keep on serving drinks.

'And you and I,' she said, turning to David, who was still on the floor, 'are going to get this dope to bed.'

'Oh, there's no need for that,' he said, getting to his feet. 'One of the lads can help.'

'Nonsense,' said Maureen, wobbling, a little tipsy herself. 'No need to tear anyone from the party.'

Behind the bar, she saw George raise an eyebrow.

'If you're sure,' said David, pulling the drunk man up and slipping an arm around his back, and waiting for Maureen to do the same. 'Okay then. Off we go.'

They guided him down the hallway and out of the house, and then along the main road towards the Braithwaites' cottage. As they reached the front door, David made his umpteenth apology.

'Ach, don't be silly,' she replied, 'We were all young once.'

He laughed. 'Once?'

'I'm forty, Mr Cox – I can hardly call myself young any more.' Without thinking she'd shaved a few years off her actual age, though she wasn't quite sure why; she'd long ago grown comfortable with the idea that her youth had totally escaped her.

'Forty!' He shook his head. 'I long for those days. I'm pushing fifty.'

'Oh, but you don't look a day over forty-five,' she said, smiling.

The drunk belched between them.

'Charming,' said David.

Inside, he settled the man in his sleeping bag while Maureen searched through the old store cupboard for a bucket to leave next to him, and finally, standing together in the kitchen, in the exact spot where the freezer now hummed, she looked hopefully at him and asked if he would come rejoin the party.

He shook his head. 'No, I think I'd just as well be calling it a night. We old fogies have to look after ourselves, you know.' The laugh lines around his eyes seemed to deepen a little.

'Goodnight then, Mr Cox.'

'And goodnight, Mrs McCloud.'

In one of her romance novels, she thought, that would have been when he leaned forward to kiss her. In her memory, sometimes, it still was. But at the time he only smiled, and she, still teetering on her feet from the drink, squeezed his arm and turned to leave. It had been enough, though – that sordid, impulsive desire – to shake her from her rut. No, nothing had happened, it was true, and during the trappers' remaining week there were no further incidents. But she had wanted something, hadn't she? Had followed him home that night out of more than her hostess's desire to keep the party going?

Of course, there was no question of pursuing anything serious. Even if she felt less sure of that now than she had at the time, she couldn't bear the thought of leaving the children. Besides, beyond her intermittent fears about handling herself on the mainland, she had real, practical problems to consider. Where would she live? What would she do? She had no money of her own, no job experience, and the few ex-island friends with whom she kept in touch seemed to be having a hard enough time scraping by as it was, without having to help Maureen as well. Assuming they even would, if she fled her family in disrepute. At best she might have been able to stay with her cousins in Perth until she found her feet, but she wasn't sure she could depend on them, either; in the years since her marriage, she'd grown convinced they liked George better.

So after David had left she'd buckled down and put him out of her head. Whatever she'd felt that night was just a silly fantasy, she told herself, and if she was sensible, there was really nothing about life at home that was particularly bad. Predictable, maybe; boring from time to time. But never bad.

Despite those rationalizations, though, the bugbears and discontents continued to collect, each one transforming David into more of a panacea. She even wrote him a letter a few months later, explaining how much she missed him and suggesting that perhaps she could come visit him on the mainland. But in the end she only dropped it off the end of the jetty and watched it float away with the waves – and then spent the whole of the following week terrified it might wash ashore again for the children to find.

As she closed the freezer now, her cheeks still tingling from the cold air, she took a wistful look around the empty kitchen, seeing herself again in the spot where they'd stood that night, and imagined that fanciful, romance novel scene for the thousandth time. She wasn't sure she'd ever quite be rid of it.

13

August, and the long trailing off of summer. It had been a brisk season, the guesthouse full most nights and the day trippers turning out in large numbers, thanks mainly to the mainland media's coverage of the cull. George in particular found the headlines hilarious (*Scottish Island Smells a Rat* was his favourite), and started a collection of cuttings that he would proudly show off to anyone who asked. He even discussed framing a few to hang up around the pub, an idea that Maureen hated. *It sets the wrong tone*, she told him. *The wrong tone for what?* he replied.

Despite the surge in customers, the business was running smoothly. Trevor was finally at an age where he could help with the easier chores, and Barry, back for the summer as usual, was more than happy to take on the daily hikes to the jetty for supplies, freeing up George for other tasks. Barry's trips were often longer than his father's, but Maureen let the tardiness pass without comment; it was the only job her son would reliably do with good humour these days, and besides, his arrivals at the back door laden with packages were more or less all she ever saw of him. Even compared to his first hermitic Christmas, he'd grown so reclusive on visits home that some days felt scarcely any different than when he was away at school. In June she had cooked him a special dinner for his birthday, all his favourite things, and invited Mr Lewis to join them – and still the boy had stayed downstairs for as little time as possible before retreating, as always, to his room.

It was a surprise, then, on his last night at home at the end of the summer – Flora's last, too, this year – when after dinner he didn't immediately disappear. Instead, when Maureen asked – as she did every night, out of some hopeless, automatic reflex – whether he wanted to stay downstairs and play a game with them, he shrugged, and mumbled an awkward yes. Flora and Trevor, who had been bickering about something at the kitchen door, froze instantly in surprise.

'Well, then,' said Maureen, clearing her throat. 'Why don't you go pick one out?'

So while she carried dinner through to George, who was manning the bar as always, the children retrieved a battered set of Cluedo from the living room, and when she returned they arranged themselves around the board at the kitchen table. As she dealt out the cards she found herself studying Barry, himself studying the tabletop intently, and wondering if there were some special reason he had consented to spend time with them this evening – or if it was simply the pre-St Fillan's jitters that, despite his usual withdrawal, she often noticed on his last night home.

'It's nice of you to stay down here tonight,' she said, distributing the players' tokens around the board. He nodded, not looking up from the splinter he was picking at on the table's edge. When it became clear he wouldn't offer anything more, she sighed and handed the dice to Trevor. 'You're the youngest, dear,' she said. 'You go first.'

As the game progressed the mood grew lighter, the outlandish mansion generating inevitable cheer at their discoveries, and good-natured despair at Flora's eleventh-hour break for the finish, and groans of defeat as she triumphantly unveiled the killer. But as they packed everything away the uneasy quiet once again descended.

'Well,' said Maureen. 'It certainly has been nice having you here this summer.'

No response.

She dropped her blue piece into a small plastic bag with the others, and the dice, and replaced the bag in the box. 'And so much easier getting things done during the day.' She smiled. 'It'll be quite a relief having you back here full-time once you finish school. Your father's got a list of projects a mile long he's been waiting for your help with.'

She saw his shoulders tense. 'Aye,' he said, fidgeting with the miniature lead pipe. 'I suppose.'

'Come on,' she continued. 'You must be a bit excited about finally coming home for good.' Even as she said it she realized how unconvincing it sounded; these days he didn't get excited about anything. And why should she expect him to miss the island, really, when she probably wouldn't either?

He shrugged.

'Maybe we can redecorate your room when you get back,' she added. 'Make it feel a bit more grown-up for you.'

He hesitated, clearly weighing something up, and at last wet his lips. 'Thing is,' he said, 'I'm not really sure I *am* coming back.'

She frowned. 'I'm sorry?'

'Yeah,' said Barry, replacing the lead pipe in the box. 'I'm leaving school next year, and not coming home.' He picked up the candlestick; Flora and Trevor gawped at him and then, after a few seconds, at Maureen. He coughed. 'I'm going to get a job.'

'A job?' Her voice was rising now. 'A job!'

Flora slowly squared the cards she'd been shuffling and set them down in the box. Trevor's face was flushed red. 'What do you mean you're getting a job?' he said.

Maureen shushed him, her eyes still fixed on Barry. 'I'm afraid that's entirely out of the question,' she said, chest tightening. 'You'll still have a year of school left, for a start. And where are you getting this supposed job, anyway?'

'I'll be sixteen next summer,' said Barry, his voice firm. 'I can leave school if I want. And one of my mates knows someone in Aberdeen – reckons he could get me signed up on a rig.'

'An *oil* rig?' Too furious to look at him, now, she began snatching up the other murder weapons still scattered around the table. 'Absolutely not!' She flung the pieces into the box and dropped the board on top of them. 'No son of mine is going to work on one of those North Sea death traps. You'll stay at St Fillan's and finish school, and then you'll come home and work for us here.' She turned back to him, waving towards the pub. 'You know your father's always planned to pass the business on to you eventually. What do you think he'll make of this?'

'It doesn't matter,' said Barry, the expression on his face serene in its defiance. 'You can't make me stay.'

'Oh, we bloody well can!'

'No,' he replied. 'You can't.' And as if to prove the point, he started for the door, ignoring his mother's demands that he stay, and marched quietly upstairs.

Safely in his room, Barry climbed into the top bunk and exhaled, his entire chest shuddering with each beat of his heart. He lay staring at the ceiling for several minutes trying to calm the pounding, trying to reassure himself he was doing the right thing, while downstairs he could hear his mother continuing to bang around.

A showdown like this had been precisely what he'd hoped to avoid when he'd settled on his decision to leave; upsetting his parents, and particularly his mother, didn't bring him any joy. But the truth was, his frame of mind hadn't changed much since that night in the orchard all those years ago: he was tired of school and tired of home – or tired, anyway, of always yearning for the home of his childhood – and he knew he couldn't stay. Couldn't sign on to a lifetime of dimly wandering around this tiny, haunted place; couldn't bear the thought of his few remaining happy memories being forced out by years more of bitter ones.

So when his geography teacher had shown the class a video about the Scottish oil fields, he'd been mesmerized, not just by the isolation of the oil platform or the hugeness of the ocean, but by the riggers' way of life: no people, no trouble, and no responsibilities beyond getting up each morning and starting work. Compared to Tam and his cronies, compared even to his family's endless, eager pleas that he cheer up, the idea of an anonymous bunk in the swells of the North Sea was too appealing to ignore. He could picture himself lying in bed on his days off and reading, uninterrupted, for hours on end, or sitting on the edge of a platform, legs dangling, watching as the sun set and the sky surrounded him with orange. It would be bliss.

Still, his plan had been to avoid telling his parents until the last second and then to slip away with as little conflict as possible, which was why he'd kept even more than usual to his room this summer: the fewer conversations he had with them, he reasoned, the less likely his post-school plans were to come up. Because he'd resolved he wouldn't lie about it if they asked, would at least grant his family that one, tiny courtesy. Indeed, it was that same distorted filial loyalty that was stopping him from running off tomorrow, even though, a few months earlier, he'd been looking up train schedules to Aberdeen as the spring term had drawn to a close. But then: Flora's visit.

He shuddered even thinking of that day in April, of the cold glint in Tam's eye as he watched Flora sit down with the other prospective students, across the dining hall. 'So, Baz,' he'd said, noticing Barry watching her as well. 'That's your sister, eh?' The sneer Barry had come to dread so much crept across the other boy's face. 'Quite the looker, isn't she?'

'You can fuck right off, Tam,' he replied, and he marvelled, still, that he'd had the nerve to talk to him like that. 'You don't go near her.'

Tam laughed, and the rest of the boys joined in. 'Touched a sore spot there, have I? Well don't worry – I wouldn't want your sloppy seconds. The way you island folk carry on the two of you probably have three spastics of your own at home already.'

More brays of laughter.

'Aye, well,' Barry said. 'We can't all be blessed with a wanking hand like yours.'

'Ho ho!' said Tam, his mouth a thin, flat line. 'You're a proper Billy Connolly, aren't you, McCloud? Maybe when we get outside later you can have a taste of that hand in your cheeky face.'

'Do what you like, Tam – just leave her be. She's off limits.'

And oh, how he'd meant that. That same fear he remembered from his early weeks at school had instantly returned that afternoon, its hard, icy edges pressing into him as he tuned out the other boys' asinine banter and looked again at his sister across the hall. She was smiling meekly at another girl, a heartbreaking, nervous naivete on her face, and all he'd wanted to do was leap across the room, tabletop by tabletop, and whisk her away.

So one more year, he'd resolved to stay, until Tam had graduated. He would keep Flora in his sights at all times, would follow her or stick to Tam or some mixture of both, always making sure they were never alone together, not even for a second. He'd make sure she kept that innocence. He had to.

The door to his bedroom opened, now, and Flora stepped quietly into the room. Sitting up half-way, Barry looked down at her from the top bunk.

'What?' he said.

She glared at him, then stomped across the room and began rooting around in the closet; he sat up further. 'What do you *want*, Flora?'

She turned for just long enough to tell him curtly she didn't want anything, then continued digging through the closet. But even without seeing her face, Barry could picture her cheeks flushing and her nostrils flaring – the same look she always had when she was lying.

'You can't change my mind,' he said, sinking back into his pillow.

She let her arms drop to her sides, and for a moment stood completely still. And then, suddenly, she turned again – he'd been right, her face was flushed – and began to shout. 'Maybe I don't want you to change your mind! All you do is upset Mum anyway, so you might as well not come back!'

He thought he might have seen a few tears appearing in the corners of her eyes, but she was already looking away again, and grabbing a stuffed bear from one of the closet shelves. She tossed it across the room at her new trunk, packed and ready for the trip to St Fillan's the next day, and hurried towards the door again, eyes on her feet. With her hand on the doorknob, she paused. 'You don't even like us any more, do you?'

He didn't answer immediately; the question caught him too off guard. He had never imagined that the compulsion he felt to leave might boil down to something quite so simple. Of course he still loved his family – how could he not? But did he really *like* them any more? Was that why home had become so unbearable?

Clearly he took too long to consider it, because Flora let out a frustrated sigh and opened the door. 'I thought so,' she whispered – and before he could say another word, she'd vanished.

Flora leapt down the stairs three at a time, still fighting tears, determined not to give Barry the satisfaction. Outside the pub door she stopped and wiped her eyes dry with the heel of her palm, blinking tightly to marshal some composure. With a deep breath, she pushed through the door and strode behind the bar to join her father.

'Dearie me,' he said, as she yanked the newspaper from his hands and started scanning the crossword. 'First it was your mother huffing around, and now you too! Is there something in the water?'

She ignored his comment and continued looking for any clues she could decipher. 'You've got this one wrong,' she said, finally, smiling faintly as she remembered her earlier Cluedo victory. '*Gathered for hearing of accused colonel*? Eight letters? It's *mustered*. Gathered. Like Colonel Mustard. One of those sound-alike clues.'

'All right, all right.' He took back the paper. 'I'll be getting you your own copy if you keep this up.' He erased his original answer from the grid and filled in the new one. 'Now come on – what's got everyone so upset?'

Flora shrugged. 'Barry.'

'Big surprise there.' He rolled his eyes. 'What's he done now?'

'Nothing.' She could feel the heat of her tears returning.

Her father shook his head. 'Not feeling very talkative tonight, are we? Okay, I won't pry. What are your thoughts on eight down?'

Flora sniffed and studied the puzzle again, but already she was losing her concentration. It wasn't only Barry's announcement; she'd been feeling out of sorts since she woke up that morning. Since the beginning of the week, really, as she fretted about her departure for St Fillan's. Or, more accurately, about her arrival there; about opening the door to a new room, filled with the metal bunks and the flimsy fake wood desk she'd seen on her tour in April. About meeting the girl she'd be living with. About meeting another girl at all.

She'd met other girls before, of course: her distant relatives in Perth, and the Kilgouries' airy-fairy niece, and a few more who'd passed through the guesthouse over the years. But taken one at a time like that it had never occurred to her that girls as a group existed as something materially that different to boys. Even after the sex-education primer she'd had from Mr Lewis, conducted just as Barry's had been, with Trevor kept unwillingly at home, she hadn't really given it much thought. It was only when she'd visited St Fillan's in April, and witnessed first-hand how effortlessly the kids from larger schools drew those strange, invisible boundaries between each other, that the difference finally made itself clear: she had smiled at one of the boys in her tour group, out of nervousness and nothing else, and immediately another of the girls – Maisie – pulled her aside, a shocked look on her face, and asked what Flora had been thinking.

'You don't fancy him, do you?' Maisie's eyes bulged. 'He's pure minging!'

Unsure what the girl meant, Flora simply shook her head from side to side, hoping it would be an acceptable response.

'Well,' said Maisie, 'if you don't fancy him you don't want to be smiling at him, or everyone will think you do.'

At that point the teacher, who was explaining something about the dormitories, shushed them – but once they were sent to lunch they were right back into it (or rather, Maisie was), scanning the dining hall for *lookers*, and speculating about which boys might have *the most pubes*, and assessing the competition from any *hoors* among the other girls. Flora, meanwhile, continued to nod or shake her head as seemed appropriate, still in a daze, and staring at where she'd spotted Barry across the room. She'd been hoping for some sign of reassurance, but it never came: their eyes met just once, and all he did was grimace and turn away towards the other boys at his table.

Seeing him in a big group like that for the first time, fitting with everybody else into the school's strange social divisions, had been unsettling, as if she were watching an actor play her brother – badly. This was a change on an entirely different scale from the times Barry had come home to visit; yes, perhaps he'd been more sullen the past few years, more withdrawn, but he had still recognizably been Barry. Now everything about him was different, his mannerisms and his posture and the shape of his mouth as he talked, and she doubted, suddenly, that even a warm smile would have been that comforting.

All those baffled fears from that first visit, though, amplified by the past months of anticipation, had faded into the background tonight, as they sat down for dinner and she realized with a jolt that, unlike when her brother had left for school, there had been no special notice made of her impending departure, no night off for her parents, no festive farewell dinner – only the usual bread and soup, with her father not even taking the night off from the pub. It didn't matter that the Kilgouries were the only people they might have invited now, and that she didn't particularly like either of them and would have complained about it endlessly if they'd been there – she just couldn't understand why her parents hadn't even tried.

George patted her on the shoulder, nodding towards the crossword. 'Any luck?'

Flora shook her head and mumbled sorry.

'Well, no matter. Shouldn't be relying on you anyway, now that you're flying the coop.'

She sniffed.

'Are you sure you're all right, love?' He frowned. 'Nervous about tomorrow, maybe?'

Looking at the ground, she shook her head again.

'Come on.' He took her chin in his hand and lifted her head to look her in the eye. 'Out with it.'

She took a deep breath. 'Will you miss me?'

'What!' His hand moved from her chin to her crown, and he gently stroked her hair. 'Of course we'll miss you, Flora! Whatever would make you think otherwise?'

'I don't know,' she said, thinking: *because we don't miss Barry any more*. She nestled her head against her father's chest. 'No one seems bothered that I'm leaving.'

He wrapped his arm around her and squeezed tight. 'We're very bothered, Flora, I promise. Especially me.' He glanced up at the few guests seated at tables around the room. 'It won't be the same around here without you.'

Her face still pressed against him, she smiled weakly, and finally sat up again, wiping her eyes.

'Does this have anything to do with Barry?' he asked, giving her a searching look. 'Did he say something nasty to you?'

'No.' She glanced at the door, then began explaining what had happened after dinner: the game, and Barry's plans to leave, and his defiant escape upstairs. As her father listened his expression quickly changed from mild concern to total dismay, and when at last she'd finished he surveyed the room again, sizing up the half-dozen stragglers still nursing drinks, and patted her on the shoulder.

'Tell you what,' he said, handing her the paper. 'We're not busy, so can you keep an eye on things while I nip through and make sure your mum's not too upset? News like that and she might be about to break something.'

She nodded and watched him hurry out. When she looked down at the page again, the black and white squares were shimmering.

When George found her, Maureen was in the kitchen, viciously wiping down a cutting board. She looked up at him as he walked in. 'Pub empty already?'

Still walking towards her, he shook his head. 'I hear Barry's been making grand plans.'

At that flippant summing up of the situation, she actually laughed, feeling a pang of relief that, in addition to all his little habits that drove her up the wall these days, the sense of humour she'd always loved about him was as reliable as ever. Small solace, though, given her despair at this further proof of Barry's drifting away, and, more than that, at her inability to convince herself that motherly concern was to blame. Because her terror when she pictured Barry on an oil rig had come only second, tonight, after a rush of other feelings that she could only describe as selfish: anger, dread. The sense of an opportunity snatched away.

She'd had those same feelings just a few months earlier, on an otherwise uneventful night just a few days after Flora's visit to St Fillan's. Mr Kilgourie had been at the pub late, stretching out his last pint interminably as she and George cleaned up around him. Once Mr Kilgourie was finished he sat at the bar not moving, portentous, until the lights were off and the chairs stacked, and George and Maureen practically screamed at him to tell them what was wrong. *I've given up the house*, he said, staring into his empty pint glass. *We're leaving at the end of the summer.*

Maureen listened in disbelief as he explained how far their finances had fallen; how they'd never completely recovered after the rats, and how they needed to move to the mainland now while they still had any money left. *Does Oonagh know you've done it?* she asked, certain it was impossible, certain her friend would have said something if she had any idea – and shocked when Mr Kilgourie nodded, and said his wife had been the one to insist. Maureen poured herself a whisky, aghast: with the Kilgouries gone, and the Mannings and the Pikes having given up over the winter, her family would be it. The last ones left. The fate of the island would rest entirely on them. She could imagine George's rallying cry as he took her hand in bed that night, and his declaration, proud and desperate and firm all at once, that it was up to them. And with Barry leaving now, that fate seemed all the more certain. Without him at the guesthouse there was even less chance of a reprieve for her, less chance of her ever slipping away, for a holiday or for good.

But to George now, standing next to her at the kitchen sink, all she said was: 'That boy will be the death of me.'

He put his hand in the small of her back. 'Ach, don't worry, Reenie. I'm sure he'll come around. This is just bog-standard teen-age rebellion.' At last she stopped scrubbing at the cutting board and looked at him, and told him that she hoped so.

He laughed. 'Trust me, he'll take one look at a rig and wilt like a daisy. Before you know it he'll be begging to come home and peel the tatties for us.'

'Maybe.' She dropped her scouring pad at the edge of the sink and began to dry her hands on the tea towel slung over her shoulder. 'It's just… He can be so bloody-minded sometimes.'

'It'll be fine, love. Really.' His hand slipped further around her waist and he pulled her closer, her body tensed in their awkward half-embrace – until she slumped, finally, and kissed him through the sleeve of his shirt.

'I'd best get back to the bar,' he said, squeezing her hip. 'Flora's probably giving away drinks.'

Maureen took a step back. 'Didn't you come in here for something?'

He winked. 'I was going to hide the knives, but you seem calm enough.'

She still just stared at him, and his playful expression disappeared. 'I wanted to see if you were all right,' he said, walking to the door. 'That's all.'

'Oh,' she replied, but by the time she thought to utter a belated thank you, he had already started down the hall.

It was sad, she supposed, that she'd assumed he must have some other motive for looking in on her. Sadder still that such an assumption didn't strike her, even in hindsight, as particularly unreasonable. Even before her most recent malaise, before the Kilgouries' announcement, before David and the rats, their marriage had slowly transformed – out of circumstance, really, rather than malice or neglect – into something more like curatorship; between the children and the guesthouse and the village, their interactions now were more functional than tender. Still, there was something else on her mind tonight that she thought probably explained her distracted response.

The night before she'd been lying in bed waiting for him to come upstairs, much as usual, the satisfying flap of her mystery novel's pages the only sound besides her occasional sighs. She hadn't looked up when he padded in, skimming forward in her book to reach a good stopping point, and when finally she did raise her head he'd already undressed and was taking off his watch.

'Late one tonight,' he sighed.

She'd set her book down. 'You are the owner, you know – you can close whenever you want.'

'As long as they keep buying drinks...' He crossed the room and climbed into bed. 'By the way,' he said, 'the wildlife chaps were on the phone today.' She instantly felt a burst of heat at the back of her neck. 'They wanted to sort out when they were coming for their follow-up on our furry friends.'

Her breath caught. 'And?'

'I put them in for the first week of October. Books were clear then anyway.'

She exhaled. 'You scheduled it without even asking me?'

He tugged the blankets towards him, and she felt a corner of her thigh come uncovered. 'Why would I ask you?'

'I don't know. I... I might have had something planned.' She pulled her nightie down to cover the exposed skin.

'Then it would have been in the books,' he said, turning over to face the wall.

'I just like being kept in the know. Is that too much to ask?'

'No,' he said. 'That's why I'm telling you.' *After you've already bloody decided everything*, she thought, but she let it drop. She wasn't even sure what she was upset about: no one had seen a rat all year, and the trappers' visit was bound to be short and uneventful; George might as well have been booking guests in for the weekend. And wasn't the fact that he'd treated it like any other business precisely what she'd wanted? Didn't that prove she'd hidden her feelings about David perfectly?

She sighed, now, taking some paper and a pen from a drawer next to the sink and sitting down at the table to make a list. The real problem, she told herself, was that she still had feelings about David at all. And clearly she did – that much was obvious from her fluttering heartbeat the night before, her churning stomach and her lying awake until three. The last time she remembered feeling that way about George had been years ago.

She scribbled out a heading on the page in front of her, but before she could actually begin the list she was looking at the wall clock and cursing under her breath: it was a few minutes past Trevor's bedtime already, and she hadn't even been upstairs to get him ready.

Trevor, meanwhile, was sitting alone on his bedroom floor, reading in the splash of eggshell light coming off his bedside lamp. Other than that, and the faint teal glow of dusk in the windows, the room was dark, and when his mother bustled in she immediately switched on the overhead bulb, clucking that he'd make himself blind.

Nodding glumly, Trevor stood up and crossed the room to where she was now pulling a pair of pyjamas from his dresser.

'You can read for another ten minutes,' she said, glancing at his alarm clock, 'but I want your lights out by the time I come upstairs again.' She was already back at the door, her hand on the knob. 'Understood?'

He nodded again, and listened to her walk off down the hallway before moving to the door himself, to check the latch was firmly shut and switch the ceiling light back off. Once he was changed into his pyjamas he returned to the spot where he'd been reading, and stared down at the book still lying on the rug. It was *George's Marvellous Medicine*, a Roald Dahl story he'd read before and not one of his favourites – but with Barry locked up in his and Flora's room tonight, as he had been so often this summer, Trevor hadn't been able to raid their shelves for fresh material. He stood for a few more seconds and considered picking it up again, but finally he shook his head and knelt down next to his bedside table. Reaching behind, he felt for a piece of skirting board he knew was loose, and carefully pried it back to pull out a small photograph.

The image was difficult to make out in the darkened room, but he knew it well enough from memory: a family portrait taken when he was still a baby, the five of them arranged around a Christmas tree in the living room, Barry and Flora glancing at each other from the corners of their eyes. He'd found the picture about a year ago, in a desk drawer in his father's office. It was tucked away in a ratty yellow envelope with a few dozen others – landscapes, mostly, and a few group shots of relatives on the mainland – but it was this particular portrait that really captured his attention: Barry looked impossibly young, and Flora, her hair longer and thicker than Trevor had ever seen it, was practically unrecognizable. Until then he'd always thought of his sister as unchanging, permanent, and to be confronted with this strange other version of her, staring him in the face as if from another world, had been captivating. He had snuck the whole envelope to his room and spent the afternoon studying its contents, spread out around him in an ocean on the floor.

The landscape shots, it turned out, were almost as fascinating as the people ones. They'd all been taken on the island, it looked like, and yet there were several that he couldn't place: close-ups, mostly, the frames filled with heather in bloom or strange rock formations in the brush. He took to studying them before bed each night, and hiking around with them during the day, consulting their fading images every few minutes as he tried to figure out their origins. Then, a few weeks later, his father casually mentioned over dinner one night that a few of his photographs had gone missing; Trevor had blushed, he hoped not too conspicuously, and the next day had replaced them all in the drawer. But he'd kept that one family shot he was gazing at now, unable to bring himself to part with it.

The thing he loved most about the picture was seeing everyone together. Though he had a few memories from before Barry had left for St Fillan's – his brother slipping him a sweetie under the table one lunchtime; the sight of their mother weeping at Barry's departure – generally he thought of the household as himself, his parents and Flora, and there was a charming novelty to the idea that at some point they had shared the space with Barry, too. Indeed, as the weeks had passed with the picture hidden in the walls, emerging every few evenings for Trevor to study it again, he'd started fantasizing about reuniting the family in that harmonious, pre-St Fillan's state. The more he'd thought about it the more he'd convinced himself it was possible, and yet tonight Barry seemed to have thrown the whole plan into disarray. Though Trevor had only the vaguest idea what an oil rig was, and the North Sea was nothing more to him than a blue patch on the other side of Mr Lewis's Scotland map, something about the tone of Barry's announcement earlier, and his mother's reaction, had left him certain of one thing: his brother wasn't coming back.

Caught up wondering why, he missed the sound of his mother's footsteps in the hallway; only as she turned the door handle did he realize she'd returned, and he frantically shoved the picture under his bed to hide it.

'Time's up, young man,' she said, as he spun his head to look at her. Apparently she hadn't noticed anything. 'Into bed.' Hands on hips, she waited for him to climb beneath his covers, then tucked him in and retreated to the door, whispering goodnight as she stepped into the hallway.

'Goodnight, Mum,' he called after her, and once the door was shut he clicked off his bedside lamp and lay there in the dark, forgetting all about the photograph and wondering instead why she hadn't made him brush his teeth.

14

There was barely time to breathe after Barry and Flora left that year: with September raining in and extinguishing the summer, the family's attention turned quickly to the Kilgouries and their impending departure. The last of the couple's crops for the year were harvested and shipped away; a buyer from Inverness relieved them of their sheep, rustled chaotically to the jetty with the help of George and Mr Lewis; and after that their house was all that remained, and its lifetime of furniture and crockery and clothing, which Maureen and Trevor helped pack over a lingering, nostalgic week. With no children of their own, the Kilgouries had no old toys to dispose of, no baby shoes or clothing, and none of the boxes of drawings that Maureen knew would have slowed her own departure. But in the absence of all that, the Kilgouries had made their belongings into offspring – their attic a mess of cast-off memories as sentimental as any parent's. Several times Maureen found them whispering sadly to each other in the corners of emptying rooms. *The old covering from the armchair, Jack!... Oh! And the paint left over from our bedroom!* They seemed bizarrely caught off guard by their attachment to the place, and when at last it was empty they sagged with relief, checking into the guesthouse for their final night ashore.

'So this is it, eh?' said Mr Kilgourie over dinner, his voice softer than usual as he stirred his soup. 'The last supper.' He and his wife were at the kitchen table with Maureen and Trevor, while George kept an eye on the season's last visitors in the pub.

'Surely you'll be back to visit,' replied Maureen, glancing more towards Oonagh than her husband. The woman had a sickly expression and hadn't touched her soup; she seemed to have aged ten years in as many days.

'Aye, well,' said Mr Kilgourie. 'We'll have to see.'

'We'll do our best, of course,' added his wife, quietly. 'Once we work out' – she cleared her throat – 'how much time off our jobs will give us.'

'You've found something, then?' Maureen asked, though she instantly regretted it. Whenever she and Oonagh had gone shopping in Fort William, her friend was always making snide, under-the-breath remarks about working wives. *Can't her husband support her?* she would always whisper, on spotting a sales assistant's wedding ring. *Has she no dignity?*

Maureen never really agreed with the sentiment – she actually saw something quite thrilling in the idea of earning her own wage – but she doubted Oonagh would want to discuss her own employment prospects now.

The woman bowed her head. 'Well, no. Not yet. There's not much I seem qualified for over in Dundee.' She adjusted her napkin ring so it was in line with the tip of her butter knife. 'Unless I want to work at the Safeway, and I'm hoping I'll not have to.' Maureen nodded, trying to imagine Oonagh scanning groceries. Trying to imagine doing it herself. 'Jack's had some luck, though – haven't you dear?'

Mr Kilgourie shrugged, and explained that he'd found some work as a farmhand outside town. 'I always thought I'd be hiring farmhands one day,' he added with a sigh, and after that the table fell silent, apart from Trevor slurping down his broth. Maureen glared at him, irritated by his indifference, and once he'd finished and waited the requisite minute or so before asking to be excused, she snapped.

'It's Mr and Mrs Kilgourie's last night!' She banged her hand on the table. 'Can't you stay and sit awhile?'

He gave her a hurt look. 'I've homework to finish, Mum. I already told you.' He had frozen in place, half-way through sliding from his seat.

'Ach, don't worry about us,' said Mr Kilgourie, with a wistful smile in Trevor's direction. 'We're not much company tonight, anyway.'

Trevor looked to Maureen again, and she told him through gritted teeth that he could go. He quickly deposited his dishes in the sink and scurried from the room.

'He's a good lad,' said Mrs Kilgourie, still staring sadly into her untouched soup. 'It's a shame we won't be here to see him grow up.'

Maureen wished she could grab the woman by the shoulders. *It's not that bad!* she wanted to scream. *You should be happy you're getting free of this place!* Then again, free probably wasn't quite the right word, given the duress of their departure and what sounded like a dismal outlook in Dundee – and yet she couldn't help but feel jealous, of the uncertainty they faced and the potential it contained, and dread at her own, inevitable future. In two days' time, she and George would be alone on the island, except for Trevor and Mr Lewis – and once Trevor finished primary school, the two of them would be gone, too. And if Trevor and Flora decided not to return, as Barry had, it would be just her and her husband, forever, and this blink of stone in the giant sea.

George stuck his head into the kitchen. 'How about we swap places for a wee bit?' he said, his eyes fixed on her. 'Give me a go with the dearly departing?'

She stood up and told him that was fine, carrying her own bowl to the sink and placing it on top of Trevor's. On her way out, she stopped where George had sat himself at the table, kissing him on the cheek, and told him to take all the time he needed.

Upstairs, Trevor had already finished his homework. Had already finished it, in fact, even before he'd excused himself from dinner – but he'd discovered that 'homework' was one of the few excuses for hiding in his room that his parents left consistently unchallenged, and in the weeks since Flora's departure he'd tried to spend as much time there as he could. The dismal, wordless dinner with the Kilgouries tonight had been painful enough, but since Flora had left even time spent with his parents felt uneven, somehow. Off kilter.

The week before, for instance, his father had coaxed him to the pub to help with one of those secret word puzzles he'd always reserved for Flora. Naturally, after so many years of curiosity, Trevor had jumped at the chance, but within minutes of his father's long-winded explanation the evening quickly soured. *Think, Trevor!* George urged him in frustration. *What words fit in the space?* Trevor kicked the side of the bar, equally annoyed. *Who cares, Dad! It's just a stupid game!* The dispute escalated: George warned his son to watch his tone, told him Flora had never behaved this way, and Trevor, already showing signs of the temper that would hobble him in later years, yelled that they *shouldn't have let her leave, then!* and swept his father's glass to the floor.

Nights with his mother were just as bad, if less dramatic. On the few occasions he strayed downstairs to find her he ended up helping clean the kitchen or doing more infernal cooking, and when he subsequently tried to weasel away she firmly called him back. *But Mum*, he'd whined once, *you cook every night! Don't we have enough in the freezer already?* She'd given him a dour look. *It doesn't fill itself, young man*. And then, more tender: *besides, it's good to have so much stored up. You never know when you might need it*.

So his room it was. He'd even started asking Mr Lewis for extra homework – *to make sure I understand*, he said – and if the man had nothing else to assign him Trevor would repeat the work they'd done in class, going through the day's sentence exercises and arithmetic problems from memory. When he tired of that he'd curl up by his bedroom window and dissolve into a book, or lately would cross the hallway to Barry and Flora's room, and sift through their belongings.

At first he was driven by a bored sort of curiosity, but quickly he found himself drawn in by the sheer amount of *stuff* he found. One night he discovered an old sketchbook of Flora's, jammed behind the dresser by the window; of Barry's, in the flyleaves of an old *Boxcar Children* paperback, a scribbled piece of what looked like years-old spelling homework. Neither item was particularly noteworthy, and clearly they hadn't been missed, but to Trevor they were a window to his sibling's secret lives; another piece of proof that the island had been more vibrant, once. A shred of hope that it might someday manage it again.

After escaping from dinner with the Kilgouries that night, he stood in the centre of his room with his fingers linked on top of his head, contemplating what to do next, schoolbag in front of him and already packed for the following morning. After a moment he let his arms drop and walked over to his closet, where he reached up on his tiptoes and inched an old shoebox from the top shelf, guiding it carefully to the floor and removing its lid. Inside were all the things he'd found in his siblings' room the past few weeks, plus the photograph he used to keep behind the skirting board, an ugly crease down its centre from when he'd rushed to hide it the month before. On top of that were a dozen or so other items filched from the Kilgouries' house as he'd helped them pack the past few weeks: a page from an ancient farm ledger, its cream-coloured pages filled with line after line of Mr Kilgourie's sloping, inky script; a heavy mortar and pestle, fragments of oat pressed permanently to its surface. And then there was the discovery that fascinated Trevor the most, the one that had prompted him to start the collection in the first place: a postcard, silken from wear, the pigment fading in its decades-old picture.

He'd seen postcards before, of course; his parents kept a small supply on hand for guests. But the ones they sold now were of scenes elsewhere in Scotland, bought in bulk from Mallaig – whereas the one he'd found last week showed a picture of *the Kilgouries' house*! The caption on the back confirmed it: *Traditional croft house*, it read; *Eilean Fìor, c.1968*. Thrilled, he'd called over his mother, who studied it for a moment with a mournful look. *Yes*, she said, handing it back to him. *The McKenzies used to sell these at the general store*. A company in Fort William had produced them, she explained, but after the McKenzies left the contract lapsed, and since it was cheaper to get the generic ones she and George hadn't bothered to renew it. She turned back to whatever she'd been packing as if no further explanation were required, and that was when Trevor slipped the card beneath his shirt. Since then he'd taken it out to look at it every night, still in awe of the world it suggested.

After a few more minutes he replaced the shoebox in his closet and moved to the window to read until bedtime. The Kilgouries popped their heads in with Maureen to say goodnight, but it was as he walked out the door for school the next morning that he said his last goodbyes, enduring awkward hugs and kisses as they wished him well in life. *I remember the day I delivered you*, Mrs Kilgourie sniffed, patting him on the head. Her wording caught him off guard; he'd always known that she'd been there at his birth, but that she had delivered him – that she was somehow responsible for his existence – was not something he'd ever dwelled on. The thought stayed with him all week, her farewell repeating in his head each morning as he left for school. *I delivered you*, she'd said. And now, he thought, she's gone.

Soon, however, his attention turned again to other things. A week into October the rat men returned, a smaller troupe than during the cull but still enough of them to fill the guesthouse's upper floor. Trevor looked up from his book one afternoon to see them approaching through his window, and crept to the head of the stairs to watch his mother meet them in the entryway. There were a few new faces in the group this time, but most of them Trevor recognized from their previous visits: a bearded giant, shoulders hunched beneath the weight of his rucksack; a lankier man behind him, with a gaunt face and a grim line of a mouth. And at the back of the crowd was the one who'd been in charge before, his silver-framed glasses glinting as he nodded at Maureen.

'You're sure you wouldn't rather we stay in the cottages again?' he was saying, as Trevor's eyes finally landed on him.

'Ach, no,' his mother replied. 'There's only a handful of you and we've no guests this week anyway. Make yourselves at home.' She smiled at the man – the first sign of happiness Trevor had seen from her since Flora had left – and he smiled back as he thanked her.

'It's our pleasure, Mr Cox,' she said. 'Let me know if you need anything.' And to Trevor's surprise, she reached forward and touched his arm then, a gesture of affection he recognized even at eight years old.

More intriguing still, a few days later: the phone call from St Fillan's.

It came in the evening, while George and Trevor ate in the kitchen and Maureen, having volunteered to give George a rest that night, manned the bar – so it was his father who hurried to the hallway to answer the phone.

'Yes, this is Mr McCloud. Yes… What about Barry?' Trevor gently laid his fork down on hearing his brother's name and strained to listen, though his father was saying little – interjecting only occasionally, between long stretches of silence, to grunt or ask a question. After a few minutes there was a click as he set the receiver down, and a long, drawn-out sigh, and perhaps, Trevor thought, unless he was imagining it, the sound of his dad running his hands down his face. Then his footsteps moved further down the hall, and the pub door opened and shut, and only in that sudden quiet did Trevor dare to take another bite of dinner.

A few moments later he heard footsteps re-emerging. 'What is it, George?' his mother said, sounding irritated. 'I shouldn't leave them too long.'

'I'm sure they can spare you for a few minutes, Reenie.' A pause. 'It's Barry.'

'Barry?' Her voice quavered. 'What about Barry?'

'He's been in a fight at school. They just called. Broke a lad's nose, apparently.'

'He *what*?'

'Broke a lad's nose! I can't quite believe it myself, but the headmaster is livid. Wants us on the first ferry there tomorrow, he said, to discuss Barry's "future at the school." His words.'

'Tomorrow?' said Maureen. 'We can't go anywhere tomorrow! Who'll look after the men? And Trevor?'

The sound of floorboards creaking.

'Don't worry, Reenie, I can go on my own. I've some banking to do, anyway.'

Silence.

'What has got into him lately, George? First all this oil rig nonsense, and now a broken nose?'

'Boys will be boys, Reenie. I dished out a few healthy knockings when I was his age, too. I'm sure it'll pass.'

'I hope so.' A sniff. 'I should get back in there.'

And as the pub door reopened, and the floorboards began to creak again, Trevor rushed to pick up his fork as if he'd been eating all along.

George left the following morning and called home late that afternoon. Maureen and Trevor were in the kitchen preparing dinner when the phone rang, and after hurrying to answer she took the handset between ear and shoulder while she dried her hands against her pinny.

'Crisis averted,' said George, his voice echoing on the line. 'Managed to persuade them to let Barry stay on, though he's suspended for a week and on probation after that. But I've had words with him – he'll behave.'

'He'd better.' She took the phone in her hand, her eyes drifting towards the pub door. 'Are you coming home, then?' It was a Friday, so there'd be a second ferry that night – one of the season's last.

'No,' he said. 'The next train won't get me back to Mallaig in time. I'll have to spend the night and catch the ferry first thing.'

Her heart beat a little faster. 'Oh,' she said. 'What a nuisance.' Another glance down the hallway. 'I'm sorry you had to go on your own.'

He assured her it was nothing, and after a few more pleasantries they hung up, Maureen's pulse now thrumming in her ears. She started for the pub.

David was there, as she'd expected, sitting at his now habitual spot and going through some paperwork. As the operation's head he wasn't doing much actual reconnaissance this trip, and had taken instead to spending the days by a window in the corner, poring over maps and his subordinates' reports, his chair tipped back, his brow ever so slightly furrowed, and an almost regal look of concentration on his face.

'It looks like you're getting the all clear,' he told her now, glancing up as she entered. 'We've still not found a thing.'

'That's a relief,' she said, pausing by the bar while simultaneously, in her head, she was walking towards him, and sitting down at his table, and taking his hand in hers. 'Can I get you a drink before dinner?'

'Oh, no. Thank you.' He shook his head. 'Have to set a good example for my rowdy lot.' As if not to disappoint her, though, he added, with one of those kind-hearted smiles she'd come to love so much, that he was getting a bit peckish for a pre-dinner snack.

'Tsk, tsk,' she said, looking away from him even as she smiled back. 'You'll spoil your appetite, young man.'

'Ah, yes, of course. And what spectacular culinary feat will I be depriving myself of tonight?'

'I'm afraid only shepherd's pie – but I've a whole salmon coming with the messages Monday.' She frowned, suddenly, and met his eyes again. 'If you'll still be here.'

'With a prospect like that,' he said, 'we may well be.'

She kept staring at him even as he returned to his work, her hands shaky, and her shoulders, and her stomach light and airy. It was the same way she'd felt when he arrived that week – and this morning, too, when George had left, leaving her standing in the kitchen on her own, with a hint of opportunity suddenly in his place. On a whim she rushed upstairs to change, pulling an old Sunday dress from deep in the closet – a relic of the days when she'd regularly gone to church – and was relieved to find it still fitted. She managed a few strokes of mascara, too, though to her dismay her rouge had grown a thin layer of mould. *My*, David said, when he saw her at lunch. *Should the rest of us be dressing up as well?* She'd beamed. *What, this old thing?*

'Mum!' Trevor was calling her from the kitchen, now, and with a start she realized she'd left him in there peeling parsnips. Flustered, she hurried away to help. They returned to the pub that evening, though, at her suggestion, to eat dinner with the men – a raucous meal that, like most nights since they'd arrived, devolved into a lengthy bout of drinks. Even Trevor stayed downstairs for a change (a curious lack of homework tonight, Maureen noticed), the visitors revelling in his attention just as much as he seemed to revel in theirs, telling him favourite jokes and performing sloppy, silly magic tricks. While the room hushed when she finally dragged Trevor to bed a few minutes past nine, it still showed no signs of emptying, and she happily alternated between pouring drinks and clearing up – until, around eleven, a few of the men finally began to drift upstairs. She dimmed the lights; the voices softened. She glanced at David. And then her mood instantly sank: he was gathering his things and standing up. Walking towards her with his empty glass.

'Goodnight, Maureen,' he said, setting it down and patting her on the arm. 'Thank you for another wonderful meal.' She grinned helplessly and said goodnight back, her skin buzzing where he'd touched her.

'And you lot,' he said, louder, turning to the room. 'This is your last round, understood? We've still got work to do tomorrow.' There were grumbles all around at that, but half an hour later the last of the men dutifully trooped upstairs, leaving empty drinks and full ashtrays, and Maureen alone in the pub. After tidying their mess and mopping the floor, she switched the lights off completely and walked through to the kitchen, retrieving a binder labelled *Inventory* from a shelf above the sink and standing over the table as she skimmed through it. Once she found the entry she was looking for she noted down the details on a scrap of paper and neatly scored through the line in the book, and then made her way to the back door and the path to the deep freeze.

When she reached the Braithwaites' cottage, she stopped. Here she was again, she thought, at the place where so many of her fantasies had started. Except that tonight, unexpectedly, they were more than fantasies; they were possibilities. Possibilities, she decided, as she stepped over the threshold, that she was going to pursue.

It had begun to seem so simple that evening, as she replayed each encounter with David over the last few days. His compliments on her appearance, his interest in her cooking... And when she set that drink in front of him, earlier, his hand covering hers as she withdrew it – that had been no accident, she was sure. She could still feel the condensation on the glass against her fingers; the absence of the wedding ring on his. It was too perfect to ignore! And though she still felt a pinch of guilt as she opened the freezer now and her own wedding ring pressed against her skin, that guilt seemed unimportant, somehow, blurry beside all she stood to gain: escape from her increasing discontent at home, and from her even greater guilt at the same. The life elsewhere that she'd always wanted. How could she not do it? The family would get by somehow without her.

Stepping back outside, a heavy tray of food balanced against her stomach, she looked towards the guesthouse and saw the light still on in his window. She imagined him in bed there, leaning against the headboard and knees bent under the blanket, turning, captivated, through a novel – his face arranged in that same thoughtful look he had while working in the pub, his features casting handsome shadows in the reading lamp's golden light. And then she was there, above him, gently pushing the book away as she climbed over his waist, pressing her hands against his shoulders and leaning forward.

In the guesthouse kitchen again, she shook her head, trying to keep herself collected as she laid down a cloth on the counter and set out the food to defrost. That done, she glanced around the room one more time, then moved to the door and switched off the lights. Still moving as calmly as she could, she stepped into the hallway and started towards the stairs.

She paused again as she reached the first landing to let her eyes adjust to the dark; picked out the hazy, monochromatic outline of the *Do Not Enter* sign on the door to the family rooms. There were no sounds behind it. No sounds upstairs. No sounds at all except her own breathing and the rush of blood in her ears. In her head she kissed him, let her hips slide further down his body, let her spine straighten as she pressed against his chest. She put her foot on the next step. Paused again. Took a last fleeting glance at the *Do Not Enter* sign. And then she started to climb, quietly, weighing each step so as not to let the wood groan, but still going, frantically, as fast as she could. Now that she'd made her break for it, she had to cling to that momentum.

As her head came level with the floor of the upper hallway she surveyed the carpet for stray slices of light from other rooms. To her relief, the only one shone out of his, and with renewed determination she pressed forward until, outside his door, she stopped – swallowed – and knocked lightly on the wood. The seconds seemed to slow and draw together, gathering like a drop of water on a leaky faucet's lip, but no one moved behind the door. Still there were no other sounds. She knocked again, louder this time, and when once more there was no answer she turned the handle and pushed inside.

The room looked as it usually did: a small dresser to her left, a wardrobe to her right, and in the far corner, flush against the wall under the eaves' sloping ceiling, a single bed and nightstand, and the reading lamp whose light she'd seen outside. Plus the crucial difference: him, lying underneath the covers. He'd been reading, just as she'd imagined, and had fallen asleep, book flopping against his chest. And just as she'd imagined, too, his knees were bent, and in his slumber had drifted sideways to lean against the wall. She closed the door softly behind her, not taking her eyes off him for a second, luxuriating in all the details of his body: his mouth hanging just slightly open; his plain white undershirt bunching around his shoulders; his glasses fogging in his steady breaths. She wondered if it were a sign that she'd pictured the scene so exactly, or if the sign instead was that he'd fallen fast asleep; if that one, simple difference was a warning she should turn away.

No, she thought. This far, she had already come. She would have the rest.

With a nervous shiver she moved forward again, striding towards him, no longer concerned with the sound of her footsteps. He stirred as she neared the bed. Opened his eyes as she knelt down beside him.

'Hello,' she whispered, and smiled at him, resting her elbow on his mattress.

He blinked a few times. 'Maureen! What—?'

And there it was, the kiss she'd seen a thousand times that night, that sigh of lips together and her eyelashes flickering against his skin. Hardly pausing, she pushed herself up, still on her knees, keeping her mouth to his, and reached across his body so she could plant her hands on either side of him. Her whole face was humming, and the nape of her neck, and her entire back, and instinctively she was standing up, still without pulling away, and sliding her leg across his body until she sat straddling him on the bed. As she held her arms out behind her and began to wriggle from her cardigan, his hands crept up her waist. She could feel his erection pressing into her thigh.

But then.

Suddenly he was pushing her away, his hands on her shoulders and their lips finally coming apart. 'What?' she whispered, breathless, tossing her cardigan behind her. 'What's wrong?'

'I won't do this, Maureen.' His face a pained frown. 'I'm sorry.'

'I… I'm… What do you mean? Why not?' She felt her face flushing and tried pushing towards him again, but he kept his arms braced against her.

'You're a married woman, Maureen. And a mother! Your son's only one flight down, for God's sake.' He squirmed, trying to slide out from beneath her.

'I'll leave them.'

His eyes bulged. 'Come on, Maureen, don't be silly – you barely know me. Besides, I'm a contractor here. If your husband found out I could lose my job.'

'He won't.'

'He might.' For a moment his face seemed to soften. 'You're a charming woman, Maureen. Maybe if we'd met in other circumstances…' He stopped, apparently thinking better of finishing the thought. 'Please,' he said, instead. 'You have to get up before one of the men hears us.'

She stared at him. 'No.'

'*No*?'

'No. You don't mean it. This isn't what you want.' She felt a tear run down the side of her nose. Tasted it when it broke at the corner of her mouth.

'It is what I want.'

She felt his arms slacken slightly, now, and let her whole weight fall against them, so that his elbows buckled and her torso finally pressed against his. 'You didn't push me away,' she whimpered, nestling her face in the vee between his shoulder and his neck. 'Not at first.' She felt the worn, velvety fabric of his T-shirt against her cheek. 'Please.'

He was silent for a moment, and then said, again: 'I'm sorry.'

All of a sudden she felt ridiculous, sprawled there simpering on this almost total stranger, for seriously thinking anything might happen. For hoping that he'd throw his arms around her and ask her to run away with him, or provide her with some rapturous moment, like those played out in so many of her books, of *feeling alive again*. For wanting something smaller, even: a soft *I understand*, with a stroke of reassurance along her back. An absolution. A promise that even though she loved her family, loved George (and she did, somehow, didn't she?), it was okay to want to leave this place. To wish for something else.

But she knew, now, as David squirmed beneath her again, that she would never leave; as he told her firmly that she had to go downstairs, she heard her final lot. She *would* go downstairs. She would sleep on her half of the bed, would get up when her alarm told her to, and would go through the next day and the next and the next knowing that she'd taken this, the biggest risk of her life, and failed.

Numbly, she allowed him to roll her to one side, and get her to her feet, and guide her to the door with his hand between her shoulder blades. Numbly, she allowed him to ease her through the door.

'Goodnight,' he said, when she turned to face him from the hallway.

'Goodnight,' she whispered, hoping one last time that he might change his mind and kiss her again. But instead he only stepped back and disappeared behind the closing door, behind the faint click of the resetting latch – behind the final thunk, this time, of the deadbolt sliding into place. She heard his mattress squeak as he climbed into bed across the room; watched the light around the doorframe vanish. And then, a few more tears starting down her cheeks, she stood there in the dark, and on her own.

2002

15

On a sunny morning in April, Trevor came downstairs for breakfast and found his mother dead. She was sixty-one.

It was a no-nonsense, practical sort of death, whose restraint she might have admired if she hadn't been its victim. She simply got out of bed as usual that morning, dressed, and stopped at the landing on her way downstairs to adjust a crooked picture – a painting Flora had given them a few Christmases earlier, the guesthouse viewed from a nearby hill, and not much more than a speck below the sky's giant watercolour sweep. She looked at her reflection in the frame, the black of her pupils swallowing up light and letting the image beneath shine through, but paused for only a few seconds before she continued, dutifully, towards the kitchen. And it was there, preparing porridge for George and Trevor, that she first acknowledged the painful twitch in her chest; there, as she sprinkled brown sugar into the bubbling pan, that at last she fell to the floor. By the time Trevor found her, fifteen minutes later, a tiny grimace on her face and the wooden spoon still gripped in her hand, the porridge was smoking on the stove; by the time the doctor arrived, half an hour after that, the whole house stunk of burnt oats.

Michael was the one to call Flora, and the rest of Maureen's relatives in Perth; Michael was the one who arranged for the body to be sent away and cremated. Michael handled everything, really, as if managing bereavement were just another part of his remit. Which in fact, they soon discovered, it was: when he contacted the family solicitor he was told that Maureen had changed her will a few months earlier and named him as executor. *She didn't think George could manage it any more*, the lawyer told him. *Said his illness was getting to be too much*.

Under other circumstances Trevor might have been piqued that his mother hadn't chosen him. He did feel, actually, when Michael explained it to him, the familiar spark of anger that would normally have set him shouting. *I'm her son, for fuck's sake! The only one who bothered to stick around! And this is what I get for it?* But a sudden flicker of regret, at so many similar outbursts inflicted on his mother over the years, left his temper dampened, and all he did was listen vaguely as Michael went through the will's few, straightforward provisions: her engagement ring to Flora, an old Stewart family portrait to Trevor, and anything else not shared with George to whoever wanted it or to charity.

The only surprise came at the end of the list, when Michael hesitated, and wet his mouth, and added that there was a savings account, too: a private one, in Maureen's name only, at a bank in Fort William instead of their normal branch in Mallaig. There wasn't much in it, Michael explained, barely £300, deposited in dribs and drabs over the past four or five years – but nevertheless, there it was, to be divided evenly among the three children. Trevor had stared at him, a blank expression on his face, and asked why she would have opened a secret bank account. *She probably wanted to keep some money separate*, Michael told him, shrugging, keeping any speculation to himself. *In case your father did something silly with their joint account*. Trevor nodded, repeating that single, collusive word. *Probably*.

The obvious difficulty with disbursing the account was Barry: in recent years he'd fallen completely out of touch, and the drilling company for which he'd last claimed to work had long since closed up shop – as they'd discovered when the last Christmas card they sent via the main office came back *Return to Sender*. And though Michael assured Trevor he'd do everything he could to track down his brother, that amounted to little more than leaving messages with every Aberdeen oil company that had a listing in the phonebook and hoping, as each day passed with those messages unreturned, for a miracle.

Trevor hardly cared, though; he felt neither sadness at the sibling lost nor frustration at his absence. He felt very little at all, in fact, in those weeks following his mother's death, beyond a tangential awareness of the basic happenings around him – Michael's tireless funeral organizing, and the mourners trickling into the village again, the Kilgouries and the Pikes and a few of the Braithwaites, and the countless flowers arriving from those who couldn't make the trip. Each day passed in an elaborate, whisky-soaked dream, so much so that weeks later he would think back and wonder if any of it had really happened. How many of the details he might have missed.

The only thing that kept his attention, in those final days before the funeral, was the village chapel. Although Michael's plan, initially, had been to hold a small memorial in the guesthouse garden and then retire for a wake inside, Trevor was seized one night with the idea that they should use the old church instead. Not because he thought his mother would have wanted anything religious, but because it would be the first time in a decade that anyone had been inside, and easily another decade before that since it was last used for worship – and opening it again seemed to him an appropriately grand gesture to mark his mother's life.

So he told Michael, anyway. Mostly he was just hoping he could block out his despair by indulging his curiosity. For as long as he could remember the chapel had been shuttered, the synod having decreed before his birth that keeping Fìor in the pastor's weekly rounds of the archipelago wasn't worth the cost. Since then it had been opened up only a handful of times, mostly for the rat hunters to lay traps and later collect them, empty – and once, on a single day ten years ago, when the Trust sent an engineer to assess a crack along the outside wall. That time Trevor actually managed to creep inside, but was quickly shooed away. He'd been waiting for an excuse to get back in ever since.

On the day before the funeral, a Saturday, when the key from the Trust arrived with the morning ferry, he went straight from the jetty to the chapel, stopping only to leave the rest of the deliveries on the guesthouse's front doorstep. Perhaps as much as curiosity or distraction, he was glad for the brief respite from his father, too. Or at least from his father's *condition* – a word he hated, but one for which he could never find a suitable alternative. *Condition* made it sound like something transient, easy to get rid of. Fatigue was a condition, he thought, or obesity, or low spirits. Not whatever was wrong with his father. Yet none of the doctors they visited on the mainland had been able to agree on a specific diagnosis, dithering between Alzheimer's and Parkinson's and Lewy Body, and settling most often for the hopelessly vague *dementia*, a symptom rather than a disease in itself, but one of the few problems they could consistently identify.

The decline had started innocently enough, with a few occasional memory lapses that everyone assumed were little more than a sign of age. Who *would* expect a sixty-year-old to get by without ever writing anything down, without waiter's pads or recipes or to-do lists, the way George always had when younger? Soon, though, there were other symptoms, too: he would drift in and out of his monthly meetings with Michael, increasingly unconcerned with the well-being of the business; he would fall asleep at odd times of the day, or at the dinner table, or even in the middle of a conversation; and he would regularly forget his chores, letting a whole batch of supplies blow away in a gale one day, for instance, because he never went to fetch it. And then his trouble moving started. Maureen had called him down as usual for breakfast one morning, and when after ten minutes he'd failed to appear she went to look for him and found him on the stairs, stuck mid-step, gripping white-knuckled to the banister with a look of impossible concentration. *Like he was walking against a riptide*, Maureen described it to the doctor later. Stranger still, when she'd asked him what was wrong, he'd looked at her serenely. *Your husband's having trouble walking, it seems*, he said. Only a few seconds later did he frown, as if snapping out of a trance. *Perhaps we should call the doctor.*

The unnerving thing was that most of the time he still looked and acted like himself – had all the same mannerisms and facial expressions, told all the same jokes – even as that well-practised exterior masked his steady disappearance. By that winter he was nothing but a charming, hollow automaton, incapable of anything beyond hard-wired routines, growing anxious whenever conversation strayed from the guesthouse or the island, and giving them unconvincing smiles to gloss over his recurring confusion. For a long time the only thing that seemed not to have suffered were his crosswords, at which he continued to toil away – until Flora came to visit one Easter and sat down with him to help, and discovered he was filling the grid with mostly nonsense. Trevor wondered how long he'd been completing them that way, cheerfully scribbling down words without any idea why. Wondered what part of his mind was compelling him to carry on.

It haunted Trevor, seeing his father so diminished, made him want to run away and cower; to preserve, at least, a memory of the functioning person who'd brought him up. Worse, though, and more often these days, his father simply irritated him, and Trevor found himself snapping at innocent acts of incompetence, or sighing loudly whenever he had to repeat himself. It was hard to tell if George noticed anything – his jovial publican's persona was his default, now, regardless of the circumstance – but every now and then Trevor was sure he caught something in the man's eyes, some distant understanding of what was going on. So as the months passed, Trevor tried more and more to withdraw altogether, leaving the day-to-day care to Maureen – it was better for everyone that way, he told himself, and perhaps until his mother's death it had been. Now, though, they'd been forced back into an awkward, faltering reacquaintance, and entering the chapel that morning, Trevor was glad to temporarily escape him.

The inside of the building was smaller than he remembered it, as if after so many years the walls had contracted at the presence of a person. He'd forgotten, too, its smell of damp stone and the bizarre arrangement of the pews, different from the chapel at St Fillan's or any other church he'd ever seen: instead of facing the pulpit the seats ran lengthwise down the small chamber, so that parishioners were forced to stare at each other, or else swivel uncomfortably to watch the pastor. The light, though, was exactly as he remembered it from sneaking in as a boy, the greyish-white of elderly hair and not quite bright enough to illuminate the hall's far corners.

Over the years a few patches of mould had grown around the joints on the wooden seating, and a thin layer of dust covered everything else, and Trevor swept and scrubbed so diligently now that he was in there well into the afternoon. His reward was the countless artefacts he discovered as he went: among the pews a black coat button, and a ballpoint pen, and a crimson hair ribbon; near the pulpit an old Bible, pages mildewed and disintegrating, and a sheet of file paper on which were scribbled and intermittently crossed out the notes for a sermon on self-reliance. And most beautiful of all, on the floor by one of the windows, the desiccated corpse of a moth, the pigment of its wings faded and its body curled inwards on itself. He added it to the pile he'd started by the door, and on his way out, once the chapel was finally ready, he scooped all of them into his hands and carried the lot back home.

When he arrived at the guesthouse, though, he found a pair of paint-flecked canvas trainers in the vestibule, and instantly forgot about his bounty. *Flora*. He looked at his watch; the second ferry had arrived while he was gone. Calling out her name, he started down the hallway, and when she called back he carelessly dropped the trinkets on the telephone table and bounded for the stairs, telling himself he'd come back for them later. By the time he remembered that evening, however, it was already too late; in the frenzy of extra helping hands around the guesthouse that weekend, somebody else had already cleared them away.

The service was short the next day; Flora wasn't sure it could even be called a service, technically, since the archipelago's new pastor, a young fellow who'd never known Maureen anyway, hadn't been invited. Instead Flora, as the oldest child present, officiated a more secular remembrance, and anyone who wanted to share a few words was welcome – which in the end meant Trevor, and one of

Maureen's cousins from Perth, and a handful of the older islanders who'd returned for the occasion.

The chapel air was cool as the two dozen or so guests filed in that morning, and Flora vaguely worried about her father catching a chill. But once the heavy doors were shut and everyone was seated, the walls began to trap the heat coming off their bodies – and by the time she stood up to start the proceedings, hands shaking and neck drenched in sweat, the room was warm and still.

'Good morning,' she said, gripping the sides of the lectern. 'Thank you all so much for coming.' Her voice cracked as she carried on reading from her notes, explaining how much the turnout meant to her, how touched Maureen would have been, and introducing the first speaker of the morning: cousin Susan from Perth. She, in turn, made much of being the only member of Maureen's extended family to stay in contact over the years, and then told a few dull but well-meaning stories about her first memories of Maureen as a child, and about the long letters they'd began to trade in recent years, and about Maureen's visit to Perth with George and Trevor the Christmas past, their first in years, and how happy a reunion it had been. Flora barely listened, alternating instead between tinkering with her notes and trying not to cry, and with each subsequent speaker – Gillian Braithwaite, a childhood friend, and Bobby McKenzie from the old general store – the routine was the same: she would stand, thank one person while introducing the next, and then return to her seat between Trevor and her father and shut out anything that threatened to break her composure.

To her surprise that didn't mean the familiar stories, the ones she remembered herself or could easily imagine: her mother mending a torn dress mere minutes before a wedding; her mother single-handedly taking over the general store's scone-baking while Mrs

McKenzie recovered from a broken wrist. No, it was the stories she *couldn't* picture that brought tears to her eyes: the book club Maureen had started for the island women, and her girlish fantasies about Richard Burton, and the impromptu ceilidh she'd thrown on the beach for her twenty-seventh birthday (or her twenty-eighth; Gillian couldn't quite remember). So while the rest of the crowd chuckled ruefully at their memories, Flora felt only regret, both that she hadn't known her mother better, and that she wasn't sure she'd ever really tried. It was a relief when at last she called Trevor to the podium for the day's final eulogy, and she returned to her seat imagining the stiff drink they could soon retire to. Her neck ached from sitting in the odd, sideways pew all morning.

Trevor began quietly. 'My mother,' he said, shuffling his feet, 'was a wonderful woman, and I wouldn't be who I am today without her.' He cleared his throat and swallowed hard, and when he continued his voice was louder, more self-consciously projected. 'But actually, I don't think any of our lives would be the same if it weren't for Maureen Elizabeth Stewart McCloud.' There were a few approving nods around the room at that, Flora noticed, and they seemed to give Trevor some extra confidence as he went on – explaining that although he was devastated to have lost a loving parent, his own loss was insignificant compared to the one suffered collectively by this crowd, and by those who hadn't been able to attend, and by the island's countless future visitors and residents who would never gain, now, from her remarkable gifts. He extolled a long list of her virtues; he told another story or two about her heroic feats helping others; and then he moved on to a reverent description of all the things she'd done with him when she'd visited for his half-term breaks: afternoons in tea rooms, and evenings in nice restaurants, and the time she'd taken him to Glasgow for a new exhibit at the Burrell.

It was a touching speech, Flora thought, unlike anything she'd expected. Since she'd left the island she'd missed, it seemed, her brother's transformation, from mercurial teenager to thoughtful, mature young man – and she cried at that clear proof of her neglect, these recent years, as much as at the speech itself. She hadn't even come home for Christmas the last three winters – part of the reason, she was sure, that the rest of them returned to Perth last year. And what a bloody mistake that was! Instead she'd spent the most recent holidays with Oliver at his family home in the Borders, out of some misguided sense of her own maturity, even after it had become clear that a break-up was inevitable. *Why can't we spend Christmas with my family for a change?* she'd asked him as they'd shopped for gifts that year along a chill, dark Princes Street. *We've been together for years and you've never even seen where I grew up.* He'd given her a bored glare, familiar from so many identical discussions in recent months. *Because*, he said, *I don't want to spend Christmas on some godforsaken rock in the middle of nowhere.*

The remark, much harsher than anything he'd said before, had stung, and she'd stormed off into the dark winter's afternoon, leaving him on his own in the middle of Marks & Spencer – and though ultimately she'd skulked back and given in, as always, the argument flared again and again, most spectacularly at his parents' house on Christmas Eve. After that they sat through a painful Christmas dinner the next afternoon, and she left on her own on Boxing Day; when he returned, a whole week later, to their cramped flat near the Meadows, they made the split official, and Flora moved into Bella's spare room again while she looked for somewhere of her own.

As Trevor finished his speech, now, she heard a sniffle beside her, and turned to see her father crying, dark splotches on his shirt where a few tears had already fallen. *Thank God*, she thought, as she stood up to return to the podium; she'd been afraid the day's meaning might escape him. When they'd walked in that morning he'd made some panicked remark about forgetting his Bible, and then a cryptic joke about how he'd rather look at Bobby's anyway – and Flora had wondered if he remembered getting married here, or if those schoolboy memories were all he had left. If he remembered meeting Maureen at all.

As she crossed paths with Trevor she whispered that he'd been brilliant, and kept her eyes on him as she addressed the room one last time, abandoning her notes and saying that she didn't have much to add: Trevor had shared a portrait of their mother more perfect, she nodded emphatically, than anything she could ever paint. She cringed as the words left her mouth – they hadn't sounded as trite in her head – but the sentiment was met with more approving nods around the room, and, grateful for that opportunity to wrap things up, she thanked everyone for coming one last time.

Michael had slipped out as she was talking, to go and set out the food for the wake, and Trevor joined him now, leaving Flora to stand at the chapel door, arm-in-arm with her father, and see off all the mourners. A woman whose name she couldn't remember stopped and patted her on the arm.

'You did very well dear,' she said. 'I'm sure your mother would have been proud.' She looked to George, who greeted her with a cheerful *How do you do?* Her face fell. 'We'll talk more later,' she whispered to Flora, and hurried away.

The wake was more of the same, streams of old islanders seeking out Flora and Trevor to applaud their poise in such hard times, and ending up grieving as much for their father as for their mother, while he sunnily chattered away with no idea who anybody was. Flora found it exhausting, and by the time the sky was darkening that afternoon, the visitors slowly disappearing to their cottages or their rooms, she was glad to spot Michael sitting alone at a table by the window.

'Penny for them,' she said, coming up behind him.

He looked up. 'Just… thinking.' She smiled and asked about what, stumbling over her words and realizing that she'd had more to drink than she'd intended. (Everyone who'd spoken to her that afternoon had insisted she take a dram.)

Michael shrugged; paused. Looked around the room. 'Things seem to be winding down.'

She nodded but didn't say anything else, scared now of slurring her words more.

'I suppose we ought to start cleaning,' he said, with a sigh. He stood up and stretched his back.

'Not yet,' she said. 'Let's take a walk.' She put her hand on his wrist. 'Before it gets too dark.' He frowned, looking around the room again, and told her they shouldn't leave Trevor on his own, which she knew was true – but in that moment she simply didn't care, overwhelmed by the desire to get out of there as fast as she could, and to take Michael with her. She squeezed his wrist where she still held it. 'Please?' she said. 'Humour me?'

And like that, weakly, he gave in.

She told Trevor they were going to the kitchen and then they snuck out the back door, taking the old byway past the chapel and away from the village. When the trail ended they crossed over to the main road for a while, and when that ended too, at the Kilgouries' old crofthouse, they carried on beyond it, into the grass, up a faint rise and over an old fence to the edge of the gentle cliffs on the island's north coast. The sky was a crisp, vernal sunset, a wash of pinks and silvers behind the clouds that were rolling in across the sea. On their left the land sloped down to the pass between the village and the Stùc, half a mile away, and to the land bridge still bulging from the water. From this angle it looked much smaller than usual, dreamlike, the merest of threads connecting the two islands.

'I didn't think it would be low tide right now,' said Flora, huddling close to Michael and wrapping her arm around his waist. She remembered, briefly, how only a few months earlier she'd wished she could stand here with Oliver; remembered the emotionless expression on his face as she told him she was leaving. Remembered how even then – even after so many years – her first thought, walking out the door, had been of Michael. Of what she might have thrown away with him. Of whether she still had a chance to get it back.

'We should go down there,' she said.

He was quiet for a moment. 'We don't have time,' he murmured, putting his arm around her. 'It'll be dark soon. And the tide's coming in.'

'Ach,' she said, letting go of him. 'You worry too much.' She took a few steps forward, and when she reached the lip of the cliff she knelt down, sizing up a rocky shelf a few feet down the cliff face and then smiling at him over her shoulder. 'Live a little.' She hopped over the edge.

Letting out a yelp, Michael rushed forward, stopping self-consciously when he realized she was fine. 'My God, Flora! You should be more careful! You've been drinking!'

'It's nothing,' she said, already scrambling onto another shelf, lower still. 'I've done this before – there's a path all the way to the beach.' She tested her footing on the next ledge and stepped across. 'Sort of.'

Michael told her again to be careful, that this was a terrible idea, but when it became clear she was carrying on regardless he lowered himself over the edge to follow, as she practically skipped ahead of him. When she reached the bottom he was still only half-way down, and she flopped on the sand to wait, watching as he took his slow, measured steps down the rock face.

She'd been thinking about him a lot since her break-up. If she was honest, she'd been thinking about him even before that, because in Oliver's latest recalcitrance about visiting the island the comparison between the two was too tempting to pass up. Why was she wasting her time, she'd asked herself, with this selfish pipsqueak who didn't care if he even met her family, when she had an admirer back home who'd already given himself entirely to their cause? Not just an admirer – someone she'd previously lusted after, for months! Why had she ever passed that up? After all, it wasn't as if she wanted to abandon the island and never return; she was glad to have gone to art school and liked the prospect of living in Edinburgh long term, but this place would always be home.

A disgruntled shearwater shrieked and flew away as Michael reached the bottom of the cliff and jumped the last few feet to the ground. Flora smiled and stood up.

'See?' she said. 'That wasn't so bad.'

He laughed. 'Still took a few years off my life.'

'Oh, wheesht.' She came up beside him and took him by the elbow. 'Come on, look: the crossing's still here. Let's make a dash for it.'

'Flora.' He looked at her imploringly. 'We can't go over there. We'll get stuck.'

He was right, of course – rationally and responsibly and emotionally she knew that. But at the same time she knew she'd never wanted anything more, not when she'd wished that Barry would suddenly show up today, not when she'd decided to go to art school, not even on that day at St Fillan's when she'd yearned to run off to Tam's room and give in to whatever he asked. So she looked at Michael now, at his eyes, sooty in the twilight, and she shook her head.

'I don't care,' she said, and, still holding on to his elbow, she raised herself onto her tiptoes, just as she had in her studio that rainy afternoon all those years ago, and kissed him. And, just as in her studio, he kissed her back. This time, though, it didn't feel like surrender, like she was settling for plan B; she simply felt calm, and happy, and decided. And for a minute or two that feeling, and his hipbone beneath her palm, and his chapped lips on hers – that was all she knew.

'I'm glad we met,' she said, when she finally pulled away. 'You've been so good to me. To all of us.' He nodded, but before he could say anything she was dragging him down the beach again, towards the land bridge, and this time he didn't try to stop her. A thin sheet of water was spreading over the isthmus as they crossed, breaking in tiny waves against their feet and then their ankles and then their shins, and by the time they reached the other side the path had mostly vanished. By then they were already looking ahead of them, though, joining hands as the amethyst clouds gathered overhead, and breaking into a run – towards the old orchard, and sanctuary, and each other.

16

TREVOR SPENT THE WHOLE NIGHT WORRIED SICK and bellowed as much at Flora when she returned the following morning, Mrs Kilgourie and several of the other elderly ex-islanders cramming into the pub to join him. (Not even their previous day's sympathy was enough to quell their love of a good scandal.) They upbraided Flora for *running off like some lovestruck teenager*, and whispered to each other disbelievingly, when she weakly defended herself against whoever's turn it was to scold, that it had been *the day of a funeral, for pity's sake*. A row of shaking heads also saw off Michael as he retreated to his cottage. *I'm just glad your mother wasn't here to see it*, Mrs Kilgourie muttered to Trevor, as Flora finally disappeared upstairs to shower.

And yet as the day wore on, as Flora offered continued apologies and forgiveness seemed to settle, Trevor wondered if they should be glad of his mother's absence, not for her sake but for theirs – because when he really stopped to ponder how she might have reacted, he doubted their reconciliation would have come so easy. There would have been far lengthier recriminations, and a week of obdurate silence, and instead of the happy dinner he had with his sister that night, all giggles and nostalgia, Flora would have pouted through the rest of her visit under Maureen's disapproving stare, hiding in her room or on the Stùc, and then escaped back to Edinburgh for months without a peep.

As it was, actually, he still didn't see much of Flora before she left, but for different reasons. Even after the other mourners trickled away, and despite a few unplanned days tacked on at the end of her visit, she was mostly with Michael for the rest of her time there. But Trevor cared less for now about the number of hours she spent at the guesthouse than about the number she spent simply on the island, contented, and acquiring more reasons to come back – because if she and Michael became seriously involved, it seemed to him, they were both more likely to keep ties there. More likely, in coming years, to settle permanently.

He had obvious reasons for wanting Flora back, of course: with Barry gone and George demented, she was effectively the last survivor among his immediate family. But he'd long been searching for a way to ensure Michael's continued presence, too, because in the man's peculiar obsession with Fìor, Trevor felt he'd found a kindred spirit – someone else, at last, who understood that the guesthouse, and the floundering way of life it represented, were both things worth preserving. And while Trevor was more than willing to bear that responsibility on his own, with his father's decline in recent years he'd realized that, unfortunately, it was much more than a one-man job.

Not that Michael had yet shown any sign of leaving. On the contrary, he'd gradually raised the amount of time he spent away from London, of his own accord, from the six or seven months when he'd started to almost eleven now. Partly it was pragmatic: letting his flat there, purchased a decade ago at the edge of what was now a trendy, gentrifying neighbourhood, brought him enormous profit. But mostly, as he'd spent more time on the island over the years, he seemed to have developed some sense of belonging there, if not alienation from the hedonistic lifestyle he'd left behind.

The turning point had been a few years ago – sometime between Flora leaving and the start of his father's illness – after Michael had cut another month off his time in London and some of his friends, in response, decided to finally visit and see what all the fuss was about. Michael had been unusually anxious at the prospect, and when they arrived Trevor could see why: they were lager louts, all of them, a pair of men and a pair of women, drinking too much and too loudly for Trevor's tastes or anyone else's. But the real disaster came on the last night, when one of the men threw up all over the bar. That was bad enough, but when Maureen went to fetch a mop and bucket she found the other man with one of the women in the public loo, she half-naked and perched on the sink, legs wrapped around him, and he telling Maureen slurringly to *fuck off and let us finish*. Maureen had screamed for Michael, who came running, aghast, and sided against his friends – and that was when the fight broke out. It took both Trevor and George and another male guest, pulled groggily from bed, to finally break it up.

Once Michael's friends left the next day he apologized profusely, even offering to give up his post in penitence – though Trevor managed, thank God, to dissuade him. *Thank you for understanding*, he'd replied, more grateful than Trevor had ever seen him. *You see why I prefer it here. Every weekend's like that back home.*

From then on Michael's whole mindset seemed to change: he installed internet on the island, both at his cottage and the guesthouse, and built a website for the latter; he began a project to replace their costly diesel generators with wind and solar power; and he persuaded the ferry company to install a phone line at the jetty to help visitors who'd missed their crossing. He even talked, though never did anything, about petitioning the Trust to rebuild the bridge to the Stùc – he wanted to convert the old schoolhouse into a museum.

For Trevor, though, the scandal that night, and Michael's subsequent talk of leaving, was a sobering reminder of how easily the man could choose to go – and a relationship with Flora seemed like the perfect way to permanently close off that opportunity. Abandoning a business partner was unfortunate, perhaps, but justifiable; abandoning a girlfriend's family – or a brother-in-law, thought Trevor, his imagination running away with him – was inconceivable. And in the meantime, their relationship would provide an equally perfect way to reel Flora back in. He was giddy at the possibilities.

When Flora finally left the week after the funeral, though, it began to look as if life on the island, at least temporarily, would be a struggle. Trevor and Michael and George – the island's three remaining residents – went to the jetty to see her off, each one giving her a long, wretched hug, and as the ship pulled away Trevor instantly felt the island grow emptier, larger, the uncluttered landscape ominous, suddenly, and the quiet claustrophobic. The other men felt it too, he was sure, because as they trudged back to the guesthouse they made incessant small talk, Michael about some new idea for the website, George about what the weather might do that night, and Trevor about anything he could think of, really, to hold the creeping void at bay. Back at home, too, they clung to each other, moving from room to room together as they busied themselves with cleaning, and then sharing dinner in the pub, frittering away the evening with more forced conversation. Trevor lay in bed that night staring at the ceiling and dreading another day of the same anxious hyperactivity. And then another. And then another.

Which was precisely what he got: when Michael showed up the next morning – after a similarly restless night, it looked like – it was with a notepad, and a thermos of coffee, and a manic, focused energy. With Maureen gone and George less helpful every day, he told Trevor, sitting him down at the kitchen table, they were going to have to make some drastic changes – and for those last weeks before the season they threw themselves into it, updating their operating manuals and filing systems and spreadsheets, and stocking the freezer past Maureen's already ample backlog, and filling every spare hour beyond that with brainstorming sessions to refine their vision of a new, improved guesthouse. Many of their changes were little more than damage control, for the time being, limiting bookings and altering duty rosters and a hundred other tweaks and stopgaps to make the place more manageable. But looking forward they cooked up more ambitious plans, of clearing out the guest rooms upstairs to make way for self-catering suites; of opening up a few old cottages as more of the same; of contracts for frozen meals from mainland suppliers; summer interns scouted from hospitality programmes; and partnerships with B&Bs in Mallaig.

To some extent it helped, actually. During the days Trevor even began to believe their plans would work, that the guesthouse would soon be great again – that years from now he'd look back on their work here as a triumph. On those lonely, sleepless nights in bed, though, he grew glummer, succumbing again and often to his funk. So what, he asked himself, if they got the place on its feet again? It still wouldn't be the guesthouse he remembered, the one he'd long pictured himself inheriting. All the improvements Michael had made the past few years were one thing – the computer, and the redecorated guest rooms, and the modern, energy-efficient window frames throughout – but now the very spirit of the place seemed dangerously in flux, transforming into something he neither cared for nor completely understood. Why would anyone sign up for one of these self-catering suites Michael was so excited about? Who would want a holiday less the care his parents had always lavished on their guests, and in a setting so sterile? The smell of soup and soapsuds from his mother's kitchen, and his father's vegetable patch, and the old half-finished Monopoly games tucked beneath the coffee table: it was all gone, his family vanished, and even if Flora did return now he doubted it would make much difference.

When they finally opened for the year and some approximation of normality returned, those concerns faded for a while; forced to assume the role of proprietor, something his father could no longer manage, he perked up considerably. In fact, despite the many extra hours cooking and cleaning, and markedly fewer asleep, he enjoyed the job that summer more than he ever had. Even handling complaints, of which inevitably there were several that year, left him with an odd sense of satisfaction.

The summer's happy reprieve, however, only made the autumn's crash more pronounced. Trevor's days seemed to settle in front of him without end, like those mornings of thick white fog he remembered from his childhood, and he spent his spare hours moping around the house, lost among spectres of his mother. All the little routines she normally had in the first weeks after the season stuck out now in their absence: the paperbacks she'd start to read, and then leave open at her place in strange spots around the house; the rich smells from the kitchen and the disappearing stack of storage tubs in the pantry; and the sound of the radio drifting from the kitchen, tuned to classical music or the world history programmes she'd more recently grown to love.

In the meantime, George was getting steadily worse, as if Maureen's death had shaken him from his moorings. One day in November, Trevor went to the jetty to fetch supplies, and returned to see his father standing motionless by the hallway telephone.

'Call heard for you as you were out,' he said, when Trevor asked him what was wrong. His faintly garbled sentences had started a few weeks after the funeral – or at least, that was when Trevor started noticing them.

'Oh?' His stomach clenched at the thought of a potential customer getting his father on the phone. 'Who was it?'

George blinked. 'Barry,' he said. 'A number left to call him up.'

Trevor's heart seemed to empty at his brother's name, but when he hurried to the telephone table and looked at his father's message on the notepad, he found only gibberish. *Barry*, it read. *Arby R. Y Arab? Bay ar(ea)* – and below that a string of numbers sloping downwards for twenty or thirty digits. Shoulders slumping, Trevor wondered if the phone had even rung. Several times in the past few weeks his father had claimed to see and speak with his dead brother James, and a handful of other islanders who had long since passed away – and even, once, to Maureen. This was probably just more of the same. Rolling his eyes, Trevor ushered him back to his chair in the sitting room.

And yet it did seem strange, he thought, as he unpacked the shopping, that his father would imagine Barry; usually his hallucinations involved people he'd known since childhood, the memories most firmly cemented. Barry seemed too recent. And his father had never imagined any of the children before, as far as Trevor knew. Or a phone call.

So once everything was put away, Trevor returned to the telephone table and studied the message again. The first ten digits in the string of numbers did look as if they could be a phone number…

He looked up and towards the sitting room, where he could hear his father humming to himself. *It couldn't be.*

Fingers trembling, he picked up the handset and punched in the number. There was the normal, brief silence as the call made its way to the exchange on the mainland – but then only the scolding, three-tone noise of a non-existent circuit, and British Telecom's haughty matron telling him the number had not been recognized. The handset still pressed to his ear, he ended the call with his thumb and frowned at the message pad again. Then he tried dialling another set of the numbers, and then another, each time with the same result, until at last, on his fifth attempt, he heard ringing. Held his breath.

'Hello?' It was a man's voice.

Trevor hesitated. 'I – um…' He hadn't thought of what he might say if someone answered. 'May I speak to Barry McCloud please?'

He braced himself.

'There's no Barry McCloud here, pal. Think you've got a wrong number.'

Trevor's eyes shut; his head sagged. He muttered sorry and slammed the phone down, suddenly furious – at himself for entertaining the possibility and at his father for putting it in his head in the first place. Down the hall the senile old coot was still humming his constantly remodulating tune, oblivious to what he'd done.

With a sigh, Trevor tore off the message and tossed it in the bin, and began yanking open drawers on the telephone table, looking for some place to hide the pad. But the first two drawers were too full of phonebooks and the miscellaneous stamps and postcards they kept on hand for guests, and in the mostly empty third he spotted something else. He moved his head closer, squinting to get a better look.

The objects he'd collected from the chapel.

He'd never looked for them again after they disappeared in April, partly because he assumed they'd been thrown out but mostly because, in the commotion with Michael and Flora, he'd forgotten all about them. Yet apparently they'd been here the whole time, thoughtfully put away by someone, and waiting for him to find them again. He fished them from the drawer, one by one. Their slight weight in his hands was soothing, somehow, disarming, and temporarily pushed aside his anger. Calling to his father that he'd be down shortly to start on lunch, he started towards the stairs, telling himself he ought to put these somewhere safe before they disappeared again.

In his room, he made straight for the closet and pulled out the most current box from his collection's three. Out of habit he sat down on the floor beside it, to sort through and savour some of its other recent additions, before he added the new ones. There was his invitation to Flora's degree show at ECA; the fuel cap from the guesthouse's old diesel generator, now replaced by Michael's solar panels; and a gnarled piece of driftwood, a rusted nail lodged in one end the only clue that it had once been part of the bridge to the Stùc. As he picked up each item, holding them to the light to look a little closer, or running his hands along their surfaces to wipe them clean of dust, he felt his temper subsiding even further, and when he came across his mother's old alarm clock he even found himself approaching a regretful sort of happiness.

The clock was an old-fashioned model, with Roman numerals on its face and two brass bells on top. A few weeks before she died it had broken, as if prompting her to give up just as insistently as it had woken her each morning, and they'd replaced it with a modern digital one she hated. This clock, though, the one that had sat by her bedside since Trevor was a baby, still felt decidedly like his mother's – and, inspired, he started rooting more purposefully through the box for anything else of hers, quickly reaching the bottom and then pulling out a second box. To his delight he found a few of the letters she'd sent him at school – mostly news about whichever ex-islander she'd heard from most recently – and a beat-up pair of the nicer shoes she always wore to see him on the mainland. Beneath all that was a lock of hair from one of the trims George sometimes used to give her, and, wrapped in plastic to prevent its smell from spreading, the wooden spoon he'd found her gripping when she died, a few dried specks of porridge still caked on the handle. He'd amassed a relatively impressive pile of stuff by the time he got to the last box – or the first one, really, the one he'd started with.

As he pulled it from the shelf he realized he had very little idea any more of what was actually in it; he'd filled it by the time he was fourteen or fifteen – *coming up on ten years now*, he realized, with a shock – and since then had hardly touched it. Unfortunately there didn't seem to be much more of his mother in it, though, and in the end he found only a few more things: the faded, family photograph he'd often stared at as a child, the image crumbling away around the crease down its centre. A painted Easter egg the two of them had made one year. And last of all, rolled up and stuffed tightly in the corner of the box, one of her old, flimsy cardigans.

He almost missed the cardigan, actually, assuming it was a blanket until he noticed the bulge of a button in the fabric and shook the thing out. As soon as he realized what it was, his spirits leapt, and he brought it to his face, eyes closed, snuggling against the soft fibres. After so many years in storage it smelled overwhelmingly of cardboard and mildew, but beneath that he thought he could still detect a few bursts of his mother's scent: the dried lavender she kept in her dresser drawers to ward away moths, and a muddy mixture of sweat, talc, and the fancy perfume she wore for special occasions. He let out a contented sigh. This was exactly the sort of find he'd been hoping for.

Letting it drop to his lap again, he tried to remember how it had come to be in the collection. There was nothing wrong with it, no stains or tears that might have made her throw it out, which struck him as particularly odd – most of his items were salvaged from the rubbish, and he would have expected his mother to miss a perfectly good piece of clothing. So where had he found it? He rubbed the collar between his thumb and forefinger, trying to jog his memory. A faint image of one of the guest rooms came to mind. *Yes*, he thought, as the details began to rise out of the murk. Flora had just started at St Fillan's, and his dad had gone to the mainland to tend to some trouble Barry'd been in at school – and with the guesthouse full of the ratcatchers his mother was leaning on him for extra help with the chores. He found the cardigan when she asked him to make the beds one morning.

He remembered balking at the job, because he'd been young enough that he'd never made a bed before and wasn't sure he'd know how – but his mother had shown little sympathy and sent him sternly upstairs telling him to use his native wit. He remembered, too, how confused he'd been at finding the cardigan there, bunched up between the bed and the wall in one of the single guest rooms; remembered rubbing it between his fingers as he was doing now, remembered feeling that thrilling, seductive mystery of an object out of place. It was a relatively dressy item, not one his mother would have worn for cleaning the guest rooms, and at the time he hadn't been able to think of any reason it might be up there.

Now he found himself wondering again. His mother had rarely fraternized with guests, and certainly never upstairs; *if they want our company*, she'd always told the children, *they'll come to us*. So what on earth could she have been doing up there in her nice clothes – removing her nice clothes, even! – on a night when her husband was away? A grim theory began to congeal as he struggled to remember more details, an uncomfortable lump forming at the back of his throat. He'd seen enough soap operas on the common-room television at St Fillan's that he could fit the pieces together well enough. A long marriage; an attractive outsider. An affair.

He shook his head. Tried to tell himself it was absurd. She had been a loyal wife and an exemplary mother. She couldn't possibly have done anything so sordid. And yet… Now other memories were surfacing, too: her late nights in the pub while the ratcatchers had been there; how she'd insisted she couldn't go to St Fillan's herself that week, despite her usual fondness for the mainland. And why *was* she always wearing those nice shoes of hers when she came to visit the school? Who had she been trying to impress? Where had she been stopping on her way?

His earlier anger was returning now, accompanied by a growing sense of horror. Which of the ratcatchers was it? How many times? Were there others, too? He flung the cardigan away from him now, tears burning in his eyes.

'Trevor,' his father called from downstairs. 'It's lunchtime.'

Letting out a frustrated sob, he banged his fist against the floor. *Not now!* He took a deep breath. Slowly stood up and walked to the door. 'I know, Dad,' he replied, trying to keep a level voice. 'I'll be down in a minute.'

'Barry phoned.'

'Yes, Dad, of course he did. You already told me.' He could feel his last shreds of patience slipping away, his blood pressure rising. His hand, still gripping the door frame, squeezed the wood tighter, until the bones in his fingers felt like they might snap.

'Trevor,' his father repeated, after a few more moments. 'It's lunchtime.'

With another exasperated roar, he stepped into the hallway. 'Fine!' he yelled. 'It's fucking lunchtime!' He jogged down the stairs, head pounding, and shoved his father out of the way as he passed him at the bottom step. That contact – his tense hand against his father's soft, ageing flesh – stirred a brief feeling of guilt, but even as he tried to take a deep breath, to remind himself it was only the Condition talking, the dementia, whatever it was, he was turning around to the sight of his father still cowering by the staircase, a pathetic look on his face. For some reason that only incensed him more.

'Trevor—'

'Don't tell me!' he shouted. 'Fucking lunchtime, is it?' He stalked back to his father. *Not his fault, Trevor.* He grabbed him by the wrist. 'Come on then,' he said, 'I'm not bloody feeding you out here!'

He can't help it, Trevor.

In the kitchen he pushed his father into a chair at the table and fetched a few ingredients from the cupboards. As he began furiously chopping an onion he could see the veins in his forearm bulging, could feel his teeth grinding painfully together, and he was asking that reasonable voice in his head why it wouldn't be better to just throw the old coot off the end of the jetty and put him out of his misery, when behind him his father croaked again.

'Trevor.'

He spun around. '*What?*'

There were a few tears running down his father's cheeks. 'I'm sorry,' he said.

And then, as if a valve had opened, all the pressure that had been building in Trevor's chest seemed to rush up towards his face, and tears began to form in his eyes, too. *Put him out of his misery?* the voice asked, fading away. *Or put you out of yours?*

It wasn't long, after that, until things with Michael began to slide, too. Though in past winters he and Trevor had seemed like close friends – spending the long evenings in the pub, or at grandfather McCloud's old card table, pulled from beneath the stairs, or simply reading side by side in the sitting room – now the man was too preoccupied with Flora to do much else. Most nights he spent at his own cottage, either at the computer or on the phone, making what Trevor could only assume were noxious declarations of eternal love. (He'd never had much taste for romance, which perhaps explained his lack of success with the opposite sex while at school.)

Trevor's waning enthusiasm for the relationship wasn't down only to Michael's withdrawal, however, or even to Trevor's subsequent loneliness: he'd also realized that, contrary to what he'd hoped in the spring, it wasn't bringing Flora any closer either. She hadn't come home any more often, and it certainly didn't seem to be increasing her attachment to Trevor or the business; the few times she did visit, for the occasional long weekend, and an entire ten days around Christmas, she didn't even spend the time at home, sleeping instead at Michael's cottage and moving her things there the way she'd once done with the mansion on the Stùc. When she wasn't there canoodling, she was sketching or on the phone scheduling some event, while Trevor, mostly on his own or chatting vacuously with his father, seemed not even to exist.

Throughout it all he stewed about his mother, too, swinging back and forth almost daily from knowing her infidelity was impossible, to knowing, just as surely, that there was no other explanation. That was the worst part: the never being sure. No longer could he call up some happy image of her to remind himself what he was fighting to preserve, or how idyllic the guesthouse had once been, or why his solitary nights in the pub that winter, crying bitterly into his whisky, were still worth struggling through – because all of them, now, came with those unpleasant questions attached.

By the time the summer rolled around again, running the guesthouse had predictably lost much of its allure. Trevor toiled through without much charm or pleasure, and Michael, his attitude towards work suddenly lackadaisical, came to view the guesthouse as more of a nuisance, it seemed, than anything else. Their weekly planning meetings grew curter and less productive, Trevor frequently losing his temper at what he now saw as Michael's arrogant obsession with the bottom line, and Michael condescending to Trevor about his untenable nostalgia. When the end of October arrived and they finally closed again, exhausted, Michael announced he'd be upping his time on the mainland again that winter, spending December through February in Edinburgh with Flora – and Trevor began to think he'd actually be better off if the two of them just left him alone and let him do things his way. Began to realize that, like it or not, that might soon be the case anyway.

So when the letter from the ferry company arrived a few weeks later, informing him they'd no longer be operating their separate summer schedule to the island – that after the usual mid-November drop to three crossings a week that would be it, all year round – he didn't mention it to Michael. Not so much because he feared that this would finally make the man give up, but from some perverse determination to face the problem on his own. Even as he reread the letter a second and third time after his father was in bed that night, he decided he had to prove to them, or to himself, or to *someone*, that he could manage without any help. So he simply hid the letter in his bedside table and went for a walk to clear his head.

It was getting late as he wandered onto the path towards the Stùc, and even with the faint light on the horizon the landscape had turned a velvet black. He'd left the house without a torch, something his father had always scolded him not to do, but he enjoyed the novelty of seeing the island this way – his eyes adjusting to the dark, the twilight giving the hills a fleeting, luminescent depth, and in the distance the whisper of the ocean growing to a roar.

Once the path opened up to the glimmer of water, he sat down on the sand and began to ponder his options. His only chance, really, was to come up with a way to change the ferry company's mind: the guesthouse itself was barely scraping by as it was, and cutting out the pub's income from summer day trippers would be the deathblow he'd dreaded for years. And yet each idea that came to him – a letter-writing campaign, a plea to his local MP, some offer of sharing the guesthouse's (non-existent) profits – seemed more hopeless than the last, and before long he'd been reduced to asking himself, sourly, what Michael would do. And worse, after that: asking himself whether Michael's help would even make a difference.

With a sigh, at last, he looked out across the water, towards the horizon, where there was still a wispy ring of gasflame blue – as if somehow, far away, the sea had caught alight.

17

THE LIGHT GOES OUT AND... What? *Title hgh. High lett. Eighth lt?*

'Fuck!'

Eighth lt. goes towards death (3, 5).

A clatter; Trevor walking into something in the dark.

The light.

'The light.'

'Yes, Dad, the light. I know. I'm trying to fix it.'

He shifts nervously in his chair. 'What's wrong?'

A sigh. 'I'm not sure yet.'

They had been eating dinner in the kitchen, when suddenly the light above the table went out. Not just the light: the numbers on the microwave, and the faint glow around the door, and the illuminated dial on the countertop radio. Other than the hiss of rain outside, all the sounds stopped, too.

In the hallway he hears Trevor jiggling the light switch up and down. Swearing again. He leans back in his chair. *It's dark to eat like this (?).*

'Sit tight, Dad,' calls Trevor. *Gorge?* 'I have to check the generator.' *Biliously?* '... Dad?'

'Okay, Trevor. I'll sit here.' *Listen: make it darker to eat less (4).*

The front door creaks open; slams shut.

Diet.

Trevor's so good to be looking after him like this. Such a splendid young man. And he's taken the reins around the guesthouse quite brilliantly, too. Has the place running like clockwork. Not many guests these days, mind. But things will pick up soon.

The front door slams again.

'Well,' says Trevor, coming back into the kitchen, a flashlight in his hand. George can smell the rain on him. 'Looks like we're finishing by candlelight.'

'Candlelight?'

Trevor walks towards him, slowly, careful not to hit anything in the dark. 'The electricity's fucked somehow. Fantastic thing to happen in the middle of January.'

There is a gloating gust of wind outside.

'I'll take a proper look in the morning – I can't see a thing out there right now.' He sighs. 'I don't suppose you remember where the candles are?'

Candles. Torches, lamps, flames. Wicks.

'I'll take that as a no.' He rummages through some of the kitchen drawers, then disappears into the hallway. Five minutes pass. Ten?

'Found some,' says Trevor, reappearing with two shot glasses from the bar, a candle standing crookedly in each. 'They were under the stairs.' He places them carefully on his side of the table. Away from George.

They finish eating; sit awhile. Before long Trevor puts George to bed. ('Not much else we can do tonight, eh?' he says, nodding towards the shrinking candles.)

George lies there for hours, not tired. It's still too early to sleep. Isn't it? These days it's so hard to tell. Time seems to stretch recently, contract, spill over, days bleeding into hours bleeding into weeks. Whole seasons sometimes pass him by.

It isn't as bad, though, as everyone seems to think. The way people talk to him now – talk *about* him, as if he isn't there, or look at him with misplaced pity – you'd think he was already dead. But what's a little confusion every now and then? No, maybe he's not as sharp as he used to be, and he knows he's forgotten things he shouldn't – and the trouble moving is a worry, too, if only because he doesn't notice it happening half the time. He'll be standing up from the table, or buttoning his shirt in the morning, and it will be as if his mind has wandered: he'll start to daydream about a flower he once saw, or a room he stood in long ago, and all of a sudden whole minutes have passed and he's still stuck mid-motion, Trevor or that nice young fellow from down the road staring at him in concern. But give him some credit, damn it! He still gets through the days in one piece, still carries on a pretty decent conversation, still manages to get a few clues in the crossword every night. As long as he sticks to his routines, he's fine.

'The only thing I feel bad about,' he says, softly, 'is Trevor.'

In the dark, his wife perches next to him on the bed. 'What's wrong with Trevor?'

'He's unhappy.' More than unhappy, really. Something harder to define. A change in the way he talks, and the way he moves, a sort of doleful blandness to his manner. Signs – signs he knows he should understand – of something Trevor won't say, but wants to. And this is where George really does rue his mental slowing down, because even if he hasn't always been the perfect father, he feels sure that in the past he would have *got it*, would have known exactly what to do – whereas now he just watches as Trevor lopes helplessly along, and feels in response some elusive, intangible remorse.

He says goodnight to Maureen, and then it's morning. Red numbers flashing above his head.

He dresses himself and goes downstairs.

'Dad,' says Trevor, standing over a pot on the stove. 'I was about to come get you.'

The fridge is humming again.

'I borrowed a part from Michael's cottage to get the power working,' he explains, dipping a ladle into the pot, 'but we'll need to pick up a new one in Fort William.' He hands a steaming bowl to George. 'Just as well we're going over today.'

George stops as he takes his breakfast. 'We're going to Fort William?'

Trevor sighs. 'Yes, Dad, we're going to Fort William and staying two nights – I must have told you fifty times. I have a meeting with the ferry people.'

Perhaps this does sound familiar. Ferry people. Yes. *Ferry people not starting to run off (5)*. He's been dreading it.

'Why do I have to go?' he asks.

'Because I can't very well leave you here alone, can I?'

'You leave me here alone all the time.'

'That's different, Dad.' He laughs, though it sounds more bitter than amused. 'You can't get into much trouble when I'm gone for half an hour to pick up the shopping. This'll be three days.'

'I can cope.'

Trevor pours the rest of the pan's contents into a bowl of his own. 'No, Dad, you can't, and you're not going to convince me now any more than the last three times we had this conversation.'

Have they really discussed this before? 'But Trevor, I—'

'Enough, Dad!' He flings the pan into the sink, where it lands with a loud clang. His face is red. 'Now eat up. We have to leave in an hour.'

George sits, sullen, and begins to spoon the oatmeal into his mouth. This is precisely the sort of coddling he can't stand. More distressing right now, though, is the prospect of the mainland – because if his routines are all he has to orient himself, now, then the mainland is a break from them beyond all others: the place is terrifying, a mess of people and places and customs as impenetrable as the radio soaps he now listens to joylessly, out of habit. The last time he went to the mainland was a year ago, for a hospital visit, and he felt so vulnerable there, so hopelessly dependent on Trevor, that he doesn't wish to repeat the experience.

He scrapes up the last of his porridge. 'Why can't you just talk to the ferry people on the phone?' he says.

But Trevor isn't in the kitchen any more; he's banging around upstairs.

George quietly takes his bowl to the sink and washes it: one of his routines, and a hard-earned one. As his seizures and tremors had worsened over the past few years, Trevor tried to stop him doing dishes altogether. *At best you'll break something*, he'd said; *at worst you'll take a finger off*. But George wasn't having it: *I'm not an invalid*, he'd shouted, and very fluidly, he thought, had banged his fist against the table. They settled, in the end, on George doing his own dishes at the end of every meal.

He places his bowl in the drying rack now, and shuts off the faucet. Routine.

Trevor appears in the doorway, telling him it's time to go, but still George lingers. Asks again why Trevor can't just call the ferry people on the phone.

'Because, Dad,' he replies, his cheeks flushing, 'this is pretty much the last thing between us and having to close up for good, and I want to make it clear how serious I am.' He squeezes his eyes shut; rubs the bridge of his nose. Tells George to put his shoes on.

George does as he's told, but sitting on the staircase's bottom step and tying his laces, he looks up at Trevor, looming over him and leaning on the banister, and makes one last plea. 'What if Michael looks in on me?'

Trevor's face darkens. 'He can't. He's fucked off to the mainland to visit Flora.' He looks over his shoulder. 'Everyone's fucked off to the mainland.'

George stands up. 'Let me stay here by myself, then. I'll be okay.'

Trevor turns to face him again, staring for a few seconds without reacting. Then he lets out a frustrated yell. 'Fuck sake, Dad! You're like a child!'

'I—'

'Okay! Fine! You want to stay here so much, fucking stay here! It'll be easier without you, anyway.' And then he reaches out with both hands and shoves George backwards, sending him stumbling on the bottom step and falling against the stairs. A sharp edge digs into his spine, and he yelps, but Trevor is already turning away, luggage in hand; the front door has slammed shut before George can think of anything to say.

He lies there without moving, his back throbbing, for what feels like several minutes, but when he eventually stands up, gingerly, and makes his way to the sitting room, he can still see Trevor in the distance, stalking away in miniature. A fine drizzle, the remnants of last night's rain, is blowing all around him.

Trevor hit him! *Every other blow a choker (3)*. But he only did it because he was annoyed, George knows that, and everybody gets annoyed sometimes. Anyway, George is safer now because of it, at home with no trip to make after all. And he *can* look after himself for a few days, easy-peasy, no matter what Trevor says.

He looks around the sitting room. Sometime recently – he isn't sure exactly when – they moved his armchair from its old position, facing into the room with the other furniture, so that now it looks out the window, over the village glen. A few of the old cottages are visible a little way off, towards the left of the glass; behind them the grey-green landscape curves and rises up into the ridge of a hill, and behind that the sky is almost white. He sits down to watch the island come awake, as he does every morning. Routine.

The rain intensifies, hissing lightly against the window. He closes his eyes. Listens. Opens them again and sees the clouds have darkened. Swivelling in his chair – his back protesting after the fall – he tries to see the time on the mantel clock, but the hands seem not to have moved since he sat down. He closes his eyes again. His stomach gurgles.

For some reason, Trevor hasn't brought him the newspaper yet. And where has Trevor disappeared to, anyway?

He's on the mainland. He's not coming back for a few days.

He's over back between the tower walls (6).

So no paper today, no skimming through the increasingly opaque news. No arriving greedily at the crossword. No routine.

Hmph.

Should he go get it himself? No. The clouds are even darker, now, the hiss of rain a growl; he shouldn't go to the jetty in that. So what instead?

His stomach gurgles again; he squirms in his seat to look at the clock and sees it's almost noon. Lunchtime. There's no food on the kitchen table, of course, nothing prepared; Trevor isn't here. He'll have to find something for himself. In front of the open fridge he frowns, and tries to think what he can make. On the top shelf he spots a plastic container labelled *Spag bol*, which he pulls out – *excellent*, he thinks, *just reheat and serve* – but once he's put it in the microwave he can only stare blankly at the controls, unsure how to start it. Eventually he gives up and eats the noodles cold.

In his armchair the sky is darker again. Sooty. The rain is still rattling against the window frames, and the wind still smacking against the walls – and as he watches, the blackness outside seems to creep in, smoke-like, around the edges of the glass. Time isn't passing; it's circling. He closes his eyes. The room is empty.

He pulls himself out of his chair and goes to the pub. The furniture is in stacks around the edges of the room, covered in dust tarps, and he twirls the lights on, full strength, to bring them out of the shadows. The air gleams.

It's the middle of the off-season, that much he knows, but he needs something to occupy him – so he moves to the closest table and carefully removes the tarp, guiding it up and over the chair legs so it won't get caught. That done, he folds it in half, corner to corner, three times, four times, five. He places the resulting bundle on the bar. Then he's back to the table again, taking down chairs, standing them right-side-up on the floor; he's pulling the table to the centre of the room and arranging the chairs around it. This is good: he's calming down again, focusing on the task. Routine.

Ringing.

Routine. He moves to another table and begins the process again, tarp off, chairs down, table out. The ringing stops.

He carries on until the whole room is set up and ready to receive guests, then moves to the doorway and admires his handiwork. The clock above the bar reads almost five. He nods. Shuts off the lights again. Outside, night has fallen, and he moves from room to room, closing all the curtains. The ringing is back.

He saves the sitting room for last, the black window there still worrying him. When at last he has no choice but to foray inside, he turns on the hallway lights first so that when he flings open the sitting room door a yellow rectangle flaps down across the floor. Quickly, he reaches around the frame and feels for the switch, and then the lights are on, expelling the darkness, and he moves to the window to pull the curtains shut. Much better.

He sits down in his chair. That bloody ringing starts again.

The phone!

He doesn't answer the phone much any more; Trevor doesn't like him to, and usually gets to it first. But George can still put on a good public face when he needs to, so out of the chair now and into the hallway he lifts the receiver from its cradle.

'Fìor Guesthouse, how can I help you?'

'Dad! Thank God! I've been trying to call for hours!'

He blinks. 'Hello?'

'Is everything okay there, Dad? Are you hurt?'

'Hurt?'

'Look, Dad, I'm sorry about before. I'm so sorry. I was just angry, and I wasn't thinking straight, and as soon as the ferry pushed away I knew I'd made a mistake – but they wouldn't go back. Said they had to get to Mallaig before the weather turned.' He swears. 'And I got off at Rum to hitch a ride back with the doctor, but with this storm, and in the dark…'

'Would you like to reserve a room?'

'Oh, Christ.' The voice pauses. 'Dad, listen to me: this is Trevor. Your son. Do you understand?'

'Trevor?'

'Yes, Dad. I'm on Rum, and I'm trying to get someone to bring me home, but the sea's too rough. I'm probably stuck here 'til morning.'

'You're stuck there 'til morning.'

'I need you to do exactly what I say, okay Dad? I need you to go upstairs to bed, right now, and try to go to sleep.'

He looks at the hallway clock. 'It's dinnertime.'

'I know Dad, and I'm sorry. I shouldn't have left you there like this. Fuck. I'm so sorry, Dad. I was just so frustrated... Dad? Dad!'

'Fìor Guesthouse, how can I help you?'

'Oh Jesus, fuck.' He sniffles; perhaps he's ill. 'Dad, please, it's Trevor. Do you remember? Your son, Trevor.' He's almost whispering.

'Trevor.'

'Yes, Dad, Trevor. Now go upstairs, please. Do you understand me? You have to go upstairs. You'll be safe that way. And I'll be home as soon as I can. Okay?'

'Okay.'

'You're going to go to bed right now?'

'Yes.'

Trevor seems to choke. 'Good. Fantastic. I'll see you soon, Dad. As soon as I can.'

'Okay, Trevor. Goodbye.'

He hangs up. Tries to concentrate. It had been Trevor on the phone. He'd said to go to bed and wait.

He looks at the clock again. It's still dinnertime, not bedtime. *I've misunderstood, somehow. I've misunderstood him again.*

His stomach rumbles and he goes to the kitchen thinking he should fix dinner, though he isn't very used to cooking any more. Something easy, then. An omelette. He can still make a simple omelette.

He goes to the fridge, trying to remember what he needs. *Omelette. Let me toe. Eel totem. Motel Tee. Motel Tee confuses breakfast order (8). Breakfast spelled out in chrome lettering (8). Let me toe scrambled egg dish (8). Egg dish.*

Eggs!

The mixing bowls aren't where they should be, so he retrieves his porridge dish from the drying rack and begins whisking together three eggs in it. The whisk *had* been in its proper place, in a ceramic jug on the counter, along with all the ladles and wooden spoons and a potato masher. The jug – glazed in a flaxen white, with thistles painted around its sides in thick streaks of navy blue – had belonged to another family, but when they'd moved away they'd given it to George and Reenie. *The Leslies!* They didn't want to take it with them, they said; were afraid it might break in transit. Were afraid it might remind them of all they'd left behind.

He blinks again. He's standing over the table, the whisk gripped in one hand and the bowl, tipping imperceptibly towards him, in the other; egg is dribbling over the edge and onto the table and down his front, and he rights it violently, dropping the whisk as he does so. More egg spatters against the cuff off his trousers. Behind him, Reenie tuts.

'Egg makes an awful stain, you know. Trevor'll have a time getting that out.'

'I can do it myself,' George mumbles. 'I don't want to trouble him.'

She shrugs, and is gone.

He needs the cheese grater. A wall of cupboards and drawers towers up in front of him, white panels and metal knobs. A few of the doors are still gaping from his search for the mixing bowls, and the dark squares and lines seem to shuffle around in front of him into a giant, lopsided puzzle grid.

No; *routine*!

He lurches forward and begins throwing more doors open, trying to rein in the kitchen. The damn grater has to be somewhere! *We hear it's better to shred all sorts of things (6).*

Frantic, he reaches deep into the cupboards, shifting around plates and casseroles and cake tins, greasy jars of mace and nutmeg; soggy boxes of bicarbonate of soda. A food processor, an electric mixer. A coffee grinder.

'Bloody hell!' he yells, slumping, his hands still hooked on the bottom lip of the cupboard. He leans his forehead against the frame.

'Calm down,' says Reenie. He spins around.

The grater is on the table.

Routine, routine, routine.

He fetches some cheddar from the fridge. Puts a pan on the stove and turns on the heat.

'Trevor wanted you to go upstairs,' Reenie reminds him, leaning on the counter.

'He's just being a fusspot.'

'He wants to look after you.'

'He shouldn't have to!' George looks up as he shouts this, hands trembling against the grater. 'I should be able to look after myself! I should be able to make myself a meal and put myself to bed without him holding my hand!' He struggles for breath.

The ringing has started again.

'Fìor Guesthouse,' he says, in the hallway. 'How can I help you?' But only the dial tone hums back. *Dial tone for your noggin? (3)*

The ringing is still there.

He's in the kitchen again. Smoke is overflowing from the pan on the stove, its skin of egg black and blistering. When did he even pour it in? He lunges for the stove and throws the pan in the sink, where it clangs against the porridge pot from that morning. There's blood on the counter. Blood on the floor. A menacing trail of pearly drops leading from the sink to the stove to the table. The grater is covered in blood too, the cheese a crimson mess. *A crimson mess. Mr Casino. Omnicars. Minorcas!*

He looks down at his hands, now covered in a cross-hatching of cuts and gruesome flaps of skin, and smeared all over with sticky, drying blood.

These birds are a crimson mess (8).

'You need help, George,' says Reenie, still in her chair.

He groans and runs his hands down his face. It stings. 'What will Trevor say when he sees all this?'

'He told you to go straight to bed.'

'I know!' A few, discouraged tears creep into his field of vision. 'I know.'

The ringing has finally stopped.

'You need help, George,' Reenie says again, and folds her arms.

And then he's by the front door, pulling on his boots. That Michael down the road is always fixing things – maybe he can help. Or Jack Kilgourie. Or Kenny Burke or John Braithwaite or that fellow who used to run the general store – there must be *someone* who can get everything sorted out. If they hurry, they can even finish before Trevor gets home, and he'll never have to know what happened.

He opens the front door. A swarm of rain and hail blows in at him.

It's dark outside. Too dark. After what feels like only a few steps, he loses his nerve, turns back to the house – but behind him, through the wall of raindrops in the sky and streaming down his face, he can't see any sign of it.

Panicking, he tries to retrace his steps, his woollen sweater clinging to his shoulders, sodden, weighing him down.

He's shivering.

The last time he'd been out in weather like this was that night years ago – or was it only months? – when the bridge had blown away. He remembers how the mud glommed to his feet, then, and how the terror crept up his neck, and how his skin felt as if it were peeling away in the wind. He remembers the wretched look on Reenie's face when he returned, and the sex and how surprised he'd been, not by the act itself but by the sense of closeness it brought him – the intimacy he hadn't realized he'd been missing. He remembers his relief when Mr Lewis had called, and his happiness at seeing the children the next morning, Trevor's enthusiasm and Flora's fealty and even Barry's awful sullenness; remembers his grief, in the years that followed, as the elder two disappeared again. Remembers his guilty fear, especially with Flora, that he was the one to drive them away.

He's standing still, struggling to move his legs forward, whether against the wind and rain or his own failing synapses, he can't quite tell. His lower back is throbbing.

'Reenie,' he gasps, and falls to the ground.

'You should know better than to leave the house without a coat at this time of year,' she says, kneeling next to him. Stroking his hair.

'Tell the children I'm sorry,' he says.

She frowns, and somehow he can see her face perfectly, even in the dark. 'For what?'

'For making them feel responsible for me,' he tells her, teeth chattering. 'For making it so hard for them to stay.' He smiles, sadly, at the touch of her fingers against his scalp. 'I suppose you must have felt that way yourself, sometimes.'

But she says nothing in response, and when he looks up again she's gone.

Reenie! He half sits up, looking desperately from side to side, but he can't see a thing in the squall. With a grunt he tries to lift his arms, to turn onto his front, to crawl after her wherever she's gone and find her one last time. But his body only seizes, stuttering, and he crumples to the ground again, into the stream of rainwater trickling beneath him, and the wet grass flocking around his head. Black clouds swirl above. His legs begin to numb.

And that's it; he won't get up again. Won't be there when Trevor returns in the morning, sprinting from the jetty and stumbling every few yards as the waterlogged ground gives way beneath him; won't be there when his son cries out at the blood smeared around the kitchen, at the single stove burner still flickering a mournful blue, at the pub set out perfectly for business; won't be there in the coming days when Barry, swallowing his pride at last, and his shame, phones again and this time Trevor answers; won't be there when all three siblings return for one more funeral, or when afterwards they leave. Instead he'll simply lie there in the dark a little longer, and finally, whispering apologies, he'll let his eyes fall shut.

Author's note

I'm afraid I must disappoint anyone hoping to visit Eilean Fìor and see the place with his or her own eyes; the place exists only in my flawed and rather questionable imagination. However, astute readers may notice similarities between my imaginary island and several other locations around the west of Scotland, from where I freely admit to having drawn inspiration. Tom Steel's excellent history of St Kilda, appropriately titled *The Life and Death of St. Kilda*, provided many valuable and haunting details about life in extreme isolation and at the mercy of the elements; Anna Blair's *Croft and Creel*, and particularly its history of Lewis, was instrumental in filling in the details of Fìor's past; and numerous other books and articles supplied the narrative with flashes of colour and atmosphere far more vivid than anything I could have come up with on my own.

More than anything else, however, Fìor owes its essential features to the Small Isles, the group of four Hebridean islands to which it putatively belongs. In particular it shares many traits with Canna, which claims the real title of 'smallest and most remote' in the archipelago. Canna also struggled with a mysterious rat infestation in the last decade, and Canna, too, occasionally finds itself split in half depending on the tides. Sanday, Canna's 'Stùc', is also home to the schoolhouse in real life, and the footbridge connecting them was torn away in a storm – though there's still an easy road crossing when the tide is in. Saddest of all, in the six years since I began this book, Canna's inhabitants – none of whom, I hasten to add, bear resemblance to the characters in this story except by extraordinary coincidence – have been reduced in numbers from thirty to just twelve.

I can't comment, though, on how the Cannans feel about all this. Indeed, given the pitiful amount of time I spent on Canna doing research, I can't really comment on their real-life plight in any capacity. Instead, I encourage anyone wishing to find out more about life in the area to take the trip and ask the Cannans personally. It is most certainly worth the effort – and, if camping isn't your thing, you will be thrilled to know that Canna, like Fìor, has a guesthouse where, at the end of your journey north, you can rest your weary feet.

Acknowledgements

Above all I must thank Kathryn Davis, the judge of the AWP 2012 Prize in the Novel, and Kate Bernheimer, one of the contest's initial screeners, both of whom picked this manuscript from a field, I'm sure, of many other deserving entries. Thanks also to the Association of Writers and Writing Programs, and all at my United States publisher, New Issues Press, who were the first to publish *What Ends* – particularly Kim Kolbe and Elizabyth Ann Hiscox, who were very patient with all my silly first-time-author habits, and Megan Lappe, who provided the beautiful illustration for the US cover.

This paragraph is a very special exclusive addition to the acknowledgements, available only in the United Kingdom version of the book – be sure to lord this over your American friends! I was extremely fortunate that the wise and always uncomplaining Adam Schear, at DeFiore and Company, was able to sell the UK rights to the book – and also to explain to me how rights work, repeatedly. I am also extremely grateful to have worked with two really splendid editors at Oneworld, Charlotte Van Wijk and Ros Porter, who finally talked me into all the changes that I should probably have known to make on my own. Also thanks to Holly Macdonald for the equally beautiful UK cover, and to Amanda Dackombe for her thorough copy-editing of the manuscript.

Dozens of people also suffered through early drafts of this manuscript, most notably Margot Livesey, my amazing MFA thesis chair and an editor more thoughtful, generous, hard-working and dedicated than any writer could hope for. Thanks also to Jessica Treadway, my thesis reader, as well as Lise Haines, Kim McLarin and the many students in their respective writing workshops, for their valuable advice on preliminary drafts. And Barb, from David Emblidge's Book Editing class – I'm ashamed to admit that I've forgotten your last name, but I will never forget your admonitions to stop explaining everything twice and not to start so many sentences with 'And then…'

While I'm thanking the people who have suffered through my first drafts, one group of people deserve a paragraph all their own: the members past and present of Write Club, in all its incarnations. Heinz Healey Schaldenbrand, Erica Dorpalen, Michelle Fernandes, Akshay Ahuja, Annie McGough, Kim Liao, Kirstin Chen, Bridget Pelkie, Taylor Shann, Jill Gallagher, Mike Dunphy, Alex Sharp… And, in the years before Write Club, Anca Szilagyi, Julian Smith, Ilya Zaychik, Danny Spitzberg and the other members of my various writing squares and heptagons. You are all saints – even those of you who only ever made one meeting.

Dozens of people also suffered through me as I wrote earlier drafts of this manuscript, and they deserve the biggest cheers of all: my family, immediate and extended, living and deceased, as well as my friends in Boston, Edinburgh, London, Montreal, New York and elsewhere.

Endless and enormous thanks are also due to Michael Kay, whose slashingly vicious editorship when I was fifteen made me the writer I am today; to Miss Carter, my high-school English teacher, whose report card my penultimate year – the one that said 'I wouldn't be surprised to see Andrew's name on the bestseller lists in years to come' – I wish I could find because I would frame it and stare at it daily for inspiration; Sean Michaels, whose own beautiful prose always makes me feel like I could be doing seven hundred times better; and everyone else who I've forgotten and forgives me for it.

And Mallory, of course. Mallory Mallory Mallory. I couldn't have done it without you.